Amelia

Life is lived forwards, but understood backwards.

Amelia 1868

Janet Kay

Dedication

For Len Fromolz, my best friend

Amelia

Life is lived forwards, but understood backwards.

Acknowledgements

There are a number of people whom I would like to thank. Without them, this book would not have been possible.

Anna Martineau Merritt (www.mistypinephotography.com) created the cover and is responsible for my author's portrait as well as other photos in my book. Autum Mist Quam served as the model for the cover, and Shana Purser provided the original image of the Victorian lady.

I am also grateful to all who reviewed my manuscript and provided valuable feedback. This includes my children—Shannon Graber, Shane Jenson, and Sherry Jenson—Agnes Kennard, Randi de Santa Anna, Peggy Roeder, Anne Rankin, and Jackie Dodson.

To my editor, Diana Schramer (www.writewaycopyediting.com), I would like to extend a heartfelt thank-you for her excellent work.

I must also acknowledge the St. Croix Writers of Solon Springs, Wisconsin for their support, the Wisconsin Writers Association, and the Alpine Artisan Writers of Seeley Lake, Montana.

Last, but certainly not least, I would like to thank the people of Virginia City, Montana; Seeley Lake, Montana; and Walnut, Iowa for sharing information about their hometowns and welcoming me into their communities. These places will always hold a special place in my heart—and I encourage you all to visit them someday.

Thank you to my readers! I hope you enjoy my story, and I hope to hear from you with any comments.

Janet Kay
janetkay@novelsbyjanetkay.com

Chapter 1
2010

The pastor cleared his throat and gazed at me with a look of concern in his steady eyes. He began to slowly repeat the question. A question that I was unable to answer. There was no appropriate response.

"Do you, Prairie Rose Johanssen, take Robert James Anderson to be your wedded husband..." he began.

My world swam before my eyes. I knew I was pale as a ghost.

"...for better, for worse, for richer, for poorer, in sickness or in health, to love and to cherish till death do you part?"

Till death do us part? Oh my God, what am I doing here? Who is this man standing beside me? Sure, I've known him all my life. Sure, I love him, but...My heart pounded as I began to sway, gasping for breath. When Bob put his arm around my waist to steady me, I almost screamed. He was suffocating me, smothering me with that lovesick look dripping from his brown puppy-dog eyes. The familiar pangs of panic consumed my body, triggering an uncontrollable need to escape. Nothing else mattered. I had to get away!

"No!" I shrieked into the silent church, breaking away from Bob. "I'm sorry, Bob." Whirling around, I tripped on my long white train. Tears of black mascara streamed down my face as I ran down the aisle and out the door of the historic church.

Frantic, I rushed out into the brick street lined with Victorian homes and century-old antique shops. An evening breeze rustled the massive canopy of gnarled trees that spread out over the street. Their ancient limbs closed in on me, trying to snag me in their branches. I felt I was drowning, tangled in floating branches.

The old globed street lights flickered hauntingly through the darkness that engulfed me. The shadows of the night were not as terrifying, however, as the demons lurking within me, urging me to run as fast and as far as I could.

Breathe deeply, I reminded myself as I kicked off my high heels, gathered up my long wedding dress, and ran into the woods behind the church. I could hear someone coming, following me into the night. I had to find myself a good hiding spot.

I heard voices calling my name as I slipped into the woods and hid behind a large boulder in a clump of trees. I reminded myself that I was safe and I was free. Nobody would ever control me again. Not even Bob, the man I loved.

Finally, the wild throbbing in my veins ebbed into a swirling eddy of nothingness. I waited, huddled on the ground in a crumpled heap of white lace, until silence finally fell upon the little town of Walnut, Iowa.

I had no choice but to leave my hometown forever.

Remembering that the side door of the church is always left open and that I had arrived at the church in jeans before changing into my wedding dress, I sneaked into the church, changed clothes, and grabbed my purse and cell phone.

Cautiously hiking down the back streets in the dark, I made my way toward the Super 8 Hotel at the edge of town. Slivers of moonbeams flickered through the trees, easing the darkness. In the distance, tiny, flashing red lights danced in the sky. They were perched upon gigantic windmill blades that methodically sliced through the night like a knife through my heart. Tonight, the windmills resembled alien creatures closing in on me.

Finally, I made it to the hotel where I checked in for the night. All alone on my wedding night. Throwing myself on the bed, I sobbed, letting the tears flow until there were no more. No more surges of panic. Just a dull sensation of numbness that crawled throughout my limp body.

Racked with guilt over what I'd done and knowing my parents would be frantic with worry, I made a quick call to them on my cell phone. Yes, I was a thirty-year-old adult…but after what I'd done to them, it only seemed right to call.

Mama grabbed the phone on the first ring. "Hello? Prairie Rose?" she cried out in her most dramatic voice. She was still wide awake at two o'clock in the morning.

"Mama, it's me. I'm okay and just wanted to tell you how sorry I am…"

"Good Lord, you will be the death of us all, young lady." She sighed a long, exasperated sigh, the kind I'd heard all my life whenever I failed to meet her expectations. This time, I deserved it. "Where are you?" Mama demanded. "Why? Why did you do this? Do you have any idea how badly you've hurt that lovely young man of yours? How embarrassed we all are? How can I ever face my friends at Ladies Aid or my quilting club? I do declare, I don't understand you, for the life of me—"

"Mama, I'm leaving for a while. I need to get away. I will be all right, and I will check in with you, okay?"

"Not again, Prairie Rose! You can't keep running away from yourself, young lady."

"Gotta run. I'm sorry. Please tell Papa...and Bob. Love you all." I snapped my phone shut and turned it off, resisting the urge to call Bob. There was nothing more to say.

Exhausted, I fell asleep in my clothes, longing to cuddle up in Bob's arms, to hear him telling me that everything will be all right. But it would never be right between us again—not after what I'd done.

Chapter 2

Early the next morning, I woke to the sound of Walnut's 7:00 a.m. wake-up siren. Then came the church bells, calling parishioners to Sunday services. My parents never missed church, so this would be my opportunity to go home and pick up my car and other things I'd need. I didn't want to face my parents, to see the hurt in their eyes, to listen to their well-meaning lectures. I still had no idea where I was going—just that I needed to get away.

Thankfully, few people were out and about yet on this late spring morning. Most were in church. Some of the regulars would already be at Aunt B's Kitchen for their morning coffee. I would have loved a good cup of coffee and one of her hot apple dumplings, but I couldn't face anyone in this town. My botched wedding would be the topic of conversation for weeks to come. I slunk down the familiar streets of Iowa's Antique City, my head hung low, trying to blend into the morning mist. I tried to absorb and memorize the look and feel of my hometown, a place I would never see again.

I passed the old brick Walnut School, which I had attended. Its Walnut Warriors logo was still proudly displayed on the front of the building—the head of an Indian chief in full feather dress. Kids here still presented the nativity pageant every Christmas. Few things changed here in my hometown. Sometimes that was a good thing.

There was the Walnut Creek Historical Museum, which Papa had worked hard to develop; DR's Kalico Kraft Shop, full of cozy homemade quilts and quilting supplies—Mama's favorite store; the old granary and blacksmith shops, now filled with an assortment of antiques; and *The Walnut Bureau* newspaper office, founded in 1878 and still printing a weekly local newspaper.

Finally, I passed Walnut's abandoned Grand Opera House before turning up Pearl Street toward our family farm. Built in 1899 when Walnut was a thriving and prosperous agricultural town, the Opera House was once an elegant structure hosting vaudeville, traveling theatre groups, silent movies, and dances in the ballroom. Today, it is boarded up, a lonely and deserted grand lady from the past. Local violinist virtuoso, Carl Hermann Carstensen, played here when he wasn't touring throughout the world or serving as court musician for the German emperor. He spent his last years living alone in a little room above the Opera House where he was found dead one day in 1924.

Rumor has it that on a still winter's night, you can walk past the Opera House and hear incredible violin music drifting out into the street. Carl's music. I believe it...because I actually heard the music one unforgettable night when I was a teenager. Bob was walking me home from a school dance, telling me the ghost story. Holding hands, we stood silently beside the spooky structure. Snowflakes swirled softly around us. It was late, and our town was wrapped in a winter's cloak of silence. Suddenly, violin music flowed through the cracks of the abandoned building—heavenly music from another time, another place. Entranced, we could not move. We felt the music sweep through us, bringing tears to our eyes. When it was over, neither one of us could speak.

Yes, Bob and I had some good times together, I sighed to myself. But after graduating from college, I was anxious to escape from the family farm and small-town atmosphere in Iowa. I wanted to see the world. I traveled to exciting places, bounced from job to job, place to place. I fell in love more than once—then terminated each relationship when it became too serious. "Commitment-phobic," my therapist called me.

Finally, I returned home to Walnut, where I moved in with my parents for a while. I reconnected with my old boyfriend, Bob. He'd grown up on a farm not far from the one that my family had owned for generations. He loved the farmlands of Iowa and had no desire to see the world. As for me, perhaps I'd seen enough of the world already and was ready to settle down and marry. After all, that's what all my friends had done. Most of them had children already...and Mama was continually asking if and when she would ever become a grandmother. I was an only child, born late in life to Mama and Papa. It was up to me to carry on the family line—something that was important to them.

Bob worked in the construction field and had just finished building our first home. Nestled amongst ancient oaks, it had a large wraparound porch where we'd planned to sit and watch the sunsets and the storms moving in. Our country home was perched high on a knoll overlooking Prairie

Rose State Park, a special place for us. As children, our families had pic-nicked there together, swam in the lake, and fished. In fact, Bob proposed to me there one night last fall as we cuddled together at a secluded picnic site. An orange harvest moon dominated the sky, its reflections dancing across the lake below. He got down on one knee and put a sparkling diamond ring on my finger. Oblivious to the fall chill in the air, we spent the night in each other's arms, wrapped warmly in our love for each other. We were so happy, so much in love.

Stop it! I reprimanded myself. This was no time to reminisce about Bob.

I turned up Pearl Street toward the old two-story farmhouse where I'd grown up. It was located on the far edge of town. As I approached, I inhaled the sweet fragrance of the lilacs bursting forth in Mama's garden. The apple and cherry trees were in bloom, and the peonies were a blaze of red, white, and pink. Spring had always been my favorite season. The perfect time for a wedding...

The old red barn was now faded and weathered. Several rotting boards hung loose, flapping in the wind. An assortment of chickens ran through the barnyard. Papa still butchered them. Mama collected the fresh brown eggs and sold the surplus to friends in town. The fields were empty these days, however. At seventy-eight, Papa was no longer able to farm or raise cattle like he did when I was growing up. Sometimes he leased his land to younger farmers who grew crops of corn and soybeans, alternating every other year.

Wistfully, I gazed at the rolling pastures I'd once roamed freely, climb-ing trees and hiding out in the tree house Papa built for me. I remembered playing with the kittens in the hayloft, riding my quarter horse down the trails and country roads, eating apples from our tree, and growing vegetables in the garden. Mama's vegetable garden had gotten smaller over the years, but she still canned tomatoes and beans and made big batches of sauerkraut and jars of jelly.

As an only child, I had an imaginary friend to keep me company. Sometimes we played together in the cemetery across the valley from our pastures. I could see the tombstones from my bedroom window.

As I walked up onto the familiar porch, I could almost see Mama rock-ing in her chair, her knitting needles flying as if under their own power. Papa loved to sit in his chair watching storms moving in from the west. More than anything, he loved to tell family stories passed down over the generations. The three of us spent many a summer's evening rocking and swinging on the porch, watching fireflies, listening to crickets chirping and the soothing sound of Papa telling his stories. I kept urging him to write a book to pass these stories down through the family. But what family? Unless I married and had children, there would be nobody to pass it down to.

Sometimes in the spring, swirling tornados moved through our area. Sirens went off, and people took shelter in their basements until the storm passed. Some of the locals were storm-chasers, using sophisticated equipment to track and monitor the tornadoes. Bob loved nothing more than chasing a storm and capturing it on film. Some of his photos had been published in *The Walnut Bureau* and the Associated Press picked up one of his shots.

I opened the door and tiptoed in. Lucky, my fluffy, white American Eskimo Dog, bounded up, thrilled to see me. He wagged his tail and licked my face when I bent down to hug him. Of course I'd take Lucky with me. He'd been my faithful companion for almost ten years.

I threw clothing and other essentials into my suitcase and grabbed my camera, laptop, journals, tent, sleeping bag, blankets, and camping gear. Lucky and I would camp out along the way to wherever I was headed. Leaving my tattered and dirt-stained wedding dress in a heap on the floor of my bedroom, I began to load my SUV.

What was that tucked under my windshield wiper? A note? Trembling, I opened it, recognizing Bob's handwriting immediately. "Never forget that I will always be here for you, Sweet Pea. Love you, Bob." Sweet Pea? Yes, his nickname for me was almost as bad as my given name of Prairie Rose... but it was his unique name for me, one he'd come up with the first time we'd made love on the moonlit shores of Prairie Rose Lake.

I sank into the cool green grass as waves of remorse washed through me. Oh my God, how could he even think about being there for me after what I'd done? He knew, of course, that I'd be leaving. What else was new? Hot tears dripped onto the note, blurring his words. Finally, I tucked it into my purse and loaded Lucky into the passenger seat. Within fifteen minutes, we were on the road.

When we reached Highway 80, I had to make a quick decision. East or west? West it was. Something about the far west called to me, compelling me to venture farther than I ever had. Maybe that's where I belonged.

As we turned onto the highway, I glanced back at the Prairie Rose State Park sign. My thoughts wandered back to my namesake, Rosa of Prairie Rose. I'd always hated my name and never understood why my parents named me after a pioneer town that no longer existed, the town my great-grandmother, Rosa Johanssen, had settled in many years ago.

I'd never forget the stories Papa told me about her, stories he'd learned at his father's knee. She was Irish with blazing emerald eyes just like mine.

Rosa was born in a bustling Mississippi River port city in northwestern Illinois in 1877. She had a strong independent streak and was not about to be confined by traditional domestic roles for women. In 1899, at the age of twenty-two and already an old maid by standards of the day, she decided to head west to the frontier prairie of Iowa, alone, which was a scandalous thing for a woman to do in those days. She talked her way onto a covered wagon train heading west by agreeing to care for the children of one of her neighbors. Their destination was a tiny country village called Prairie Rose not far from Walnut, where her neighbor was going to work at the local creamery. He agreed to let Rosa stay with them in the log cabin until she found a place of her own—or married.

Founded in 1895, Prairie Rose was nestled around a knoll where waves of prairie rose flowers grew profusely across the windswept prairie. Surrounded by acres of farmland, the village boasted one of the finest creameries in Shelby County. By the time Rosa arrived, there was a general store that served as a post office, a blacksmith shop, and an implement shop, even a dance hall. The storekeeper and butter maker had large homes to house their growing families. Other employees lived in log homes they'd built or on nearby farms.

Rosa loved to join the children running barefoot through the fields, basking in the fragrance of wild anemones, trilliums, sweet william, and bloodroot. Sometimes they picked bouquets of flowers to brighten the darkness of the little house they were all crammed into. In the fall, they gathered wild grapes and made pies.

It was a quiet life disturbed only by the train chugging by on its way to the Walnut Creek Station. Everyone ran out to watch the train and to wave at the conductor. The other source of entertainment was the activity at the dance hall. Farmers and their families came in on Saturday nights to dance to the local fiddlers. One thing that most settlers insisted on bringing with them when they traveled west was their fiddle. Music and the sounds of hands clapping to the music drifted across the prairie, rising above the wind into a steady crescendo. Laughter rang out. An occasional fight broke out in the dirt-rutted street. Late at night, the farmers would hitch up their wagons once again and drive home, with children fast asleep, before it was time to milk the cows again.

Rosa continually stretched the limits of propriety: Running barefoot in the fields. Reading novels of questionable repute. Writing poems filled with passion. Attending barn dances without a chaperone. She was known to dance a mean Irish jig or hornpipe dance, clogging to the fiddle music while people gathered around clapping. Now and then she even took a swig from the flask of one of her suitors. While there were few eligible bachelors in the territory in those days, she managed to find an adequate supply of dance partners. Her dance card was always full. She learned to ignore the occasional glares from some of the farmwives whose husbands were all too eager to dance with the young and lovely Rosa.

Rosa wanted to learn more about her world and to make a difference in it. She loved to join the men who discussed the politics of the day around the potbellied stove in the general store. At first, she pulled up a crate and seated herself near them, just listening. They cleaned up their language out of respect for the lady, but they weren't sure how to treat her. They'd never before had a lady join them. Women simply had no interest in politics—not until this one came along. Before long, she dared to ask questions and express her opinions. Shocking behavior, they thought, but the more they listened to her, they grew to respect her ideas. Sometimes they even asked her for her opinion on various matters of the day.

Finally, she began writing letters to the editor of *The Walnut Bureau* newspaper, expressing her opinions on political issues. The editor began publishing her letters. People began talking and asking questions. Who was this Rosa person? Was she really a woman?

One day, a fine black horse and fancy buggy pulled into Prairie Rose. A handsome, well-dressed stranger with gleaming black hair emerged, bidding his chauffeur to care for the horse while he attended to business. He cut a smart figure, as the story goes, strolling into the general store where a group was gathered around the stove deep in conversation. Silence fell upon the room as the stranger entered.

Rosa looked up, her heart catching in her throat at the sight of this handsome, well-dressed man. She flushed as his gaze fixed upon her. "I'm looking for a Rosa Peterson," he began.

"For what purpose?" one of the men by the fire inquired of him in a protective manner.

"I wish to meet the lady who has written such thoughtful and inspirational letters to *The Walnut Bureau*," Franz Johanssen replied. "I am a great admirer of hers."

The rest of the story is history. Franz and Rosa fell in love, married, and lived happily ever after. At least that's the way the story goes, I thought to myself. Oh to be a fly on the wall...

The town of Prairie Rose soon died after a series of prairie fires destroyed most of the town. Franz and Rosa moved into Walnut, which was then a booming town. In addition to The Grand Opera House, Walnut contained a flour mill, lumberyards, elevators, agricultural implement stores, blacksmith and harness shops, carriage shops, hotels, saloons, drugstores, groceries, millinery stores, shoe shops, a jewelry store, churches, doctors, and lawyers.

Rosa continued to write letters to *The Walnut Bureau* and was finally assigned to write a well-read column documenting significant events in the lives of the citizens of Walnut. Not bad for a woman in those days.

My namesake. I grinned to myself. Perhaps there was a reason I was named after this independent woman. Maybe I should take pride in my name instead of hating it as I had all my life. Maybe I could learn from Rosa. I wished I could ask her some things. Was she happy as a married woman? Did she not feel smothered and confined? Or had she found a way to balance that independent streak with the love of a good man? Franz did, after all, apparently allow her to write for the newspaper, and he obviously respected her intelligence. That's why he sought her out in the first place. The more I thought about it, my Bob seemed to have many of the same qualities as my great-grandfather did.

Chapter 3

Lucky and I cruised into the sunset, listening to soothing classical music on National Public Radio. Windows rolled down, sunroof wide open, my long hair whipping wildly in the wind. I was free. No destination, no schedule, no commitments stressing me out. I breathed a deep sigh of relief, tempered by a sense of remorse that I refused to acknowledge.

My big dumb dog, as I affectionately called him, flopped his head onto my lap. He didn't care where we were going as long as he was with me. He trusted me—much more than I dared to trust myself.

As the miles rolled by, I searched for interesting towns along the way, sometimes detouring off the highway to explore them. I wondered what it would be like to live in some of these places and where I'd find a job. I had a bachelor's degree in creative writing and some experience as a feature writer and reporter for various newspapers and magazines. My dream was to write and publish novels. Someday. Of course, I couldn't rely on supporting myself this way, and my money wouldn't last forever. I'd need to find a job before long.

We traveled cheaply, setting our tent up every evening at campgrounds along the way. My cooler was filled with bread, packets of oatmeal, peanut butter, cheese, bottles of water, apples, and dog food. Gas for my SUV was my biggest expense.

Sometimes we stopped at a coffee shop with Internet access so I could do some research on the places we were passing through. Nothing seemed to fit. Something kept pushing me farther west, as if something was waiting for me there. I only hoped I'd recognize it when I found it.

"Where would you like to live, Lucky?" I carried on a one-sided conversation with my faithful friend. He never talked back, never argued with me. What more did I need in life?

By the time we arrived at the old western town of Cheyenne, Wyoming, we began to see mountains. Spectacular sunsets bathed the mountains in shifting shadows of golden light. It was beginning to feel more like home. On a whim, I decided to head north toward Montana.

Montana! I was full of anticipation as we crossed the state line. Mountains, lakes and streams, ranch country, wildlife. The scenery was spectacular as we wound along mountain roads, descending into delightful western towns.

As we crossed the Continental Divide, 8,510 feet above sea level overlooking Butte, Montana, I saw a huge, white statue on the East Ridge. Built in the likeness of Mary, Mother of Jesus, she stood ninety-feet tall and weighed eighty tons. Our Lady of The Rockies, I learned, was dedicated as a tribute to women everywhere, especially to mothers. Mothers—a special group of women that I may never be part of...

I continued winding through the valleys and mountain passes, absorbing the sheer beauty of the mountains and the rushing streams around me. When I stopped for gas at The Town Pump at the junction of Highways 90 and 200, I decided it was time to branch off the interstate. I was on my way toward a little mountain town called Seeley Lake. I had to stop to let a few bighorn sheep cross the road. Signs warned me that this was grizzly bear country.

I was breathless as we descended into Seeley Lake, nestled beside sparkling lakes and surrounded by mountains. We found a campground on Salmon Lake just as the sun was slipping into the lake, the mountains on fire. It was time to check in for the night. Luckily, I found us a secluded campsite, #22. Right on the lake, it had a fire pit, a sheltered picnic table, and was near the toilets and showers. Perfect.

"Maybe we will stay here for a while," I told Lucky as I set up camp and made a peanut butter sandwich for dinner. I made a fire in the pit to celebrate our new home and sat beside the crackling fire late into the night, breathing in the fresh mountain air. I marveled at the brilliant stars lighting up the pitch-black sky. They reminded me of the fireflies back home and of the nights we spent sitting on the porch watching them flicker through the sky. I sighed wistfully as Lucky snored beside me. I wondered if Bob was also gazing up into the Universe, rocking alone on the porch of the house he'd built for us. Stop it! I scolded myself once again.

I was up at dawn the next morning, boiling a pot of coffee on the camp stove. An early morning mist hovered over the lake, breaking up as the sun's rays streaked through a filmy blanket of fog. Sick of oatmeal and peanut butter sandwiches, I was hungry for real food. Counting my dwindling cash reserves, I decided it was time to explore Seeley Lake and find a job.

Seeley Lake, Montana was a charming little town with everything a person would need—grocery and hardware stores, restaurants, gift shops, churches, cabins, a library at the high school, even a huge quilting store. The people were friendly and very helpful when I inquired about a job. However, there were not a lot of full-time jobs available unless I wanted to work at the mill—and they'd just laid off a number of workers due to the struggling economy.

Finally, I found a part-time job at The Grizzly Claw Trading Post, a rugged old western store featuring locally made products, including log furniture, Indian blankets, jewelry, bins of beads, clothing, artwork, photographs, and books. I loved browsing through the book section and the art and photography displays. The owners frequently went on buying trips and came back with antiques, which they also sold in their store. I'd never get bored working here, I thought to myself.

Lucky and I settled into our tent and fell into a new rhythm of life. I worked mornings at The Grizzly Claw and loved it. Lucky was allowed to come to work with me. He greeted the customers and played with the children. Afternoons, Lucky and I explored, hiked the trails, and canoed on the lake.

I dug out my good camera and began taking photos—*lots* of photos. Evenings, I'd chase the light along the winding mountain roads, trying to capture the surreal reflections of the sinking sun upon the many faces of the mountains. No two sunsets were ever alike. It was therapeutic to absorb the beauty of nature in what had to be God's country. My goal was to supplement my income by selling framed and matted prints at the store. After seeing some of my best work, the owners agreed to let me have my own display wall and sell my photos. Things were looking up.

Nights, I sat in my lawn chair by the fire, Lucky at my feet. I wrote endless pages in my journal, trying to make some sense out of my life. There seemed to be an endless pattern of failed relationships. Looking back, I'd fallen in love a number of times, or what I thought was love, only to panic and run when things got too serious. I struggled with issues of trust, expecting others to betray me, to break my heart. While I'd worked with several therapists to try to get to the bottom of my anxieties, I'd not yet been successful.

My life seemed to be haunted by a sense of restlessness and by persistent nightmares. As far back as I could remember, I'd been terrified by a recurring dream in which I was drowning. And I'd always been fascinated with and drawn to the West. Perhaps I'd find the answer here to the mysteries that seemed to plague me. Hopefully, there was a reason why I'd been drawn to Montana.

My thoughts frequently drifted back to our family farm, to the stories Papa told—and retold—about growing up as a country boy in Walnut, Iowa. Maybe there was a connection that I needed to explore. By getting in touch with my ancestors and family history, I hoped to discover things about myself in the process.

Nagging thoughts crept into my head, keeping me awake late into the night. I had unfinished business to attend to but no clue what it might be. It will come to you if you quit pursuing it so desperately, a voice whispered from someplace deep within. You're not there yet.

"But where is *there?*" I cried aloud into the starlit night. The only response I got was the gentle lapping of the waves upon the rocky shoreline accompanied by the lonesome cry of a wolf in the distance.

"I give up, Lucky." I extinguished the dying embers of our fire and crawled into the tent. Sleep did not come easily that night, however. Maybe I needed some diversion, something to occupy my mind instead of chasing that elusive butterfly. If I could focus on something else, perhaps the butterfly would light upon my shoulder and point me in the right direction.

Chapter 4

Gradually, it dawned on me. I knew what I needed to do to begin the process of finding myself. The key may be Papa's family stories of life in Walnut, Iowa. They needed to be written down by someone. If he was unable or unwilling to do so at his age, maybe I needed to be the one to do it. After all, I was a writer, wasn't I? I knew his stories by heart, and I had too much time on my hands. Maybe I'd even publish the book someday and finally be an author.

As the summer progressed, I spent many a night tapping the keys of my laptop beneath the hanging lantern in the tent and usually worked until my battery ran out. The next day, I'd recharge it at work. Some days, I took my laptop in to the Stage Station and worked there.

Papa's stories were coming to life, shedding light on my own life in the process. As I wrote, I could see him clearly—sitting in his favorite chair on the porch, his eyes smiling into the night, lost in memories of the good old days.

As he rocked, he would slip back in time, back to his years growing up on the family farm near Walnut. Papa's early memories, and his character, were shaped by his years of hard work as well as a deep sense of independence and connection to the land. There were cows to be milked in the chilling darkness of early winter mornings, eggs to gather, chickens to butcher and dress, corn to shell, haying and harvest time. Harvest time was always exciting when threshing crews came from miles around to help out. The ladies prepared loads of food, including cakes and pies, to feed the hungry farmers twice each day. They helped each other out, moving from farm to farm, sharing equipment.

Every winter, they butchered their own hogs. Neighbors helped each other dress the hogs, render the lard in a big iron kettle, and make sausage. Nothing was wasted. They cooked the heads, feet, and ears to make into headcheese, mincemeat, and pickled pig's feet and ears. Papa and his siblings were active in 4-H, and as they got older, they were allowed to go to movies at the new Walnut Theatre in town.

Those were the days when families hitched up the wagons on Saturday nights after the farm chores were done and made their weekly trek into town. The merchants stayed open late that night so farm families could purchase their supplies.

The dirt-rutted Main Street was framed by an umbrella of American Elm trees. Trains sped through the town, whistles blowing, aglow from the firebox illuminating the night. Papa and his friends loved to watch the trains speed past, wondering where they were going. Papa dreamed of hitching a ride like the hobos did, of exploring the world beyond his little town.

As Papa and his friends played, their fathers delivered loads of grain to the elevators before reloading the wagons with goods. Sometimes, especially during the Great Depression, locals trapped muskrat, mink, and skunk. They traded the furs as well as eggs and farm goods for groceries. One favorite stop was the Moritz Meat Market with sawdust on the floor, pickle barrels, and the aroma from the smokehouse in the rear wafting through the store. Men huddled around the potbellied stove at the Rock Island Depot, playing checkers. Women shopped for bolts of fabric, which they used to make the family's clothing. Scraps were assembled into crazy quilts or friendship quilts during quilting bees when all the farm wives got together.

Papa had attended a one-room country schoolhouse, Monroe District #8, located near the family farm. There were eight grades in one room, all taught by one teacher. In addition to teaching, the teachers shoveled snow, carried in cobs and coal for the potbellied stove, disposed of ashes, and cleaned the schoolhouse. Students helped pump water from the outdoor well and carry pails of water into the schoolhouse. They all drank from the same metal dipper.

In the winter, the children put on boots and coats to trek out to the outhouse. They dried their mittens by the stove. During recess, they played hide-and-seek, Kick the Can, and Andy Over. They had snowball fights, built snow forts, or went sledding. Of course, they all walked to school, sometimes several miles each way.

In 1949, the country school closed. Abandoned, it began to crumble slowly into the past. Country schoolhouses were rapidly disappearing from the landscape, replaced by big city schools that kids were bused to. It bothered Papa every time he drove past this important part of his history.

Years later, in the 1990s, the Walnut community learned that the schoolhouse was going to be demolished. Not about to let that happen, the Walnut Historical Society took action. Papa helped organize a community-wide effort to move the old schoolhouse to the downtown area of Walnut. Funded by spaghetti dinners, Victorian teas and style shows, bake sales, and concerts, the move was made in 1993 and restoration efforts began. Today, the old structure is open to the public as a school museum. Stepping inside brings back memories of yesteryear. The original chalkboards and several of the original desks with inkwells are even there. Papa still spends time wandering through the building, reminiscing of days long gone.

Papa's memories of Walnut were far different from my own. While Walnut was a thriving agricultural market center up until the mid 1970's, things soon began to change. Rural towns everywhere were struggling to survive as the world changed. Walmarts moved in. Transportation increased accessibility to larger cities and people began to commute to work. Businesses began to close. Finally, in about 1983, the town adopted a new vision based on tourism, primarily antiques, and re-created itself into "Iowa's Antique City."

I realized that I already missed some things about my hometown. The friendly people who knew everyone else's business—and then some. An Antique Christmas Walk was held every year during Thanksgiving weekend. Storefronts were beautifully decorated with greenery and old-fashioned lights. A towering live Christmas tree always stood at attention on the brick street in the center of town, surrounded by antique shops offering hot, spiced apple cider and cocoa. Christmas carols and holiday laughter filled the air as children laughed and played in the snow.

As I wrote Papa's stories, I began to appreciate all that my hometown had to offer. Yet, I also loved living in the mountains of Montana, especially Seeley Lake. One day, I discovered Alpine Artisans, an organization of regional artists and writers. They had a performing arts program, even a local writers group which I joined. We met every other week at one of the member's homes, read our work, and offered feedback as well as support. It felt good to bond with my fellow writers who soon became good friends. As we shared our writing, we shared our lives with each other.

Chapter 5

I spent many long hours working on Papa's book over the summer. Finally, "Memories of a Country Boy: Memories of Growing Up in Walnut, Iowa" was finished. This would be a gift to my father, one I knew he would cherish forever. I was proud of myself as I signed off my computer and saved the manuscript on a flash drive for safekeeping. I'd actually finished something—and something important at that, instead of flitting away to another project or place. It was time to celebrate, I decided. Since I arrived in Seeley Lake, I'd saved my money carefully, knowing that winter would be setting in and I'd soon need to trade my tent for a cabin someplace.

But tonight I would splurge on a good meal at the rustic Double Arrow Ranch, something I'd always wanted to do. I drove through the massive log arches, past the golf course, and took the road to the historic main lodge where the Seasons Restaurant was located. Built of logs in 1929, it boasted a massive stone fireplace in the Great Room. The warmth of the fire on this early September evening felt good. I could sit by the fire with a good book forever, I decided, but my growling stomach led me to the intimate dining room with its linen tablecloths, rustic log walls, and French windows overlooking the golf course. The lodge was nestled in the valley between the Mission and Swan Mountain ranges, offering dramatic views of mountain peaks. The lacy tamarack trees were already turning to gold—a sign that winter was just around the corner.

After ordering a glass of red wine and reading the extensive menu, I settled on the Rattlesnake Fettuccini Alfredo. Yes, rattlesnake! I simply had to try this dish, which was made with rattlesnake and rabbit sausage. It was delicious, but I secretly wished I had somebody to share this experience with. For dessert, I had heavenly huckleberry swirl cheesecake.

The sun was sinking into the lake beyond the campsite by the time I returned. Lucky, as always, was anxiously waiting for me. I'd saved one piece of the rattlesnake sausage as a treat for him. There was a definite chill in the night air, so I put on warm socks, pulled on a hooded sweatshirt over my pajamas, and climbed into my sleeping bag.

The wind began to howl late that night, slapping against the sides of the tent, threatening to blow it down. I buried myself deeper into the warmth of my sleeping bag, cuddling up to Lucky. It was bone cold in the tent when I stumbled out to grab my flashlight. Unzipping the flap of the tent, I looked out to find heavy flakes of snow falling. The ground was already white. Snow in early September? Of course it would melt by the time the sun rose in the morning and bathed the world in light. For now, we were settled in for a long, cold night. I braced stacks of books and boxes against the inside walls of the tent to secure it. It was time to think about packing up and finding a real place to live—perhaps a cabin on the lake.

By morning, the snow had ceased, and I woke to a clear, crisp day. The lake was shrouded in mist, the trees frosted with a glistening coat of ice as the sun broke through the low-hanging clouds. A beautiful day to be alive, I thought to myself as I bundled up, grabbed my camera, and went out to capture the beauty of the day. Every day was different here in Montana—different angles of light, changing reflections dancing across the lakes and mountains. Nature calmed my soul and made the world right once again.

Lucky trudged along beside me as we walked along the lake. He nudged me gently, reminding me that it was time to eat and perhaps time to think about finding a warm place to live. Thankfully, it had warmed up by the time we left for work.

As I walked into The Grizzly Claw that morning, the other employees greeted me with looks of concern. "Rose, are you all right?" Little Bird blurted out.

"Of course. Why?" I replied, heading for the Jitterbug Java Café in the back of the store. All I needed was a hot cup of coffee—maybe even a mocha latte on this chilly morning.

"We almost drove out to your campsite last night to bring you home with us," Dee confessed. "You know, you really need to find a place for the winter."

These were my new friends, and I appreciated their concern. They would be happy to help me find a cabin to rent. In fact, they soon began giving me leads, which I scribbled down on the back of an envelope in my purse—the letter I never sent to Bob.

Dee and Susan had just returned from another antique buying trip and were busy hauling in their treasures, entering them into inventory and arranging them around the store. I loved working here. There was always something new and different, and I met the nicest customers.

I spent the next few hours showing and selling locally made jewelry. Susan, Little Bird, and other locals made beautiful jewelry from a variety of gemstones. I'd always admired the beautiful green malachite stones assembled into pendants, necklaces, and earrings. My favorite was a perfectly shaped oval pendant set in a lacy silver frame. Streaks of green swirled through the stone. Someday, when I could afford it, I planned to buy that necklace. I always breathed a sigh of relief when customers moved on and selected other pieces.

As my last customer left with several pieces of art in his arms, I turned to find my coworkers gathered around one of Dee's new acquisitions. He was hanging an antique clock on the wall. I approached as if in a trance, my heart racing. As I got closer, I could make out an old wood pendulum clock with an ornate porcelain dial. Well-worn spindles protruded from the antique clock, which had a bronze head of a bearded man at the top.

"It's rare, one of a kind," Dee boasted. "Probably from an Old West saloon."

My head began to swim. I struggled to breathe as I forced myself to move closer. I had to see if there were any initials on the pendulum and if a small piece of the man's nose was missing. The letters "A. J." screamed from someplace deep down. "Please, not A. J.," I whispered silently, over and over again.

The inscription on the pendulum had faded with time, but there was no doubt that the letters, in a fancy Old English script, were A. J. And yes, there was a small piece of the man's nose missing as I knew there would be.

I grasped the counter as the store began to spin in circles. I was swirling down, down, into a deep hole. Then everything went black.

"Rose? Rose?"

Distant voices called me back. Someone was checking my pulse. At first, I did not recognize the name they called me. Rose? I was somebody else, someplace else. I was dancing in a beautiful, low-cut, old-fashioned dress. The overwhelming scent of musk filled the air.

Shaking my head, I soon regained my senses. I was back, listening to my friends and the local doctor mumbling around me, giving me a drink of water, helping me off the floor and into a chair in the back room where the good doctor joined me. He asked questions. Had I ever had a panic attack or suffered from anxiety? How often? What triggered my feelings of anxiety? He offered to prescribe something.

But I had few answers. Sure, I'd had a number of experiences in which I couldn't breathe, felt I was drowning, and had to get away. It usually happened when I was getting too close to someone or something, losing myself. But how could I explain to him that I'd just freaked out because of that antique wall clock? That was insane. Maybe I *was* insane. I accepted his prescription, thanking him. Maybe I'd try one of his magic pills the next time I was tempted to leave my fiancée standing at the altar…if there ever was a next time.

Regaining my composure, I returned to the store under the watchful eyes of my coworkers. All I could think of was that clock on the wall. I knew that clock…I'd seen it someplace long ago, although I had no idea where that could have been. It seemed to have eyes that followed me around the room, ticking slowly, loudly, calling me. I could hear a fiddle playing in my head although I realized that none of my coworkers could hear the music. My initial shock and dislike for the old clock turned into intrigue. I had to know more about it.

As I snapped photos of the clock, Dee informed me that he'd purchased it at an antique auction in a little Montana town called Ennis about two hundred miles or so southeast of Seeley Lake.

Ennis. I could hardly wait to begin researching the town on my laptop. Located in the Madison River Valley of southwestern Montana, Ennis was once the home of Shoshone, Flathead, and Bannack Indians who hunted the valley each spring. The town was born in 1863 shortly after gold was discovered at nearby Alder Gulch. Today, it is known as "the world's best fly fishing country." A colorful, authentic western town, it was surrounded by ranches, farms, and mountains. The main street had an assortment of art galleries, antique shops, and restaurants. There was even a Cowboy and Indian Antique Auction that had recently taken place. Maybe that's where Dee had purchased the old clock.

Just thinking about that old clock sent shivers up and down my spine. My bizarre reaction made no sense, but I was obsessed with finding out where it came from. Perhaps it would lead me to my ultimate destination, to discovering my mission and putting my life back together again. Nothing else mattered at the moment. I felt bad leaving my job and my new friends, but I had no choice.

I arrived at work early the next morning after taking the tent down and loading Lucky and all our gear into the SUV. A chicken at heart, I planned to leave a farewell letter, explaining that an emergency had come up and I needed to leave. I wouldn't have to face anyone if I got there early enough.

But I found Little Bird quietly waiting for me with a strange look in her eyes. She knew I was leaving; I could sense that. This intuitive Indian woman seemed to have special powers and a great deal of wisdom that she'd learned from her ancestors. I often felt she could read my mind, which was slightly unnerving. She knew things about me—things I had not yet discovered.

"You're leaving, aren't you?" she inquired sadly.

I nodded and tried to explain. But she already knew there was no family emergency. She knew that I was really leaving because of that clock and the strange power it seemed to hold over me.

"There are secrets from long ago that you must discover before you will ever be at peace," she spoke slowly. "Your mission will finally be unveiled, and then you may need to make some difficult decisions. Trust that you will make the right ones." Tears welled in her troubled eyes as she turned to open the jewelry case. She turned back to me with the malachite pendant in her hand. "This is for you, from me, for wisdom and understanding on your journey."

I was shocked. "I can't accept that, Little Bird, although I greatly appreciate your offer. I've always loved that one."

"I know," she smiled. "But you will take it. You must." Her eyes turned very serious. "You will need the protection of this gemstone on your journey. It will ward off danger and will bring harmony into your life—finally. Malachite has been used for spiritual, emotional, and physical healing since recorded history began. It still works its magic in the world today."

I gave her a hug, thanking her profusely. As I walked out the door for the last time, she called out, "Ennis isn't that far away, you know. Please come back to see us." I should have realized that she'd know exactly where I was headed.

I proudly clasped the striking green pendant around my neck, trying to absorb its power as I drove out of Seeley Lake. Bob would say the pendant was the same color as my eyes.

Chapter 6

I had no idea what to expect in Ennis. All I knew was that I was following that clock, tunneling back into an unknown past that was calling me and almost holding me captive. As strangely as I'd reacted to seeing the clock, I was apprehensive about what I'd encounter when I arrived in Ennis.

I tried talking some sense into myself as the miles ticked by. I absorbed myself in the rugged landscape of the Old West. Rolling past ranches nestled in the valley beside the rushing Madison River, I finally arrived. It was a charming town all right, but I felt nothing unusual as I drove through town back and forth several times.

I needed to find a place to stay. My natural inclination always was to get as close to water as possible, be it the sea, a lake or river, even a duck pond. I had mixed feelings about water, however. As much as I loved it and needed to be near it, I also feared it. All my life, I'd had dreams in which I was drowning, struggling against a force that pulled me down beneath the waves. My fears, however, had compelled me to learn to swim, and I'd become an endurance swimmer in high school.

On the edge of town, beside the rapidly flowing Madison River, I found The Riverside Cabins with a vacancy sign in the office window. The cabins had flower boxes overflowing with an assortment of native flowers. There were wide-open green spaces dotted with massive trees and lawn chairs overlooking fertile ranches. The surrounding mountains glowed in shades of pink and lavender as the day came to an end. Several deer wandered past my car, calmly grazing on the grass, as I pulled in.

My cabin was cozy and warm and had everything I needed, including an efficiency kitchen and bathroom, a bookshelf housing an assortment of books, and a homemade quilt on the bed. The quilt, of course, reminded me of home. I hadn't checked in with my folks for a while, I realized, so I went out to sit on a lawn chair beneath a blanket of stars and made the call.

"Prairie Rose?" My mother's voice was tinged with her usual dramatic flair as if she was shocked to hear from me.

"Mama, I just wanted you to know I'm safe and sound in a charming little cabin in Ennis, Montana. Yes, it's nice and warm…no, I don't have a job here yet, but I will. Mama," I tried to get a few words in as she chattered and asked questions.

"Mama," I interrupted her. "I thought of you when I found a lovely quilt on my bed here in the cabin I'm renting." It was true, and I thought that would give her some pleasure. "Are you still making your beautiful quilts?"

Instead of answering, she went off on one of her tangents. Sighing in exasperation, she informed me that she still had the wedding quilt she'd made for me, and that she cried every time she walked past it. "Maybe I should just destroy it, Prairie Rose—or give it to Bob when he someday finds a woman who loves him properly. Oh, child, do you have any idea how much you've hurt your poor old parents? And we aren't getting any younger, you know." She sighed once again.

I rolled my eyes. Here we go again. "I've told you I'm sorry, Mama, but I have to live my own life." I tried to change the subject. "How's Papa?"

"If you want to know the truth, young lady, he's not good. He's heartbroken over what you did. All he ever wanted before he dies was to see you married off to a nice local boy. All he ever wanted was to hold his grandchild in his arms before the Good Lord takes him away. Now it may be too late." Mama hit hard, projecting her own feelings onto my father.

"What's wrong? Let me talk to him, Mama."

"I'm not sure he is up to talking with you, Prairie Rose," she began as I heard Papa in the background.

"Give me the phone, Anna," he instructed in a firm voice while she obviously protested, her hand half-covering the receiver on the old telephone. They argued for a little while before Papa got on the line. He assured me that he was just fine, told me the latest news in Walnut, including how some of the farmers were having a bad harvest this fall, terrible yields due to the flooding over the summer months. Some of their farmland was still under water. Papa was having a hog butchered and putting up meat for the winter. He was also looking forward to going deer hunting with his buddies, an annual tradition he'd enjoyed all his life. Perhaps it was also a way for him to get away from "the wife," as he called her, and enjoy some peace and quiet.

"Ken next door is splittin' a load of firewood for us, and we're gettin' ready for what the *Farmers' Almanac* says will be a cold, snowy winter," Papa was saying when Mama called out in the background, "Ask her if she's coming home for Thanksgiving."

"I'm afraid not, Papa," I said sadly. "I can't afford another trip right now, not until I get settled in a new job here. I can't just take off until I've earned some vacation time." What I didn't tell him was that I had no idea what kind of job I'd find or if I'd have any vacation or other benefits at all.

"It's okay, Rose, we understand," he said softly as Mama grumbled in the distant background. Papa did understand. But Mama didn't and never would. "Now you just never mind your mama, ya hear? She means well, but...you know how she works herself up. We love and miss you, Rose."

"Love you too, Papa. Mama too." I hung up the phone and sat for a while staring out into the night. Why did relationships have to be so difficult? Why couldn't I have been content to marry Bob and give my parents the grandchild they wanted?

꿁ꛯ

The next morning, I was up early on my mission to track down the clock. I carried the pictures in my purse, planning to show them to the local antique dealers. Hiking down the main street, I realized I was starving, so I stopped for breakfast at the old-fashioned Ennis Café. Red vinyl stools lined the wraparound counter in the center of the wood-paneled dining room. I settled into one of the booths and ordered a western omelet with a side of hash browns.

Sipping on black coffee, I watched a group of local men come in and cluster around a large table in the back of the restaurant. The regulars, I figured. A friendly waitress with a badge that read "Sally" slipped into the booth across from me to visit and welcome me to town. Of course everyone knew I was a stranger in town. They all wondered who I was and what I was doing there. I apparently didn't look like one of the fishermen who would be arranging fishing trips with the local outfitters.

Sally chattered about the town, places I simply had to visit, and then asked if she could answer any questions for me. I showed her the picture of the clock and asked if she'd ever seen it. She hadn't, but she jotted down the names of several local antique dealers on the back of a napkin.

"Sally, how about more coffee?" one of the men in the back called out loudly.

"Get it yourself, Fred," she teased before grabbing the pot and trotting off to take care of her customers. "They'd sit here and drink all day if I let them," she grumbled to me with a twinkle in her eye. "Ya'll come on back, Rose, ya hear?" And I did go back for breakfast every morning that week. I enjoyed visiting with Sally.

In the meantime, I made the rounds to the antique dealers. Nobody recognized my clock—yes, it had somehow become *my* clock, whether I liked it or not. I was referred to others who referred me to others yet. They all promised to spread the word and get back to me if they had any news about the clock.

Finally, on Friday morning, an old man with a long, gray beard and a wide-brimmed cowboy hat stopped into the Ennis Café and immediately sauntered over to my booth, taking off his hat in a gentlemanly fashion as he nodded at me.

"Ma'am, are you the stranger in town asking about an old clock?"

"Yes!" My eyes lit up. "Please sit down." I immediately pulled the pictures from my purse and showed them to the cowboy, holding my breath.

"Hmmmm," he stroked his beard, examining the photos carefully. "Yup, I think I've seen this clock just a few weeks ago, as a matter of fact. See, there was this big auction just out of town, and I think some feller from Seeley Lake bid on the clock and got it—"

"Yes!" my heart was pounding now. "That's it! I need to know where the clock came from. It's very old."

"I reckon it was Paul Dubois who brought it to auction." He paused. "Yup, I'm sure it was Paul. Now I ain't got a clue where he got it, but you can ask him."

"Where can I find this Paul Dubois?" I held my breath.

"He lives here in Ennis, in a big, old house on the Madison River. But he's not around during the week. He works at the library in Virginia City, curator or some such fancy title. A strange feller."

Absorbed in our conversation, I didn't notice Sally coming over to our booth, coffeepot in hand. "You can find Paul here on Saturday mornings, precisely at ten o'clock." She winked at me. "And, yes, Bill is right. Paul is a little strange, but a nice guy."

I had to know why Paul was strange. After all, he may hold the key not only to the clock but to the secrets I was supposed to discover so I could find harmony in life. Wasn't that what Little Bird told me?

According to Sally and my new cowboy friend, Paul was a loner. Never married. A guy who read lots of books and did research, or some such thing. He worked at the library in nearby Virginia City, an old ghost town. People said that he believed in ghosts and was a "ghost hunter." Although he stayed pretty much to himself and had few friends, he did come in for coffee every Saturday morning. Sometimes he just watched people, sitting quietly by himself. Once in a while, he visited with his old high school friends and fishing buddies.

Paul DuBois. Even his name was intriguing. I was already fascinated with this "strange feller," as the old cowboy called him. Strange indeed. A ghost hunter? Of course it was ridiculous to believe in ghosts.

Little did I know what a critical role this man would play in unlocking both my past and my future.

Chapter 7

For some reason, I took time Saturday morning to curl my long, dark hair, put on makeup, and selected a green silk blouse to wear over my best pair of jeans. It complemented my green malachite pendant as well as my eyes.

Settling into my usual booth at the Ennis Café, I sipped coffee, nervously waiting for this Paul DuBois character to show up. Ten o'clock came and went. Ten-thirty. Sally assured me that he would show up. I wondered if he'd gotten word that some stranger was asking questions and had decided not to come that day.

Suddenly, the door swung open, framing a large, handsome man of about thirty-five years of age. He could have been a ghost from the past. Black, well-trimmed beard, piercing black eyes, and longish, black hair curling around his ears in a way that made me want to wrap his windswept curls around my little finger.

He stopped abruptly, staring at me as if confused, and shook his head. "Do I know you?" He spoke in a low whisper, his black eyes flashing.

I shivered, looking away. Those eyes...there was something about those eyes that were so familiar. They evoked conflicting feelings within me and an overwhelming sense that I had once known this man. I had no idea when or where.

The restaurant fell silent as all eyes focused on the obvious tension between us. Sally finally injected herself into this strange standoff by introducing me to Paul DuBois and signaling him to join me for coffee. He hesitated as though he wanted to flee, but it was obvious he had no choice in the matter. He slid into the booth across from me, removed his cowboy hat and plopped it on the table.

"Do I know you?" he repeated his question, shaking his head as if trying to get a grip on reality.

"I...I don't know." I refused to look at him directly. "You seem very familiar, but..."

Do not trust this man, a tiny voice within cautioned me. Yet I could feel waves of long-lost love and desire flowing across the table between us. Something was not right here. Had someone slipped a drug into my coffee? Was I losing touch with reality?

His piercing gaze did not waver. He waited patiently, drawing me to him, seeming to enjoy the fact that I'd turned a ghostly shade of white and was trembling. "Are you cold?"

I shook my head. Pulling myself together, I retrieved the photos of the clock from my purse. It was time to move beyond this nonsense and get down to business. I saw him tense up when I spread the photos in front of him.

"That damn clock," he snarled. "What about it?"

"I need to know where it came from. It's very important," I whispered, trying to keep my voice firm and steady instead of squeaking like a mouse. This was not the time to break down in tears or have a panic attack.

For some reason, Paul opened up to me, a complete stranger, as if he'd always known me. That clock, he told me, had been in his family forever, and he'd always hated it. After his grandfather died in their family home, he had inherited the place and the clock.

He went on telling me about his family home on the banks of the Madison River. He'd been raised there by his grandparents. It was an eerie mansion, he said, tucked into a maze of ancient cottonwood trees that seemed to live and breathe. Sometimes late at night, the wind would howl and churn the river into a whirlpool of angry waves. On those nights, he sometimes saw in his dreams a ghostly image of a woman drowning in the river.

A spooky place, he told me, but the scariest part of all was that damn clock hanging on the wall in the parlor. The eyes of the bronze man on the clock followed him around until he could no longer stand it. He felt he was suffocating with remorse and a sense that he had found but lost his true love forever.

I listened intently, drawn into his story, as he fell into a silent world of pain. "So did you lose your true love forever?" I finally asked to break the heavy silence between us.

He emerged from his reverie. "I never found love, never married. I've always belonged to the past somehow."

Nodding in understanding, I decided it was time to bring the conversation back to the clock. "So what did you do with the clock that you hated?" I tried to smile, hoping to soften the pain this man was experiencing.

"Oh, well," he came back brusquely, his gentleness a mere memory. "I moved that damn thing down into the cellar so I wouldn't have to look at it anymore. But you know what? It didn't work. I could still feel it down there, tormenting me, making me mourn for something lost, something I destroyed. Making me feel guilty for something I will never understand. God, I hated that clock. That's why I decided to put it up for sale at auction, to get it out of my house.

" And now you are here, asking questions. Why?" he whispered as his hand crept slowly across the table toward mine as if he could not help himself.

When his fingers brushed mine, my heart melted. Struggling to compose myself, I focused once again on the photos, avoiding his eyes. Silence ensued, but it was a comfortable silence; the kind that wrinkled old lovers shared as they held hands, smiling at each other, after fifty years of marriage.

Finally, I broke the silence, remembering the reason I was here. "Paul," I began gently. "Do you know where your grandfather got this clock? I really need to know."

"Why?" His eyes flashed in anger, forcing me to turn away once again.

"Because...because knowing this may help me put my life back together again. I don't understand it anymore than you understand why you hate that clock. But something is driving me to find out where it came from."

"All I know," he finally confided to me, "is that it once hung on the wall of a hurdy-gurdy dance hall in Virginia City sometime in the 1860s during the Alder Gulch gold rush days."

"Virginia City. Isn't that where you work?"

"Yes, at the library."

"Would you mind if I came there someday to do some research?"

"Be my guest." He smiled as he stood up, towering over me. With a gentlemanly bow, his cowboy hat over his heart, he bid me farewell and sauntered out the door of the restaurant. I had to pinch myself to control my surging emotions. I'd struck gold, I thought, as far as tracking down the roots of the clock that brought me here. But this Paul DuBois character had rattled my world in ways I did not understand. While I had to follow the trail to Virginia City, I decided there was no way I'd see this man again—even if that meant I wouldn't be able to do my research at his library. He was dangerous.

Chapter 8

I tossed and turned most of the night, images of Paul flittering through my mind. Trying to figure out when and where I could have known this man. Trying to understand why my feelings about him were so conflicted. They shifted from love and desire to fear and anger.

Early the next morning, I put on the coffee and took Lucky out for a walk. A chill was in the air, reminding me that if I was going to settle in for the winter, I'd need to get a job soon. But first, Virginia City was calling.

It was a fourteen-mile trip from Ennis to Virginia City, a scenic drive winding through the mountain pass. I stopped at an overlook to snap a few photos of the Madison valley far below, framed by ragged mountain ranges. The aspen trees were turning gold and the pastureland, blowing in the wind, into amber waves.

Soon I was descending into the old western ghost town of Virginia City, Montana. The main street was lined with weathered historic buildings dating back to the 1860s gold rush days. A boardwalk with hitching posts ran the length of the main street.

I was stepping back in time...way back...when déjà vu suddenly ripped through me like a bolt of lightning. This was the place I'd been seeking all my life. I suddenly realized I had unfinished business here, although I had no idea what it could be.

Virginia City looked like the sketches I had drawn as a little girl—something I'd forgotten about until now. Mama always thought it was strange for me to draw sketches of an old western town with fancy Victorian ladies and cowboys. My sketches included mountains, a stagecoach, even a young man hanging with a noose around his neck. Poor Mama had been quite upset over that drawing as she tried to figure out where I'd gotten such strange ideas. She had certainly never exposed me to such things, and I wasn't old enough to go to school yet.

My first doll was a fancy lady dressed in a long, red satin Victorian dress with lace trim. It was a large doll with long, curly hair, almost as big as I was.

I was eighteen months old when Mama took me shopping for that doll. She was determined to buy me a cuddly baby doll that I hated. I threw it on the floor and began to sob. "No, no, no!" I'd shouted as she tried to interest me in another baby doll. I hated baby dolls. They made me cry. Finally, Mama gave in and bought me the Victorian lady. That doll became my best friend.

Today, years later, I found myself sitting in my parked car at the edge of Virginia City. Shaking, I grasped the steering wheel tightly, trying to calm myself. As I gazed down the main street, images of long ago seeped into my mind. While some things had changed over the past century and a half, I recognized some of the old, weathered buildings. The rutted dirt road was now paved. There were no horses, buggies, stagecoaches, or covered wagons—just a few cars. The mountainsides were no longer dotted with a haphazard collection of shacks and hand-hewn log cabins with mud roofs. I could no longer hear the ring of the blacksmith's anvil or the clanging of picks and shovels as the miners scoured the gulch and foothills of the mountains for gold.

Where had all the people gone? There were no women in long dresses and wide-brimmed Victorian hats. No cowboys, outlaws, or miners. No music blaring from the saloons and dance halls. The silence was deafening. A pulsing sensation of heightened energy seemed to reverberate from the surrounding mountains, sliding down into the valley.

I looked up at the old cemetery overlooking the town and valley and shivered silently. An image of five men standing on tall crates with nooses around their necks flashed through my mind. "Men, do your duty," a harsh voice echoed from the past as bearded men kicked the boxes out from under the road agents. They hung lifeless now, swinging in the bone-chilling squalls of a gray January day.

The Vigilantes had made an example of these outlaws, a warning for others who might also think of robbing stagecoaches and killing anyone who got in their way. They had taken the law into their own hands, trying to ensure the safety of rapidly growing communities springing up along the gulch where gold had been discovered. Now five men were dead, soon to be buried in the cemetery overlooking Virginia City.

Tears filled my eyes as I remembered one of these lifeless men—a young man who'd come west to make his fortune panning for gold. Instead, he found an easier way to get rich in the company of the road agents gang.

What a shame...he had seemed like a nice lad, although I had not known him well...

Another flashback rushed through my mind as if it had finally escaped from captivity in my subconscious. I was dancing with this man, one of my regulars, dressed in a long, bell-shaped, red satin dress with a low-cut bodice. My jewels glistened in the candlelit saloon as we danced a schottische number together. One of the town's ministers stood outside the open doorway, preaching about the evils of dance halls and saloons—as his beady eyes bored through my elegant dress.

A car whisked past, pulling me back to this century. Something strange was happening to me here. I had to get out and walk to clear my head.

I strolled down Wallace Street past a large, two-story, brick building, the Thompson-Hickman Library and Museum. I didn't remember this impressive building—probably because it wasn't built until 1918, according to the sign. This must be where Paul worked. My heart flip-flopped as I tiptoed past the library, praying that he wouldn't look out and see me. I didn't need any more weirdness in my life today.

One step at a time, I floated down the street as if in a trance. I began to focus on the oldest structures as some of the newer ones disappeared into the recesses of my mind as if they no longer existed. My world was spiraling backward in time, back to the early gold rush days of the 1860s. Head held high, I bent demurely to scoop up my long skirts and petticoats, protecting them from the muddy ruts as I dodged the inevitable piles of horse droppings—until I looked down at the clean paved street and realized I was wearing jeans.

Detouring down Hamilton Street, I recognized the old Gilbert Brewery and the Gilberts' rambling family home perched just beyond Daylight Creek. I could almost see the Gilbert children playing in the yard and in the beer park across the muddy road. In 1863, Gilbert Beer had been produced and bottled in this old brewery. Today the building was closed, although it was used in the summertime for old-fashioned performances of the Brewery Follies. Today, a lopsided antique wagon was parked beside the building. An image of a ghost loomed eerily from a cobweb-framed window on the upper level. Ancient trees spread out across the property and over the meandering creek, their massive trunks and limbs contorted into shapes that resembled faces and spirits of the past.

Back on the main street, I recognized the old Allen and Millard Bank, built in 1864. But something was missing. The French doors and tall windows were gone. I almost expected to see a dashing man of particular interest to me peering out the Gothic windows, watching me stroll past on the boardwalk. He would check his expensive pocket watch, counting the minutes until he could be with me once again. He had to be careful to conceal our illicit relationship, as it would not be appropriate for a successful banker, not even in the context of the Wild West. Certainly not in the particular situation he found himself trapped within.

Ahhh…the old Creighton Stone Block, constructed in 1864 of locally quarried stone. Wasn't this where the weekly newspaper was once published and where the first telegraph pole was planted? The entire block housed businesses of all sorts to meet the needs of this rapidly growing town. It was hard to believe today that some thirty thousand people had once lived in Virginia City and other nearby communities stretched out along Alder Gulch.

I was once again jolted back to reality as I passed several people on the street, friendly people who nodded and greeted me warmly. A stranger in their midst, I felt welcomed although I knew I would also be the object of ongoing conversations throughout the town. Who was I? Why was I here? Did I understand and love the historic Virginia City culture as much as they did? Or was I here to try to initiate change, to destroy all that these good people had worked so hard to preserve for the past 150 years?

Summer tourists long gone, the residents of Virginia City were settling down and going about their daily business in the heart of the ghost town they loved. Shopping at Rank's Drugs for gifts, vintage clothing, or a few groceries. Picking up mail at the post office. Having lunch at the Outlaw Café where they discussed town business and politics. Slugging down a few beers at the historic Pioneer Bar. Sharing memories and ghost stories that continue to haunt this area. Aside from that, this boomtown from yesterday seemed to be closed for the winter. A hush from the past whispered through the deserted streets, escalating as the winter winds whipped through the mountain passes.

I felt compelled to continue my journey into the past, picking up speed as I headed down Wallace Street. Along the way, I stopped to read historical markers on the old buildings. I was searching for a saloon where that clock once hung on the wall. Hopefully I could find it without having to find Paul to ask for more information.

My heart began to race as I approached an old frame building with a western-style false front where two pairs of double French doors were topped by a transom of windows and an ornate wooden cornice. A faded sign identified it as the Sauerbrier Blacksmith Shop. Just a blacksmith shop? My palms were sweating as I began to feel woozy. I settled on a nearby bench on the boardwalk, unable to take my eyes off the shop.

Having calmed down, I strolled over to the building and peered through the windows. A variety of old blacksmith tools, horseshoes, and a wooden bench filled the room. But there appeared to be another small structure within, as if the blacksmith shop had been built around a small log cabin.

My face pressed against the glass, I could almost hear music floating out through the seams of that V-notched log cabin. "All hands round," a male voice boomed as dancers shuffled around the room. I was dancing in an elegant dress, aware of a handsome gentleman standing at the bar. He watched me intently before opening his poke and dumping gold dust on the bar. He paid to dance the remainder of the night with me. He was obviously a wealthy man, impeccably dressed, sporting a handlebar mustache. It was rare for a man to purchase more than one dance at a time. I hoped he was not looking for favors that I was unwilling to grant.

Lost in my fantasy, I was startled to hear a man's voice behind me. "Ma'am?"

Whirling around, I found a trim, elderly man smiling at me. He wore dusty cowboy boots, a belt with a large silver-and-turquoise buckle, and a black cowboy hat over his longish, gray hair.

"Well…ah…hello," I stammered, returning to this century.

Introducing himself as John the local historian, he asked if I had any questions about this town that he knew backward and forward—and loved with all his heart.

"I find myself intrigued with that log cabin inside the blacksmith shop," I began. "Can you tell me what it is?"

He chuckled. "It once was a hurdy-gurdy dance hall, way back in 1863. Have you ever heard of a hurdy-gurdy girl?"

"A what? Do you mean a prostitute?"

"Some of the girls were also prostitutes. More weren't. Hurdy-gurdies were dancing girls for hire in the dance halls back in the 1860s," John explained. He proceeded to explain that these dance halls opened every night after the miners and businessmen were done working for the day. In those days, there were few women in Virginia City. Most wives and children were left behind in the East until there was adequate housing here and until conditions were safe enough for them to travel. Meanwhile, the men were starved for the attention of a woman. They would clean up, learn to dance, and pay for the privilege of dancing with the hurdy-gurdies. They also purchased and drank whiskey at the dance halls. The girls made good money, enough to buy the finest silks, elegant dresses, and dazzling jewels.

"Once the wives arrived, however," John grinned, "they tried to run the girls out of business. The wives looked down on them as women of questionable repute. I'm sure they resented the fact that many of their husbands had probably paid to dance with these fancy ladies."

"Interesting." I pulled the photo of the old clock from my purse and showed it to him. He was fascinated but not sure where the clock would have come from, as there had been a number of saloons and hurdy-gurdy houses here in the past. But he did suggest that I contact Paul DuBois at the library. He had a collection of photos of the various saloons and dance halls.

I could not seem to get away from Paul DuBois.

The sun was already hanging low, blazing across Montana's big sky, by the time I bid my new friend good-bye. It had been a long and puzzling day, and I'd only begun to scratch the surface of all that I needed to do and learn here. I was intrigued with this town, a place that haunted me with strange memories of the past as if I was tapping into history itself.

Before heading back to Ennis, I drove around the residential area that included lovely old Victorian homes and quaint little cabins. Maybe I could rent a place here. Maybe I could even get a job here.

Chapter 9

Finding a job was not an easy task this time of the year. The tourist season was over, and many businesses were closing down for the winter. People were hunkering down for the season of solitude.

I pored over the sketchy want ads in the local newspaper with little luck. Sally at the Ennis Café agreed to keep an ear out for any possible jobs in the area. She knew everything that was going on in town, as she had the ear of all the regulars who stopped in for morning coffee, lunch, or dinner.

Early one morning, I set out again for Virginia City. I could not stay away. I stumbled upon The Outlaw Café, the only restaurant that was open all winter. It was a charming place filled with antiques. Black-and-white photos of local historical figures and notorious outlaws lined the walls as if these ghosts of the past were still watching over the town, reminding residents and tourists alike of their places in history. An ornate wood-carved bar with a mirrored wall dominated the room. In the backroom, a variety of antiques were for sale along with gently used toys and cowboy boots and books documenting Virginia City's notorious history.

Sipping my coffee after a hearty western-style breakfast, I gazed out the window. While I could feel a pervasive sense of the Old West flowing through the streets and buildings, I was determined to keep my head on straight today. I would not give in to the strange fantasies that had consumed me the first day I'd arrived in Virginia City. There was no explanation, I decided, aside from my overactive imagination. After all, I was a writer, wasn't I? And writers had a tendency to flip back and forth between the real world and the fictional worlds they created in their novels. And sometimes the boundaries between those worlds blurred. Sometimes things were not all they seemed to be...

"Hey! You must be new in town!" My petite waitress slipped into the chair across from me, introducing herself as Maria. She was probably about my age with short, curly, blond hair, deep blue eyes, and a flawless ivory complexion. She looked like a china doll. Her eyes sparkled with curiosity as if she welcomed anything new or different in what was probably a fairly boring town during the long winter months. With a population of about 150 people, Virginia City was rather isolated from the rest of the world once the snow fell. You couldn't always count on making it through the mountain pass to Ennis. And Sheridan, the closest town in the other direction, was about fifteen miles away.

Maria and I hit it off right away. She filled me in on what life was like in Virginia City, the place she'd lived her entire life. A single mother, she had a little girl to support, so she worked here at The Outlaw Café and picked up other odd jobs around town. She claimed to be happy with the little she had in life, focusing on her daughter. Still, she admitted she was bored to death at times. She had no life of her own. And frankly, this was not the place to meet a good man. The men, she said, were all one hundred years old, married, or obsessed with ghosts and the history of this town. Someday she would leave and venture out into the world. Someday she would find some excitement in her life. But for now, she was doing fine.

She proudly showed me several wallet photos of her "pride and joy." The toddler's name was Mia, short for Maria, and she was adorable. As Papa would say, the child was "the spittin' image of her ma." A wistful smile spread across my face.

"What about you?" she finally asked, coming up for air as she got up to fetch the coffee pot. "What are you doin' here in Virginia City?"

"Well." I hesitated. "I'm fascinated with this old town. The minute I arrived, I felt like I belonged here. It was as if I'd actually lived here many years ago." My mind began to slip down that slippery slope into the past. Catching myself, I continued, "I plan to take some photos—I frame and sell some of my work—and do some research and learn more about the old West."

"Hmm…research sounds a little boring to me. But I'd love to see your pictures. Are you staying here in VC?"

"I'd like to if I could find a place to rent. But first, I need to find a job."

"Not much here in town that I know of." Maria wrinkled her brow, deep in thought. "It's not the season, you know. The tourists are gone. Businesses are closing for the winter—except for our café, Ranks General Store, and the Pioneer Bar. That's about it. Unless you're a secretary or something. Maybe you could work for the county offices here. But I think they just laid a few gals off last month."

"Doesn't sound too promising, huh?" Despair filled my soul. I belonged here, and I needed to do something important here—once I could figure out what it was.

"Wait! You said you liked research, right?"

I nodded.

"Do you write?"

"Well, yes." I began to brighten up a bit. "I have a degree in creative writing and journalism, and I have written for several newspapers. Why?"

Maria clapped her hands in glee, leaning in across the table to share her exciting news. "Yes! I have the perfect job for you, Rose. The library is looking for someone to help the director with his research. He plans to write a book about Virginia City and the gold rush days."

My heart leaped and then sank. It *would* be the perfect job for me. A dream come true to get paid for the work I already planned to do here. But the library? The place where Paul DuBois worked?

Maria was already scribbling a name on the back of a napkin. "Paul Dubois," she announced proudly. "He's the one to contact, the director. Tell him I sent you, okay?" She grinned, obviously pleased with herself. "It would be great to have you here in town, Rose. I think we'd be good friends."

"I think so, too, Maria," I replied warmly. I could use a friend in this world. She was so open, so genuine, and so easy to talk with.

"What do you know about Paul? What is he like?" I had to ask.

"Hmmm..." She paused to collect her thoughts. "A nice man, I'd say. He comes in for lunch almost every day. Kind of keeps to himself—one of those deep thinkers, I guess. He works hard on his research and things like that. But..." She paused again. "He's a little strange in some ways."

"How's that?"

"Well, they say he's a ghost hunter. He sets his equipment up around town sometimes, even up at the cemetery in the middle of the night. He tries to find and talk with ghosts from the past." She eyed me cautiously to see my reaction, if her words had frightened me. It was obvious that she didn't want to lose her new friend.

She had my attention. "Ghosts? Do you think there are actually ghosts around here? Have you ever seen one?" I had to know.

"Can't prove there are or aren't ghosts here." She fiddled with her paper napkin, twisting it around her little finger. "Some people swear they've seen ghosts here—but they are usually friendly ghosts. You know? They don't mean no harm. It's like they have something they still need to do here on earth, or maybe they don't know they're dead, or they just like to hang around the places they used to live. I know it sounds crazy."

Maria shrugged her thin shoulders and sipped her cold coffee, waiting for my reaction.

"Very interesting. How do you know they're friendly, that they won't hurt you?"

She opened her mouth to speak but then quickly closed it as if wondering whether or not she should share something with me.

"Can you tell me more?" I asked. "I don't think it's at all crazy. We have so much to learn, and I'd really like to know everything I can possibly learn about this place—even about the ghosts who may still hang around."

"Okay." She decided to trust me and leaned closer across the table. She began to speak in a hushed tone of voice but became more animated as she told me the story of Sarah, the little ghost resident of The Outlaw Café.

For years, the staff of the café had been baffled by things that happened here, especially during the night when the cafe was closed. Somebody was moving things around—especially the toys in the back room. It was as if a child had been playing there during the night, sometimes strewing a few old marbles around the restaurant. But there was one toy in particular, a battery-operated musical clock shaped like a rocking horse, that was apparently the favored toy. Coming into work in the morning, the cook frequently found the rocking horse playing music, despite the fact that it had been turned off when he left the previous night. Thinking it strange, he would take the batteries out, only to find the toy playing again the next morning when he arrived at work.

One gloomy winter day, Maria and several of her coworkers were startled by a cold burst of air sweeping through the kitchen. Turning around, they saw a filmy apparition of a little golden-haired girl floating through the restaurant and back into the toy section. She wore an old-fashioned cotton frock. Suddenly, the image disappeared.

A happy but displaced little girl, she seemed to love playing tricks and rearranging things in the café. Sometimes they could hear her giggling in the back room as she played. Of course, nobody was there when they went to investigate. The room would be empty, yet toys would be scattered about the room.

The owners of the café decided to ask around town to see if anyone else had ever encountered a spirit like this. Sure enough, they found an elderly man who'd once lived in an apartment above what was now The Outlaw Café. He recognized the little girl as Sarah, a child who had died in this building many years ago. While he'd lived there, Sarah was a frequent visitor, leaving antique marbles and sometimes wild daisies around the room. He was pleased to hear that Sarah was still around.

"But," Maria concluded solemnly, "although we enjoy her company, I wonder sometimes if it would be kinder to help her move on, to go to the light, you know, so she can finally cross over into the next world. Just sayin'…"

"Or," it suddenly occurred to me, "do you think she could live in both worlds? Maybe she just likes to come and visit sometimes."

Maria sighed, a shy smile lighting up her face. "I hope so. Maybe she has messages for someone or unfinished business to take care of before she moves on."

The bell over the doorway tinkled as a group came in for lunch. Maria excused herself, grabbing a handful of menus and making her way to the table. Her customers greeted her warmly, asking about Mia.

The morning flew by. As I paid my bill and walked out, Maria winked at me. "Come on back, ya hear? We can talk more."

I was all the more convinced that I simply must find a way to stay here in Virginia City. I was drawn here for some reason, tugged back into another era that was long gone. Maybe I was the one who had unfinished business here. And maybe the ghosts of Virginia City could help me figure out what I needed to accomplish.

Chapter 10

Lost in thought and blinded by the sunlight, I almost bumped into a large man in the doorway of the café. I was leaving as he was coming in for lunch. Strong hands grasped my arms in an attempt to avoid a head-on collision. A shock surged through my body as I looked up into the amused face of Paul DuBois.

His hands remained on my arms longer than necessary, stirring up conflicted feelings in me. His touch was so familiar, so comforting. Yet I was also angry with and afraid of this man.

"Well, well. I was wondering when I'd run into you again, darlin'." He laughed as I pulled free from his grip. "I thought you'd have more questions about that old clock."

Of course I was dying to find out exactly where it came from. But I was too shook up to respond. Why did he just stand there staring at me, enjoying my obvious discomfort? I shielded my eyes, hiding from the light flickering in his. My feet seemed to be glued to the boardwalk, despite the fact that my mind was screaming at me to leave now.

"I'd ask you to join me for lunch," he spoke softly now, "but I've got a business lunch here today. Trying to hire an assistant at the library, and I finally got a lead that may or may not work out. Not easy finding what I'm looking for."

He must be talking about the job that Maria told me about, perhaps the only job available in this town, I thought to myself. And now he was hiring somebody else. Not that I would ever in a million years want to work with Paul DuBois. But maybe I had no choice.

"So, maybe I'll see you around?" he asked hopefully as he swung the café door open.

"Paul," my voice squeaked reluctantly.

He swung around to face me. "Yes?"

"I'm looking for a job here, and, well, I don't know if it would work out, but what exactly are you looking for in an assistant?" God, I hated myself at that moment. I felt I was about to sell my soul to the Devil.

"You're kidding!" he beamed down at me. "Here, sit for a moment. Let's talk."

He held a chair out for me at the wrought-iron table on the boardwalk and plopped down across from me. "I need someone to help me with my research about Virginia City, including some of the ghost stories from the past. You see, I'm writing a book, and truth be told, I'm not the best writer. I'm looking for someone who can write, edit, and organize information. If it works out, I may also be looking for someone to help with book publishing and marketing strategies. I know it's a lot, and I may not be able to find anyone who can do all of that." He paused. "So tell me about yourself. What kind of work do you do?"

"I write, and I research." My voice was so soft that he leaned closer to hear, too close for comfort. The brim of his cowboy hat brushed against my forehead, and I felt my face flushing. I needed this job. This is your only chance, I scolded myself. Speak up and sell yourself. Forget about your foolish feelings. You will find an appropriate way to handle them. Just lock them away like you lock up everything else that you don't want to face in life. You can do this.

So I proceeded to tell him about my skills, my degrees, and the articles I'd published. He grew more excited as I talked. When another man came out of the restaurant, wondering why Paul was late for their business lunch, he brushed him off. "Sorry, Sam, but I'll need to take a rain check. Something's come up, and I think I've filled the position. I'll call you later."

"You are perfect—for the job, of course," he blurted out. "You are hired, darlin', if the terms and salary are acceptable."

The terms and salary were even better than I'd hoped for. It was my dream job. I should be thrilled, but a nagging feeling churned through my gut. Run, Rose. No, don't run, Rose.

"Well?" he interrupted my internal struggle. "Is there something more that you need from me? I may be able to offer you a raise after your first month on the job. I'm flexible as far as hours and time off. Rose, I really hope you will accept my offer." His dark eyes pleaded with me.

"Isn't there something you need from me? Like a resume, references, samples of my writing?"

"You can bring in whatever you care to share when you report for work tomorrow morning at nine o'clock, okay? My gut reaction tells me that you are for real, Rose, and that I'd be a fool not to hire you. I suspect you are hiding or running from something...just a sense I get. But aren't we all in one way or another? It's okay by me, and I'm not one to pry. You ran to the right place, and I'm glad you're here."

"I'm not running," I began to protest and decided it was time to change the subject. "But I am looking for a place to live here. Any recommendations?"

"You're not staying in Ennis?"

"I am, but I'd like to move to Virginia City if I can find a place. Not sure my little SUV will make it over the mountain pass this winter. Do you ever have trouble doing so?"

"Oh, yes," Paul grinned. "But I have a solution. I keep a sleeping bag, extra clothes, and a few grocery staples in the back room of the library. Yes, I've spent more than a few nights camping out there when the weather sets in and closes the pass. It's not bad...you're welcome to join me." He winked at me.

I stiffened. He noticed.

"Hey, I'm just kidding. I have a strange sense of humor sometimes. I'm sorry. It probably would be a good idea for you to look around Virginia City for a rental. You may want to check out Karen's Cabin up on Idaho Street, less than a block's walk from the library. Now that tourist season is over, you may get a good deal over the winter months. It's located right behind her Victorian Gingerbread House."

He paused, carefully gauging my reaction. "Rose, I can give you an advance on your salary if you need it to settle in." Once again, his eyes tried to penetrate mine, to bore into the core of my being.

Looking away, I blurted, "No, thank you, but yes, I will accept your job offer. I do need to clarify one thing, however, before I do so."

"Anything, darlin'. You name it."

Taking a deep breath, I made my wishes clear. "I need to be sure that this remains a professional relationship. If we are going to work together, there must be clear boundaries. Crossing those boundaries can destroy a good working relationship."

That was apparently not what he wanted to hear. "But, of course," he replied in a professional tone of voice. "Does that mean I can't call you 'darlin'? Meant no harm. Didn't mean to offend you, Rose. It's just an old western figure of speech."

I had to grin at him as we shook hands across the table, ignoring the sparks that flared between us.

Paul rose from his chair, tipped his hat in his usual gentlemanly fashion, turned sharply, and sauntered down the street toward his library. He was a vision from the past in his dusty cowboy boots and tight-fitting jeans. And he'd apparently forgotten all about lunch.

I had a job and would start work tomorrow. Anxious to get back to Ennis so I could tell Lucky about our good fortune, I decided I first needed to take a drive around Virginia City to find a place to live. Lucky would have to wait for his walk.

Idaho Street? Yes, that was what Paul said. I drove past the impressive brick Thompson-Hickman Library and Museum where I would be working, turned right up the hill, and found myself on a street lined with Victorian homes of yesteryear. I passed the Gothic-styled Elling House. While I had no memories of this house, it looked haunted with its vine-covered stone walls and ornate black wrought-iron fence.

Just down the street, I found several intriguing Victorian bed-and-breakfast inns. Someday when I could afford to do so, I promised myself that I would stay at one of these places. I fell in love with The Bennett House, built in 1876. It was surrounded by lavish gardens, a porch filled with old wicker furniture, and a recently added outdoor hot tub. I could imagine soaking in the tub with someone special, beneath a star-studded sky, surrounded by the majesty of the mountains. Or sitting in the antique-filled parlor reading one of the great classic books.

Across the street, I found the Gingerbread House that Paul had mentioned. A vision from the past, this pastel Victorian lady was decked out in ornate gingerbread trim. I stopped my car, gazing in awe as a brunette middle-aged woman emerged from the garden, her basket overflowing with an assortment of fresh flowers. I inhaled the sweet scent of her delicate roses. The smell brought me back, way back, to another time.

"Hello, can I help you?" she smiled at me, obviously knowing I was a stranger in town.

"You have a wonderful place here. Your flowers are lovely."

"Thanks. It's going to freeze tonight already, and I'm trying to save everything I can. Covering plants. Cutting and bringing flowers in for my guests to enjoy."

"I'm looking for a place to rent for the winter," I informed this friendly hostess, "but I can't afford your lovely Gingerbread House. I start work at the library tomorrow, and Paul told me that you may also have a cabin for rent?"

Karen deposited her baskets of flowers on the ornate porch of her Victorian home and led me back behind the house to a little cabin overlooking the valley below. It had a spectacular view of the surrounding mountains.

This was it, my dream home. I knew I had to have it, even before she opened the door and showed me around. It had a little porch where I could watch the sunset and where I could look across the valley at the town's cemetery that was framed by mountains. Shadows of light began to play across the ever-changing craggy faces of the mountains. Aside from the aesthetic beauty of this place, it made sense. I could walk down the alley to the library every day in less than five minutes.

The interior of the cabin was cozy and had everything I needed, including Internet access and a fireplace to take the chill off cold winter nights.

"I'll take it," I announced before I even had the presence of mind to ask the cost.

"I figured you would," Karen smiled. "Paul has already called to provide an excellent reference for you. He has, in fact, charged your first month's rent to his account."

"I will pay my own way," I protested indignantly. "I do not need my employer's help."

"Work that out with him, okay? I'm pleased to have you here, Rose, and want you to know that I'm here in the Gingerbread House anytime you need anything or if you just want to talk and hang out."

Lucky and I moved into Karen's Cabin in Virginia City that afternoon, just in time to watch the sun set over the mountains. I sat in an old rocking chair on the porch overlooking the valley below, in awe over the beauty and serenity of the views from my new home. There was something almost spiritual about this place, an intense connection with the past, as if the past still lived here within the present.

Chapter 11

I quickly settled into an almost comfortable routine. Lucky and I rose with the sun and went out for an early morning walk. I had the old ghost town almost to myself as I hiked along the boardwalk, peering into the old buildings, imagining what life was like in the early days. A chill filled the air these days as snow clouds sometimes appeared on the horizon. I breathed deeply, taking it all in. I felt I belonged here, and that was a good feeling— although I sometimes had to stifle feelings of panic and terror. Something strange lurked deep within my soul, I feared. Whatever it was, this was not the time to acknowledge or deal with it.

I was becoming a firm believer in the concept of timing. Timing was everything, some important person once said. I began to believe that when the time was right, critical information would be revealed to me. It would bubble up from someplace deep inside. Until then, I would enjoy my life and absorb all that I could of this special place.

After our walks, I sat on the porch with a mug of steaming, hot coffee, thinking and preparing for my day at the library. I loved the research I was doing. In the process, I learned fascinating things about the history of Virginia City. The people who'd lived and died here were beginning to come to life for me. That was good, since I would apparently be doing most of the writing for Paul's book. A ghost writer...in more ways than one!

As for Paul DuBois, he was an unusual person. He did remain professional in his dealings with me and treated me well. But I sometimes felt him watching me as I worked. When I looked up, he would avert his glance and erect a wall between us. Still, I felt strange sensations emanating from him. It was as if he was lost in the past, puzzled, trying to figure something out.

I, of course, had my own peculiar reactions to him ever since the day we'd met at the Ennis Café. But unlike Paul, I'd buried those feelings in my hidden vault and thrown away the key. This was one of my talents.

Paul's eyes revealed a great deal of conflict. They conveyed a deep love and passion as well as a profound sense of loss, sorrow, and hopelessness.

Spikes of anger and hatred occasionally flared from the depths of those eyes. I learned to look away quickly. I felt him trying to draw me into those eyes, into a deep connection that I knew would ultimately destroy me.

While I was intrigued with him, I was also fearful. I knew he was dangerous. Sometimes I dreamed of him at night, of falling into his arms. Other times, he generated unwarranted feelings of anger, fear, and deep sadness within me. I really didn't know him at all—nor did I want to know the dark secrets that seemed to consume him.

I loved working in the old library with its massive arched French windows and old stone fireplaces. It was peaceful listening to the ticking of the old grandfather clock. When the library was busy with library patrons, I moved into my office in the back room and shut the door.

I got to work early, usually several hours before Paul arrived. I understood that he worked late some nights doing paranormal research at various locations. He was a ghost hunter. He didn't talk much about this part of his research, but he was obviously engrossed with his findings. After a good "hunt," he would furiously document and analyze evidence of the haunting he had uncovered. I was quite curious about his findings but was not about to ask him.

Most days, we buried ourselves in our respective research and had little need to converse. That was all right with me. I didn't even ask him about that old clock, the one that brought me to Virginia City. I instinctively knew where it came from—the old hurdy-gurdy dance hall that I'd been drawn to my first day in town. Someday I would confirm that. Meanwhile, the research I was doing, supplemented with several more conversations with John the town historian, was helping me to understand what those hurdy-gurdy girls were all about.

One day, Paul pulled up a chair across from me as I sat working at my desk. He smiled warmly.

"Yes?"

He glanced at the piles of books scattered haphazardly across my desk and the notebook I was making notes in. "You look busy."

I nodded.

"I'm curious why you haven't asked me more about that clock," he began quietly.

Part of me wanted to bark, "What clock?" and turn away from him in anger. Well aware that my strange reactions to this man made no sense, I bit my tongue and replied, "Well, I already know where it came from."

"You do?" He sounded surprised.

"Yes, the old hurdy-gurdy house inside the Sauerbier Blacksmith Shop."

His eyes widened in disbelief. "Well, I'll be damned. How do you know that? There were many hurdy-gurdy houses here in Virginia City, thirteen of them."

How could I explain to him that some strange force had drawn me to that place? Should I tell him or was it best not to? Do not trust this man, a weakening little voice within tried to warn me once again.

The words began to flow anyway. "This may sound weird to you, but the moment I arrived in town, I felt like I'd been here before. I recognized places and things. Something guided me to the old blacksmith shop. It was as if I remembered that place. I don't know why, but..." I stopped in midsentence. What had I done? Where was my common sense? I gasped, holding one hand over my mouth.

"Hey." Paul reached out to touch my shaking hand, his eyes full of understanding and relief. "All I can say is I'm glad I'm not the only one around here who has experienced things like what you've just described."

"Really?" I relaxed, aware of the warm sensation of his hand on mine. This time, I was unable to pull away. I was frozen in time.

"Rose, I think we have a lot more in common than either of us realize. I would like to know you better, but, of course, we need to keep this professional." He seemed to be teasing me, tempting me.

Abruptly moving my hand away from his, I nodded formally. "But, of course."

"However," he was not about to dismiss me yet. "I do know more about that clock, if you are interested."

"I thought you hated that clock and did not like talking about it."

"That's true, but do you want to know or not? I prefer never to talk of it again after today." A dark shadow flickered across his handsome face.

"Yes, I want to know everything that you know about it." I grabbed my pen and notebook to begin making notes.

"My late grandfather, the one whose house I live in, had a story about that clock that had been passed down through the generations. It happened before his time, of course. Well, there once was a special hurdy-gurdy girl who was a favorite at the dance hall that you know of. She had her pick of all the miners and merchants in town. But she fell in love with a prominent businessman who happened to be married. Unable to marry her, he still wanted to monopolize her and was jealous of the other men who spent time with her. He wanted her to think only of him, so he had that clock made for the hurdy-gurdy house and insisted it be hung on the wall in a place where his beloved would see it and hopefully think of him. He wanted to prevent her from having relationships with the other men who stalked her. She would have to walk past that clock every night when the hall closed. He wanted to be sure she didn't even think about leaving with anyone else. He even had her initials engraved on the clock."

"A. J.?" my eyes widened in shock.

"Yes, A. J. How did you know?"

"I…I don't know. I've seen that clock before someplace, and I know the initials. What was her name, Paul…this A. J.?"

"I have no idea. There are few records of any of the girls who worked in these places, and I haven't been able to figure that one out."

"What happened to her?" I held my breath. This story had to have had a sad ending.

"They say she committed suicide."

"Because of him? Because he wouldn't marry her?" I was horrified.

Paul shrugged. "I don't know. All I know is that evil lurks in that clock, some kind of spiritual residue from the past. I have no idea why my ancestors kept it in the family all these years. They cherished the damn thing. The clock must have liked them. I'm the only one that it doesn't like."

His eyes suddenly hardened as if he was embarrassed to have told me more than he planned to share. "Now that we're done discussing that god-awful clock, I have something to ask you. You know, there will be some local ghost stories in our book—"

Our book? So it was now *our book?* I couldn't help grinning.

"Is something funny?" he snapped, shifting his emotional gears once again. I seemed to have that effect on him.

"No, I'm sorry. I was just thinking about something else."

"Well, if I could have your attention, I would appreciate it. As I was saying, I think you may want to accompany me on one of my paranormal investigations so you can learn more about it. You will be the one writing and polishing my words. You need to understand the process and get to know some of the ghosts."

I hesitated, as a warning light went off in my head once again. It was blinking red, shouting "Stop!" But a green light was also pushing me forward into high gear. This could be an incredible opportunity.

He cleared his throat. "You need not be afraid. I am an expert in this area and will keep you safe. I do not take chances. Besides, to be honest, I suspect that you have the ability to sense and communicate with spirits of the past. Working together, we may discover some very interesting things."

He was right.

"Rose, I need you." His tone softened. "The success of our book depends on it. By the way, I'm giving you a raise, $100 more per week, if you agree. And, of course, you will have comp time off during the day for any night work we do."

I knew he worked nights. Red flags again. However, I impulsively decided to take him up on his offer, throwing caution to the winds. Sometimes you had to take a few risks in life.

Chapter 12

A full, orange moon lit up the black sky as it cast shadows over the gravestones and monuments scattered throughout Hillside Cemetery. Half-naked trees rustled in the breeze, their fallen leaves of many colors dancing upon the graves of spirits from the past.

I gazed in awe, huddled in a warm winter jacket, while Paul unloaded his gear. "Look at that moon," I marveled, compelled to speak. It was entirely too quiet up here in the middle of the night. I could see the lights of the sleeping town winking in the valley below.

Paul grunted, preoccupied with setting up his equipment. He had cameras, a video recorder, an electronic magnetic field detector, thermometers, infrared thermal scanners, a spotlight, and a number of flashlights.

It was spooky enough up here, I thought to myself, but all the more so since it was just several days before Halloween. Visions of ghosts and goblins seeped into my overactive imagination.

"Do you know that's the Hunter's Moon?" I continued to chatter. Papa knew all the moons and what they represented. He'd learned some of this by reading the *Farmers' Almanac*, his faithful companion. He religiously sought out weather forecasts from this annual publication before deciding when to plant and harvest his crops. In my heart, I knew that Papa and Mama would be out on their porch tonight, looking up at the same moon I was watching.

And there was Bob...yes, I still thought about him, especially on a night like this. We'd watched many a full moon together. But tonight I watched the moon with a relative stranger in a haunted cemetery that seemed to be at least a million miles from home.

Home...where was home? I thought I belonged here in Virginia City although my hometown of Walnut, Iowa tugged on my heartstrings at times. Home was supposed to be where your heart is, but what if your heart is divided into pieces that reside in different places?

Paul took time to respond, breaking into my reverie. "Why do you call it a Hunter's Moon? Isn't it a Harvest Moon?"

"It's both." I was relieved to have someone to talk with, realizing that we'd need to be quiet soon—as still as the sleeping spirits who lingered here. "But the Native Americans called it the Hunter's Moon. It represented the time of the year when they began storing up meat for the long winter."

"Okay, we're set." That was my clue to stop talking, I realized. "Are you okay?" he asked gently.

"Of course. I'm not afraid of ghosts," I teased, although I was careful to stay close by his side.

We sat side by side on a blanket in the darkness of the night, just waiting, watching his meters, checking to be sure the video recorder and audio equipment were working properly. My eyes searched for any signs of life—or death—or something that fell someplace in between the two extremes. Paul used a night light device of some kind and frequently snapped still photos into the darkness. Trying to capture orbs of psychic light or ectoplasm, he told me.

I heard his steady breathing close beside me as I watched my breath curling into the chill of an almost-winter's night. A wolf howled in the distance. Otherwise, it was deathly still.

Minutes ticked by slowly, cautiously, unwilling to wake the dead who rested here in this mountainside cemetery. I occasionally glanced back across the winding road toward Boot Hill Cemetery. The five road agents were buried there after they were hung in January 1864. After that, nobody in town wanted their loved ones buried in the same cemetery with those murderous criminals. So Hillside Cemetery was created a safe distance away from them.

Suddenly, Paul came to life. "Okay, we've got action," he whispered to me as he checked his equipment and began snapping more pictures. His EMF detector was registering strong disruptions of the electromagnetic field, and the motion detector was picking up signals of something approaching as the temperature dropped dramatically.

"Hello?" Paul called out into the darkness, startling me, as he fiddled with the settings on his audio equipment. "Who are you? How can I help you? I'm Paul, and I have Rose here with me. We're here to help. We want to know about your life, what we can do to help you complete your business here on earth."

Paul waited, hoping for a response. I held my breath, my heart pounding so loudly I was afraid that Paul or the ghosts in the cemetery would hear.

"Hello? Do you have a story about your life that you want the world to know? We can help. If you're not sure you want to talk to us yet, that's okay. We can come back another time."

Suddenly, Paul's equipment went haywire. The batteries abruptly died. He'd apparently lost communication with a spirit who didn't feel like talking.

"Damn!" he exploded, grabbing a flashlight. "Rose, I need to get a few backup things from my truck. Stay here. I'll be right back." He turned on a powerful spotlight to keep me company while he ran to his nearby truck.

"Paul!" I whispered into the darkness as he disappeared. I was alone with the ghosts of the past, but I knew he'd be back within minutes. Even if he didn't care about me, he'd never let this ghost get away if he could help it. Breathe deeply, Rose, I reminded myself. Breathe deeply.

I had to get up and stretch now that the silence was broken. It was cold—in more ways than one. I walked cautiously, staying within the beam of the spotlight, swinging my flashlight from side to side to see where I was going, trying not to step on the graves surrounding me.

I was awed by the monuments erected to honor important historical figures of the past. Angels reaching into heaven. However, I soon discovered a long-forgotten area of crumbling, tilting, and broken stones. No flowers on these graves. They were stifled with rambling weeds, crumbling into the dust. Names of the deceased were barely legible.

Something gripped my heart, urging me to venture farther into the depths of the cemetery. Fear was no longer an issue. I was on a mission although I had no idea what it was. I thought I could hear Paul's voice calling to me, frantically, through the melodious voices of the winds that were now singing in concert over the cemetery.

Darkness descended as the moon disappeared behind the clouds, refusing to illuminate Planet Earth any longer on this night of the moon. I swung my flashlight in circles and suddenly felt compelled to drop to my knees before a simple gravestone. It was crumbling into the earth, pockmarked from years of neglect and covered with an assortment of weeds that I impulsively began to pull out by the roots. I had to dig deep to uncover the inscription, to find out who laid buried beneath this particular stone. My fingernails were encrusted with dirt, and my fingers began to bleed.

"AMELIA 1868" it read. That was all. Nothing more. No last name. No date of birth.

I shut off my flashlight and began to sob uncontrollably, alone in the dark. I had no idea why I was reacting so strongly. I was enraged somehow, feeling that I needed to pursue justice on behalf of this long-forgotten woman.

As I sat there in a crumpled heap on the freezing ground, streaks of dirt running down my face, I became aware of another figure lurking in the dark. He sat in the shadows beside Amelia's grave, not far from me. Paul had apparently found me, but he was not speaking or acknowledging my presence.

I could barely see him in the dark, but I felt overwhelming grief pouring out from his soul. His love for Amelia was beyond anything I'd ever known—the kind of love that transcends lifetimes. But why was Paul brooding in such a heartbroken fashion over this Amelia person? Pangs of jealousy ripped through my soul before I had time to logically dismiss them.

As the moon and stars reappeared in the skies above, I glanced over at Paul, but he was gone. He had magically disappeared. There was no sign of another human being. I tried to turn my flashlight back on. It was dead. What was I doing alone out here in a haunted cemetery in the middle of the night?

"What the hell do you think you're doing?" Paul's voice suddenly thundered from behind me. He was nowhere near the place that I swore I'd just seen him grieving beside Amelia's grave. I tried to find the image that had just disintegrated before my eyes, but I could not. All that was left was the real, live Paul DuBois who was moving in from another direction—and not the least bit happy with me.

"I'm sorry, Paul," I began. Why was I always apologizing to this man, even if he was my employer?

"You know you've just ruined tonight's investigation, don't you?"

"But I've found something else that we need to pursue," I began hesitantly.

"Something more important than the presence we just picked up? Get real, Rose. What do you think you are doing?"

He was not happy with me. Hadn't he told me that I had paranormal abilities? Well, maybe I'd just discovered something important. I had more questions, however, than answers: Who was Amelia? Why was I drawn to her so strongly? And...who was that grieving man beside her grave? It *had* to have been Paul.

I was not happy with him either. "Why did you sit there by Amelia's grave, grieving for her?" I had to know.

"What? Who the hell is Amelia? And why would I be sitting by her grave?" Paul shook his head in confusion and then stiffened, swinging his flashlight around with a sense of urgency. Trying to see into the shadows. "Look, we need to get out of here. Something is wrong. I do not like this part of the cemetery."

Paul grabbed my arm and began pulling me along with him. It was useless to protest. He seemed angry and scared.

"Are you trying to tell me that wasn't you sitting there near me in the darkness?"

"Absolutely not! Look, your imagination must be playing tricks on you. There's nobody here."

"Not even a ghost?" My eyes grew huge. "Isn't that what we're looking for?"

I tried to tell him about Amelia. He expressed no emotion aside from well-concealed shadows of pent-up anger and loss. "Look, Rose, she was probably just another prostitute in the gold rush days. She died in 1868. So what? Let her go."

"Never!" I exploded, surprising myself. "I can't do that, Paul. I need to find out who she was and what happened to her. I will not let it go."

"I'm telling you to let it go!" He raised his voice. "We have more important things to do, do you understand?"

"No, I do not, and I will not quit until I've discovered the truth. Fire me if you like, and I'll do the research on my own."

"Why are you so obsessed with this? You're not making any sense," he scolded me. He was obviously fascinated, yet angry, over my reaction. But his curiosity about all things related to the paranormal realm eventually overruled his anger.

"Why, Rose? " His tone softened into a more professional mode. "I need to know what you've discovered, what you think about all of this."

"Amelia was not a prostitute." I glared at him as he threw his equipment into the back of his truck. We climbed in, sitting as far away from each other as possible.

"How do you know that?"

"I just know. That's all. I can't explain it, but I need to find out who she was and what happened to her. It was not a happy ending."

"I'm sure you have proof of that," he challenged me. "You have a lot to learn about paranormal investigation. We don't just make things up or let our imaginations run wild. We need proof, documentation."

I ignored him. We rode in icy silence until he pulled up to my cabin.

"So am I fired?" I had to ask, suddenly worried I'd gone too far. I loved my job, and I needed to hold onto it.

"No, you're not," he sighed in exasperation. "I expect you to report for work tomorrow as usual. It's two a.m. Sleep in tomorrow morning, and plan to be at the library by noon. I expect you to write down everything you thought you saw or felt tonight. I'll need it by tomorrow afternoon."

Paul did not look at me. I felt a heady blend of passion and sorrow beginning to erupt within him as he surrounded himself with a wall of ice. A wall designed to protect him from something I did not understand. Maybe he didn't either.

"Okay, but you need to know that I will be pursuing the identity of Amelia and helping her accomplish her mission. I heard you tell the spirits in that cemetery that you'd help them complete their business and move on, right?"

"Yes, I did."

"So, why can't we help Amelia accomplish her unfinished business?"

"I don't want to go there. Believe me, she was a whore, not worth your time. Otherwise, she would have had a proper tombstone and burial."

I began to bristle once again but was not about to let him know that. I had no idea why he was so hostile toward Amelia and no idea why I was I so eager to help her.

"I will prove you wrong." I attempted a weak smile, but he wasn't looking. He had a death grip on his steering wheel as he stared straight ahead into the night.

Conflict seemed to permeate the world that Paul and I shared together. Yet it seemed to be our destiny to work together.

Chapter 13

My head was reeling as I climbed into bed that night. Nothing made sense. I thought of Amelia and that strange ghost-man grieving at her grave. And then there was Paul.

Tossing and turning, I finally remembered Mama's age-old advice. "Sleep on it," she'd tell me whenever I was struggling to figure something out. I desperately needed sleep. Maybe things would become clearer by morning.

My last thought was of Amelia. As I slipped into the world of my dreams, memories of the past began to bubble up into my mind.

I was a little girl again, playing with my imaginary friend. I bolted upright in bed when I remembered that I'd named my little friend Amelia! A strange name that I'd never heard before. "Where did you ever come up with a name like that?" Mama had asked. I had no answer.

Amelia and I used to play in the cemetery just beyond our rolling fields. We played hide-and-seek among the tombstones, monuments, and gnarled old trees that resembled ghosts and witches. We told ghost stories, although I did most of the talking. Amelia wasn't real, but she was my best friend in those early years. She loved mountains, lakes, and rivers, although she couldn't swim and was terrified of drowning.

I suddenly remembered a special tombstone in that old cemetery. Amelia loved this one because the inscription on the stone said simply "AMELIA," with no last name. It did include dates of birth and death, however.

I could still see that old gravestone in Walnut's South Cemetery. It was located right between two family plots. We never knew which family Amelia belonged to or if she belonged at all. But she'd been buried just south of a beautiful white angel statue. That angel was taller than I was and seemed to watch over Amelia's grave. I always believed she had magical powers connecting us to God and that she could hear our prayers. We sat at her feet sometimes, absorbing a deep sense of peace. Other times, a pervasive sadness seemed to radiate from her angelic face as she looked down at Amelia's grave.

When she was sad, we'd pick wild daisies and place them beside Amelia's grave and at the feet of the angel. There was an inscription on the angel that said something like "Gone but not forgotten," if I remembered right.

I tried hard to remember the dates on Amelia's stone back in Walnut. Then it hit me. She'd been born in 1868, the very year that Virginia City's Amelia died. A chill ripped through me. This was eerie.

Amelia...the name haunted me.

I remembered a story my parents told me, one I'd long forgotten. I was a toddler, just learning to talk. Mama was trying to teach me to say my name. "Rose," she repeated slowly, over and over again.

"No, no, no!" I'd screamed, shaking my head as my eyes filled with tears. Upset, I kept pointing at myself and screaming something that sounded like "Melia."

Mama thought I was referring to myself as "me." She was surprised at how upset I always got, and that I seemed to hate my name. Now, looking back, I wondered if I could have been trying to say "Amelia." After all, that's what I later named my imaginary friend.

I began to fear I was losing my mind as I obsessed over this name and all of the strange coincidences surrounding it. For some unknown reason, this was very important to me. But a part of me felt like I was getting in too deep.

I needed to ground myself in the real world, I decided, instead of focusing on ghosts, imaginary friends, and unexplainable events.

❧

Gazing out the window, I watched the sun peek over the mountains. It was going to be a beautiful day, I decided. Throwing on a pair of jeans and a warm hooded sweatshirt, I ran a brush through my tangled mass of hair, brushed my teeth, and woke Lucky.

"Time for your walk, buddy." I ruffled his fur. He yawned, stretched, and wagged his tail, eager for our morning walk.

"We have the entire morning to spend together," I chattered to him as usual. "I don't have to go into work until noon."

Lucky's tail wagged harder and faster, thumping against the door. I wondered sometimes how much dogs actually understood.

Virginia City still slept as far as I could tell. An occasional light filtered out from several of the houses. I could see that Karen, my landlord in the

Gingerbread House, was already up. She poked her head out the door as we walked past.

"Good morning, Rose!" she called out.

"Morning, Karen." I liked her and hoped to get to know her better.

"Everything okay at your place? Just let me know if you need any-thing."

"Thanks, I'm lovin' it. It's perfect for us. If you'd like to come over for coffee someday, let me know."

"As a matter of fact, I was thinking the same thing. Thinking of asking you over for coffee—say tomorrow morning? I make some mean huckleberry scones and would love to show you my house."

"That sounds wonderful, but I need to be to work by nine."

"How about eight then?"

As I accepted her invitation, she grinned. "I see you had a late date last night with that handsome young Paul DuBois."

Blushing, I informed her, "We were just doing some research. I'm not dating my boss." I wasn't, after all. So why could I feel my cheeks turning red?

"Hmmm, research in the middle of the night? I personally think that the two of you would make a very nice couple." Her telephone rang, and she excused herself. "See you in the morning."

A smile spread across my face as Lucky and I walked down Idaho Street admiring the Victorian houses and old cabins. Most of the places in town were on the National Register of Historic Places. Many had plaques provid-ing information on the history of the house or business. I stopped to read several of them, appreciating all that this town had to offer.

Instead of hiking down the boardwalk on Wallace Street, I impulsively decided to head up the hill past the old Gilbert Brewery, all the way up to the cemetery. I wanted to see it in the light of day—and to visit Amelia's grave again.

It was an invigorating hike on this chilly, late fall morning. Snow clouds hung in the distant sky, just waiting to officially begin the long winter season. I could see my breath in the air.

Finally, we stopped at the intersection between the two cemeteries— Boot Hill where the road agents were buried and Hillside where Amelia and the rest of the town were buried. The valley shimmered in the early morning sunshine far below. Ripples of light flickered through the trees, illuminating the historic ghost town buildings. Turning around in circles, I was surrounded by mountains.

Moving on, Lucky and I marched through the old wrought iron gate and began to wander around the cemetery. We stopped to look at the stones and monuments and to read the inscriptions. I recognized the names of some of the town fathers and early pioneers from the research I was doing.

Our final destination was Amelia's grave. I stood quietly, honoring this unknown woman, thinking thoughts to her. Who are you? How can I help you? I repeated these words in my mind, over and over again.

Suddenly, Lucky began getting restless as if something was scaring him. He began to whine as his fur stood on end. Strange. He was tugging hard on his leash, wanting to leave.

I looked around cautiously. Nobody was there, not even a squirrel to excite him. My big, dumb dog loved to chase squirrels although he probably wouldn't know what to do if he ever caught one.

"Okay, Lucky, I guess it's time for us to leave, huh?" I gave in. "Just let me snap a few pictures first." I pulled my digital camera from my pocket and shot Amelia's grave from several different angles.

Lucky continued to whine and strain on his leash. When we headed back down to the valley, he calmed down and was fine once we left the cemetery. Was there something up there that he could sense but I couldn't see?

We proceeded down Wallace Street past all the stores. Maria was right. Most places were closed now that tourist season was over. I saw that Rank's Drug Store was already open. It looked so familiar to me, almost as familiar as the blacksmith shop. There were a few changes, but I became so intrigued that I decided to go in and look around. I tied Lucky up to a hitching post on the boardwalk and went in.

A friendly older woman with a name tag that said "Emma" greeted me as I wandered around in awe. It was as if I'd stepped back into another lifetime. Victorian clothing, hats, jewelry, shawls, even lace parasols and crocheted gloves filled the store. Bloomers. Lace fans. I could imagine myself shopping here long ago, buying some of these beautiful items. There was a fascinating collection of Western American history books, including some about Virginia City that I simply must buy someday.

"This place is incredible." I beamed at Emma. "How old is it?"

"It was built in 1864, and it's the oldest operating store in Montana," she replied proudly.

1864. Amelia may have shopped here...

"The clothing we carry is what the Victorian ladies and gentlemen would have purchased here in 1864. People today purchase these items to wear at Virginia City's Grand Balls."

"Fascinating," I murmured as a haunting image from long ago spiraled into my mind. As it did, I gripped the counter to steady myself. "Jack Slade?" My words surprised me as they tumbled out.

"Why, yes," she brightened. "This is the place where he was hung in 1864, hung from a post out back behind the store. He was arrested right here in this store."

1864 again...

Emma continued to tell the story, one I'd not yet heard, although I recalled that Jack Slade's name was on the list of chapters for the book Paul and I were writing. Perhaps Paul was handling that one.

Slade, Emma informed me, was a handsome and courageous man whom some once felt was a true hero. He was an Overland Stage agent and gunfighter who fearlessly protected his passengers from robbers and attacks by the Indians. He had many friends and a devoted wife, but he was also a hell raiser, especially when drunk. While on a drunken bender, he'd terrorize the town, racing his horse up and down the main street, shooting into the air. He'd ride his horse right into the saloons, shooting his pistol, busting up doors and furniture, and harassing the girls in the brothels and dance halls.

Finally, after one particularly ugly episode involving his refusal to obey orders issued by the sheriff, the Vigilantes arrested him and hung him promptly—even before his wife, Virginia, had time to come to his rescue. She was not one to be reckoned with. But the town had had enough of her husband's drunken terrorism. He'd finally crossed the line.

"The town folks and history itself can't agree on whether Slade deserved to be hung or not," Emma sighed. "Poor Virginia was devastated and furious. One of her husband's friends had raced out to her place to warn her about what was happening, thinking perhaps she could talk some sense into the men who were already preparing to hang her husband. Virginia, an expert horsewoman, mounted her black stallion and raced furiously into town.

But she was too late. Her beloved husband was dead, swinging from a noose right behind this store."

Chills rushed through me as a tear trickled down my cheek. "How sad. Mr. Slade could be a perfect gentleman when he was not inebriated," I protested delicately. "Truth be told, he cut a dashing figure, one that was difficult for any woman to resist."

Emma looked at me curiously as she adjusted her wire-rimmed bifocals, hoisting them farther up on her nose. Nodding eagerly, she leaned in toward me, glancing around the store to be sure we were alone.

"They say that Virginia never really left Virginia City," she whispered. "Some of the old-timers swear they've seen her on very still nights when the moon casts reflections over the mountains that stand guard over this valley. They hear the sound of hoof beats racing down the mountainside into the valley, getting closer and closer. Then a cloud of dust materializes, and suddenly, a ghostly apparition of Virginia Slade emerges, illuminated by the shadows of the moon. She's riding her wild black stallion, her black skirts billowing out behind her as her raven hair flies wildly in the wind. A low moan of agony and desperation emerges from her throat, building into a deafening scream. They say her bloodcurdling wails echo throughout the valley and the surrounding Tobacco Root Mountains."

I tried to comprehend Virginia's pain, to understand how she could have loved this man so much that she remained here after death, reliving the tragic past. Was she still trying to find her beloved husband?

"So, that's the story of Jack and Virginia Slade in a nutshell," Emma sighed. "I have some great books about them if you're interested."

"I am, and I will be back, Emma. Thanks so much, but I have my poor dog tied up outside. I'd better run now. Oh, my name is Rose. I'm the new assistant at the library, and I'm doing research about Virginia City."

"Pleased to meet you, Rose." Emma extended her hand, which I shook warmly. "I suspected that's who you were. Small town, you know. I've lived here all my life...seventy years or more, but who's counting? If you want to talk someday, I can tell you tales to make your hair stand on end."

I grinned at her, excited to have found such a wonderful source of information. "Thanks, I will take you up on your offer."

Lucky was anxiously waiting for me. Our morning together was going all too fast. I decided not to take time to stop at the blacksmith shop/hurdy-gurdy hall today as usual. I'd had enough ghostly excitement for one day.

Walking past the post office, I almost stumbled into Paul, who was coming out with a large package under his arm. "We seem to have a habit of running into each other, don't we?" He grinned as if he'd forgotten all about last night.

"Morning, Paul." I grinned back. "I guess we do."

"Did you get any good photos at the cemetery this morning?" He raised his eyebrows, enjoying the opportunity to surprise me once again.

I frowned. "What? How did you know I was there?"

"Small town, Rose. You may want to take a look and see how your pictures turned out. I'd like to see them."

As I pulled my camera from my pocket, he set his package on the bench, sat down beside it, and motioned for me to join him. I did.

"Not sure I got anything much," I began as I scrolled through the photos. "It's an awesome cemetery, and I was just trying to capture the views."

"Sure...especially Amelia's grave," he sighed with a hint of exasperation. "Wait! Can I take a look at that?" He reached for my camera. He began zooming in, looking closely. Then he extended the camera to me, grinning from ear to ear. "Do you see anything unusual?"

I looked closely. All I could see was a blob of transparent light, apparently a reflection from the sunlight filtering through the trees.

"You've captured an orb, Rose—ectoplasm, or psychic energy. You were right, there is at least one spirit lurking around this Amelia's grave. Good job!" He patted me on the back and then impulsively ran his big hand across my shoulders, massaging them gently.

I trembled as waves of hot and cold streamed through me. Suddenly, he jerked his hand away as if he'd been jolted by a bolt of electricity. Shaking our heads in tandem, we rose from the bench, bid each other good-bye, and went our separate ways.

I arrived at the library promptly at noon to find Paul absorbed in his research, furiously tapping the keys of his laptop. After exchanging pleasantries with the library staff, I slipped into my office and went to work. But I could not stop thinking about Jack Slade.

Finally, I knocked softly on Paul's door. No answer. I knocked again. He was obviously deep in thought. "Hello?"

Bringing himself back into the present, he swung around to find me standing in his doorway. A pleased but puzzled expression spread across his face before he shut down. "Yes?"

Be professional, I cautioned myself as I handed him several pages I'd just printed off from my laptop. "You wanted documentation of what happened last night at the cemetery. Here it is."

"Hey, thanks, Rose. Anything else?" He was obviously anxious to get back to whatever he was working on.

"Just one thing. Jack Slade."

"What?" Paul's large frame stiffened in his chair as his eyes hardened into solid lumps of coal. Sparks of anger flared across the room. "What *about* Jack Slade?" He clenched his fists, trying to hide them from me.

"WOW! So you don't like him anymore than you like Amelia? Why is that, Paul? What is going on here?" Stunned, I was unable to contain my questions.

He turned away from me, glaring at his computer screen. I waited. Finally, he swiveled his chair around to face me. He was not smiling. "Why do you ask so many questions?"

"Because I thought I was here to help in your research."

"You are, but you keep coming up with irrelevant things…like Amelia, the whore."

"She was not a whore!" I exploded once again. "And I will prove that to you. For now, all I want is to know about this Jack Slade. Isn't he on the outline for our book?"

"He is, and I will handle that chapter. Why do you care about him?" From the look on his face, I could have sworn that he was consumed with a misplaced sense of jealousy over poor Mr. Slade.

"I just heard about his tragic hanging, Paul. To me, he seems to have been a kind and courageous gentleman—except when he was drinking."

"And how would you know that, darlin'? You've sure as hell changed— and that's not a compliment," he spat.

I was bewildered. "I've changed? Since when? And how would you know? You have no idea who I am, Paul."

His eyes widened. He shook his head as if to clear the cobwebs from his brain. "Not sure why I said that. Guess I was thinking of somebody else. You remind me of somebody else, that's the problem."

I waited silently, sensing he was still simmering inside.

"You should know that this Slade was a bastard. He devoured innocent women and ruined their lives—as well as the lives of all who loved these women."

"How do you know that? Where's your proof?" I hotly contested his unwarranted accusation. Something within me knew beyond a doubt that Paul was wrong. Jack Slade was not the kind of man to abuse any woman. His wife, Virginia, had loved him dearly, and he had loved her.

Silence dominated the room once again as Paul's eyes glazed over. He seemed to retreat into a world I was not yet a part of and hopefully would never be. The only sound was the rhythmic ticking of the grandfather clock in the main room of the library.

"Paul, you may know things I do not know. But you need to realize that I also have inner knowledge and very strong intuition. Sometimes I feel like I can go back in time to relive history. Who is to say that I'm wrong? And what makes you think you know the truth about Mr. Slade, or about Amelia?"

"You don't give up, do you? Maybe we're more alike than I thought. Maybe our differences of opinion will actually help us come up with a better book. Maybe…if we don't kill each other first." He ran his fingers through his mass of unkempt hair, sighing in frustration.

"That's an awful thing to say!" I shuddered. "I will leave you alone." I slipped out of his office, my emotions flipping back and forth between fear and desire. There was something about the wild streak in this brooding man that made him all the more handsome—and irresistible.

"Come back tomorrow, Rose, please?" His eyes softened into pools of swirling dark chocolate, pleading with me, begging me to understand.

I did not answer him. Closing the door behind me, I left the library. For the life of me, I did not understand this man's strange behavior or my intense reaction to him. But I knew I would be back. I would never turn my back on Paul…or would I?

Chapter 14

I needed a break from this insanity. Maybe a walk would do me good, I decided, and stopped home to pick up Lucky. We hiked up into the hills and through the residential sections of town.

On Idaho Street, just a block from my cabin, I paused outside the historic Saint Paul's Episcopal Church. A beautiful English Gothic-style church constructed with sandstone blocks, it had a number of intriguing arched stained glass windows. A sign said it was built in 1902. I was suddenly homesick for my little church in Walnut. I hadn't been to church since I left home four months ago, and I missed it. My parents would be appalled if they knew.

Maybe this church would become my new church home. Maybe I'd go to services here this Sunday. With my luck, Paul was probably a member. I hoped not...or did I actually hope he was? I couldn't seem to make up my mind.

Enough, I scolded myself as I walked up the stairs into the church and tried the massive wooden door. It was open, so I tied Lucky up outside and entered. Alone in the entrance hall, I peeked into the church. The stained glass windows glowed in the darkness as beams of sunlight filtered through them, casting shadows of light upon the ornately carved wooden pews.

As my eyes grew accustomed to the semi-darkness, I walked down the aisle toward the front of the church. I paused before the sunlit windows, engulfed with a profound sense of peace and hope.

Suddenly, I felt a presence behind me. I spun around to see what looked like a nun in a black robe kneeling on a prayer bench, her head bowed. I could not see her face, and she did not look up from her prayers. Not wanting to bother her, I tiptoed out, my eyes glued to her form. As I passed her, I was almost overwhelmed with a sense of comfort that flowed through me. Still, she did not speak or lift her eyes. Then she suddenly disappeared, leaving no trace.

Was I losing my mind? I hadn't taken my eyes off her. I searched the church but found no signs of anyone having been there.

Strange things seemed to be happening here in Virginia City, things that I learned some of the locals simply took for granted. Maybe I'd stop at the café to see if Maria was working. I could ask her about what I'd just encountered without feeling like a fool.

Maria was glad to see me when I came in and sat down with me at my favorite table by the windows. I could keep an eye on my dog from here. He was stretched out on the boardwalk, sniffing the smells of home-cooked food wafting from the restaurant.

"Just coffee today, Maria. I was hoping to see you."

She grinned, sensing I had a burning question to ask her. "What's up?"

After telling her about my experience at the church, she smiled. "You've just met Sister Irene."

"Who? But she disappeared before I could speak with her."

"Of course. She died in 1880. She's one of our best-loved ghosts, Rose."

"That figures. What is it about me and ghosts?" I sighed, beginning to accept that I seemed to attract them.

Maria shrugged her shoulders. "You know, it's an honor to see Sister Irene. She seems to show herself to those whom she wants to comfort or protect. It's a good sign. Anyway, she arrived in Virginia City on a stagecoach when she was only eighteen years old. She and several other nuns came to work in the crude Saint Mary's Hospital.

"Everyone loved her. She was full of enthusiasm and zest for life, in spite of the harsh conditions here. She taught the children about religion and the Bible. While the nuns had no medical training, they provided basic first aid. But mostly, they provided sympathy and spiritual inspiration."

"It must have been a hard life here in those days." I was intrigued.

"Oh, yes. The sisters carried heavy buckets of water from the well, made their own soft soap, used washboards to clean their clothes, and had to carry wood and coal for their heat stoves. They got by with very limited medical supplies. Still, Sister Irene never complained. She always had a smile on her face, they say, and would help anyone."

"You know a lot about her, Maria. But why do you think she lingers here?"

"I think she still feels a responsibility to help the people of Virginia City. It's like she senses when someone needs something from her. Then she comes back, like a guardian angel. She's been seen praying in the church before. Others have seen her walking down the street where she used to live or sitting beside their sickbeds."

A troublesome thought entered my mind and a frown wrinkled my forehead. Maria noticed and waited for my question.

"So," I began cautiously, not sure I wanted to hear the answer, "should I be worried that Sister Irene appeared to me? Is she trying to protect me from something bad?"

"Maybe." Maria hesitated. "Or maybe she's here to guide you on your journey. Maybe just to comfort you. I can't say, but I wouldn't worry about it. I'd be glad she's here for you. She won't be hanging around, Rose. You may never see her again. But I believe that if you need her help, she will be here."

"Wow, I feel like one of the chosen ones," I grinned. "How do you know so much about her?"

"Because she was here for me once when I was at the end of my rope. She saved me." Her eyes grew misty. "But that's not a story for today. Maybe I'll tell you someday...just not here in the café. Maybe we could meet for a beer some night down the street at the Pioneer Bar?"

"I'd like that. See you later, Maria. And thanks."

"Anytime. Take care, ya hear?"

Chapter 15

The sun was setting in a fiery blaze behind the peaks of the Tobacco Root Mountains by the time I returned to my cabin. A winter's chill was in the air, so I bundled up in my red winter jacket and black fur cap. I could not resist sitting out on my porch with a glass of red wine, watching the glorious spectacle unfolding before me. One by one, the lights of the town turned on around me, reminding me that I was not alone in the Universe.

As shadows of the night began to creep across the landscape, I noticed that the lights of the library were still on. I could see Paul's office from my rocking chair. Rocking harder to keep warm—or to fight my conflicted feelings—I continued watching his window. Perhaps it was my imagination, but I thought I saw him peering out his window, watching me.

Suddenly, the lights of the library went out, the door swung open, and a man stepped out into the dusk. It was Paul, of course. He hiked down the alley that led to my place. Before I could escape into my cabin, he called out, "Rose, wait. Please."

I froze in place as heavy, wet snowflakes began to fall around me. I'd always loved the first snow of the season. It would be beautiful up here in the mountains, I thought, as I captured a snowflake on my black glove. Admiring the delicate shapes of the snowflakes swirling around me, I felt like a child again. I felt like making snow angels, like dancing in the snow.

Despite myself, I was grinning from ear to ear by the time Paul arrived. He leaned heavily against the railing of my porch. His eyes smiled, watching my delight over the falling snow. "This is the real you," he whispered hoarsely. "An innocent child, a beautiful young lady."

I felt my cheeks turning pink.

"Maybe someday we will dance in the snow together or go for an old-fashioned sleigh ride followed by an oyster feed at midnight. And after that…"

"What?" I found my voice at last, breaking the spell that he seemed to be lost within. "Isn't that what the young people did back then in the 1800s?"

"Why, yes. Oh, to have lived then. That's where I belong, Rose. Some-how I think you also belong to that era. Have you ever felt that way?"

I had to admit that I'd always been entranced with the Victorian age, that I also longed to have lived then, and that I seemed to know more about life in those days than was probably good for me.

The snow came down harder and harder. While I was sheltered by the overhang on the porch, Paul stood in the alley with layers of snow covering him. He looked like a snowman. I couldn't help laughing.

"What's so funny?" he asked, oblivious to the fact that he was covered with a thick layer of pure white snow. His black hair and beard had even turned white.

"You look like a snowman," I giggled.

With that, he scooped up a handful of snow, shaped it into a snow-ball, and playfully hurled it at me. The snowball fight was on. We chased each other around the yard, tossing snowballs, and finally collapsing on the ground beneath a huge tree that had been disrobed of all her summer fin-ery. Paul pinned me down, washing my face with snow as my arms and legs flailed in all directions. I tried to get away...but not very hard.

Suddenly, our playful antics gave way to an insatiable fire that burned deep within our souls. His mouth found mine, hungrily devouring me, as I responded in like. It was as though we'd been waiting forever for this mo-ment, but also as if we'd done this many times before. I knew his kiss, one I'd never forget, one I'd longed for since the day I was born.

If it wasn't for the neighbor's car driving past, I don't know what would have happened. The headlights jolted us back to reality. Reluctantly, we part-ed and stood up, brushing the snow off our clothes.

"I'm...I'm...sorry. I don't know what got into me. It just felt so right at the time."

"It's okay," I whispered, my heart still racing.

"Are you sure?"

"I'm sure, but...I guess I better get in and feed my dog." I looked down at the ground, wondering if it would be so wrong to invite him in.

He waited, obviously thinking the same thing. Minutes ticked by. Nei-ther of us spoke.

Finally, he broke the silence. "I know. We need to keep it professional, right? It's the right thing to do. We will do that, if that's what you want..." His eyes searched mine hopefully.

"I...I don't know what I want," I blurted, avoiding eye contact with him.

"So maybe there's hope for us, someday?"

"I can't answer that, Paul. I'm sorry. For now, can we just work together?"

"Of course." He hung his head.

"Why did you come over anyway?" I asked gently, digging the heels of my boots into the snow.

"Oh, I almost forgot. I came to tell you that a major snowstorm is moving in. Hopefully, you can walk to the library in the morning. If it's too bad, wait until it is safe to do so."

"What about you?" I was suddenly concerned.

"I'm spending the night at the library, in my sleeping bag," he grinned. "Not safe to drive over the pass to Ennis tonight—or back in the morning."

"Have you had dinner, or what will you eat?" That was dumb, I reprimanded myself. But it was too late. The words had already escaped from my mouth.

"I'll get by with a few candy bars and my bottle of water," he sighed dramatically. "There are no restaurants open in town at this time of night, you know. Not in the winter."

Throwing caution to the winds, I invited him for dinner. It wouldn't be much, I told him, but I was planning to make Italian spaghetti, garlic bread, and a salad. He gladly accepted.

After we'd dried off by the fireplace, I made dinner. I could not help noticing his rippled muscles that throbbed beneath the wet shirt that clung to his body. They made me shudder.

We shared a bottle of wine by the fire, talked easily about anything and everything—everything except Amelia and Jack Slade, that is. Without their interference, we seemed to get along just fine—as if we'd known and cared about each other forever.

Paul insisted on doing the dishes while I chilled out on the sofa by the fireplace, trying to convince myself that I was not falling in love with this man.

With a gentle kiss at the door, he bid me good night and ventured out into the blizzard, trudging his way back to the library. I watched carefully, making sure that he made it back safely. Back to a sleeping bag that awaited him in the back room of the library. While he tried to sleep there, alone, upon the hardwood floor, I would sleep comfortably in my cozy bed, also alone.

Emotionally and spiritually exhausted, I headed back to my sofa, feeling almost giddy about this man who had somehow wormed his way into my life. Yet I remained deeply troubled on a spiritual level. I was satisfied in some respects, happy but restless, yet scared of the future and somehow still thinking about my old life in Walnut, Iowa.

As I settled into the sagging pillows of the sofa, I noticed the pile of mail spread across my coffee table that I'd been ignoring for the past few days. As I shuffled through it, I discovered two letters from home.

I was not surprised by the first letter from my folks, written by Mama. Was I coming home for Christmas? When was I coming home and forgetting the foolish notions that had sent me west? Did I know that Bob, my former fiancée, might be dating other women? Not confirmed, she admitted, but how much longer could he be expected to wait for someone who had abandoned him? He deserved so much better. What a shame that she, Rose, had not recognized Bob as the devoted spouse who would always be there for her.

Trying to regain my composure, I moved on to the next letter. There was no return address, just a postmark from Walnut, Iowa. But I recognized the distinct handwriting immediately. A letter from Bob.

I had not heard from him in months, not since I left him on our wedding day. While I'd written several letters to him since then, letters that I never dared to mail, this was the first letter I'd received from him.

Dearest Rose,

I hope you don't mind that I got your address from your folks who, of course, love and miss you. Yes, you must follow your own dreams. I understand that, but I must admit that I'd hoped for so much more from you. I'm still here, fixing up the house I built for you. I spend many a night sitting on the porch just thinking of times we shared together. Just hoping you may someday come to your senses and decide to come on back home where you belong. We all miss you.

Always,
Bob

Confused, I fed the letters from home into the embers of the dying fire and dragged myself into bed. As I drifted off into a fitful sleep, I found myself romping through a snow blizzard with Paul, melting into an inferno of love and lust. Suddenly, Bob thundered onto the scene, riding Daisy June, my childhood horse, and rescuing me from disaster.

Paul? Bob? I jolted upright in bed, heart pounding. I seemed to have two men in my life…although I did not really have either one of them. If I had to choose between them, what would I do? Any sane woman, I realized, would choose Bob. He was steady like the Rock of Gibraltar, loving, forgiving, and always there.

But perhaps I was not completely sane these days. Sometimes I questioned my grip on reality. But nobody had ever kissed me the way Paul just had—a hungry and hauntingly familiar kiss that seemed to transcend lifetimes. However, I could not deny that Paul was dangerous, dark, and totally unpredictable.

Chapter 16

The blizzard of the century raged on for several days, isolating Virginia City from the rest of the world. All roads were closed. Not even a snowplow dared to venture out into the howling winds and whiteout conditions. Businesses and schools were closed. Cell phone coverage was sporadic, and people relied on their emergency radios for updates on the weather.

Somehow, the dangerous weather conditions created a sense of excitement and community. stranded in their homes people called to check on their neighbors. The braver ones, who seemed to thrive on the excitement of a good old-fashioned winter blizzard, bundled up in fur hats and scarves and ventured out of their homes. They shoveled snow to clear paths from their doors to the street in case they had to get out fast—not that any emergency vehicle could have gotten through the main roads anyway. Several hours later, their cleared paths were once again covered with mounds of drifting snow.

Karen, my landlord, called to be sure I was okay. I told her I was...just before my cell phone went dead. In fact, I was almost enjoying this snow day. I immersed myself in a fascinating book, *Witness to History*, about the history of Virginia City and nearby Nevada City. It was written by John Ellingsen, the local historian I'd met by the hurdy-gurdy house.

Intrigued with all that I was learning, I tuned out the rest of the world for much of the day until I heard a scraping sound on my porch. Looking out, I found a barely recognizable man sporting a fur hat, parka, and a scarf over his face. He was shoveling my sidewalk and porch.

I tried to shove my door open to greet my helper, but it was blocked by massive drifts of heavy, wet snow. When I realized it was Paul, my heart flip-flopped. I waved at him through the glass door, as he continued shoveling. Finally, he cleared the doorway, and I shoved the door open.

"Now you really look like a snowman," I laughed as he came in, trying to stomp the snow off his boots. Instinctively, I brushed the snow off his parka as puddles of melting snow accumulated on the floor. I ushered him toward the warmth of the flaming logs in the fireplace and got him a hot cup of coffee. As I watched him, I could not help but notice the way his eyes glowed with excitement and the color in his cheeks. He was obviously enjoying this storm and the challenges that it provided. A true Montana pioneer.

Until now, I hadn't even thought about food, as I'd been too engrossed in my book. But what about Paul, stranded in the library, probably without an adequate supply of food? "Are you hungry?" I asked.

"Well, starving, if you want to know the truth. Out of candy bars and snacks. Even the Pioneer Bar and Outlaw Café are closed. Not that I could get there in this storm. It was enough of a challenge trudging my way down the alley to your place, step by step, through many feet of snow."

"I do appreciate your valiant efforts, sir." I curtsied demurely, totally uncharacteristic of me. His eyes registered strong recognition as I turned away to warm up leftover spaghetti from the night before.

We ate together by the fire and drifted off into a comfortable silence. Every so often, I'd get up to look out the window and check the status of the blinding storm. I could no longer see the cemetery where Amelia slept beneath a heavy blanket of snow. Paul was obviously not in a hurry to head back to the library. He tuned into the emergency radio broadcasts on my weather alert radio. It was going to be a hazardous night. Dangerous wind-chill readings and blinding snow.

Suddenly, the power went out. No light, no heat. I scrambled for a flashlight as Paul peered out across the valley, noting that the entire town was shrouded in darkness.

"What do we do now?" I was suddenly terrified of the dark.

"We will need to keep this fire going throughout the night," Paul said as his solemn gaze met mine. He was not planning to go anyplace, not even back to the library, where he belonged. I was not about to protest. "Where's your woodpile?" He sprang into action. "We need more wood in here."

"But it's dark and dangerous," I protested, not sure if I was referring to the storm—or to him.

Ignoring my protests, he pulled on his parka and boots and headed out to the woodpile with the flashlight. I held the door open against gusting winds as he brought in armloads of wood and stacked them beside the fireplace.

Finally, he came in, shut and bolted the door against the fierce winds, took off his snow-laden garments, and joined me on the sofa by the fireplace.

He shut off our only flashlight to conserve battery power. It was just the two of us, all alone, basking in the flickering flames of the fire as Lucky snored beside the fireplace.

"Look, I don't want to impose, Rose. I can make my way back to the library, I think."

"Stay, please stay," I blurted out the words before I realized the possible repercussions of my bold statement.

His eyebrows arched in a questioning manner as if he was wondering what my words meant. His eyes followed me closely, almost seductively, as I got up and wandered into the dark kitchen, trying to compose myself. Pretending that I was shutting off the coffeepot, putting leftovers away. I was simply trying to shut down the feelings that were seeping through me.

Paul took control of this uncomfortable situation immediately. "Look, Rose, we will need to take turns keeping the fire going. I'll sleep on the sofa and will do the first shift. Go to bed. I'll wake you when I need you." He turned from me abruptly, staring into the flames licking the knotty-pine walls of my cabin with flickering shadows of light. The shutters shook as my little cabin stood its ground against the raging storm.

I'd been dismissed in my own home. Exhausted, yet somehow trusting Paul to take care of things, I disappeared into my bedroom where I collapsed on the bed after locking the door and shoving a heavy chair against it. Somehow, despite my best intentions, I fell into a deep sleep, totally unaware of Paul's presence on the other side of my locked door.

Before long, a glowing vision appeared to me in my dreams. It was Amelia. I recognized her immediately, instinctively knowing that this was the woman whose grave I'd been led to. Amelia 1868. She stood at the foot of my bed, gowned in the identical red Victorian dress that I'd imagined myself wearing the first day I arrived in Virginia City, Montana.

She seemed so real that I was not sure if I was dreaming or not. Her sorrowful eyes pleaded with me, drawing me in, deeper and deeper, until I felt myself becoming one with her. I was disappearing into her life in the last century. I held onto my mattress for dear life, trying to stay grounded. Trying to escape from the dream that did not seem to be a dream.

"Help me, please help me!" she cried out to me as she suddenly disappeared from my bedroom and then reappeared as a vision in the midst of a raging river.

Struggling and flailing wildly against a force that was dragging her down beneath the churning waves, her green eyes registered shock and fear. "Help me! I can't swim!" Her panicked cries echoed throughout the Madison River Valley. Her wild eyes focused on a shadowy figure disappearing into the fog. Gulping water, she struggled to come back up, but her long hair became entangled in twisted tree branches that spun her around in the current, sucking her down into the depths of the river. Soon, she was gone.

"Amelia?" I bolted from my bed, drenched in sweat. Turning on my flashlight, I searched the room for some sign of the vision I'd just seen. Nobody was there.

I threw on an old bathrobe, carefully unlocked the door of my bedroom, and tiptoed out into the main room. I found Paul sound asleep on the sofa beside the fire, snoring softly as reflections from the flames of the fire played across his rugged face.

I tread lightly, as if in a trance, toward the window. Peering out through the frosted window pane, over the mounds of snow, I tried to see across the valley into the cemetery where Amelia's grave lay. I was trying to find Amelia. All I could do was think my thoughts to her, as forcefully as I could.

Come back, Amelia, I pleaded with her. I will help you.

Finally, I tiptoed past Paul again, resisting an impulse to touch his face and run my fingers through his hair. Back in bed, I struggled to fall asleep. Amelia was heavy on my mind, and my heart raced just thinking of the man sleeping on my sofa. Eventually, I drifted into a beautiful dream in which I floated into Paul's arms, lost in his kisses. Our bodies melted together...

The ring of my alarm clock suddenly brought me back to reality. I could smell coffee brewing and bacon frying. Paul was already up and apparently making breakfast. Grinning to myself, I dressed for the day and slipped out into the kitchen.

"Good morning, sunshine." He handed me a cup of coffee. "Storm is over, electricity's back on. So I decided to make us some breakfast."

My heart sighed. I could get used to this kind of treatment, I decided. It might be nice to have a man in my life, someone like Paul. "Thanks, Paul." I touched his arm gently. "You forgot to wake me for my turn tending the fire."

"I thought you needed your sleep," he grinned lazily. Putting down the spatula, he turned and pulled me into his arms. I could not help responding to his kiss. He released me to tend to the bacon before it burned.

The rising sun streamed through the window over the breakfast table where we sat together eating breakfast. I almost told him about my dream, but something stopped me. Despite my feelings for this man, I could feel myself beginning to withdraw from him. He was getting too close. I was enjoying his company too much.

Chapter 17

Do not trust this man. That nagging little voice taunted me all day at the library. I hid in my office, avoiding Paul, trying to figure out what was preventing me from trusting him and why I was so conflicted. One minute I was ready to go to bed with him. The next, I wanted nothing to do with him.

I pretended to be preoccupied with my research every time he poked his head through my door. He looked puzzled, and rightfully so. After all we'd shared last night, I had shut down my feelings.

I worked late, waiting for him to leave so I wouldn't have to speak with him. But he apparently had no intentions of going home until I did. Finally, about seven o'clock, he came into my office and plopped down in the chair across from my desk. A deep frown creased his forehead.

"So what is it, Rose? Did I make the coffee too strong for you this morning?" He tried a light approach.

"I've been really busy today," I lied.

"Seems to me that you've just shut me out of your life, haven't you? What in the hell do you want from me?"

"I...I don't know."

"I don't understand you. You're like a schizophrenic, like two different people. As soon as I feel we've got something special happening between us, you slam the door in my face. Why?"

"I wish I knew. I'm as confused as you are, and I'm sorry about that." I stared down at my desk, avoiding his gaze. I could feel the sparks flying between us—a heady mixture of desire and fear.

"For God's sake, what do you want from me?" His voice was laced with anger.

"I think I need some space, Paul, some time to figure things out. It scares me when things move too fast, when I feel like I'm losing control. I'm just not ready. It has nothing to do with you. In fact, I do care for you. I think you know that, don't you?"

"I'm not sure about that, and I don't think you are either. So we're right back to square one, back to a working relationship? I'll respect that. Maybe we both need some time and space." While he was obviously disappointed, he seemed sincere in respecting my need for space.

"I appreciate your understanding," I sighed. "I will think of you as a friend for now, okay?"

"Some things in life may be worth waiting for." He got up to leave. "Friends it is."

Paul and I managed to maintain an almost-comfortable working relationship at the library for the next month or so. As long as we avoided the ghosts of Amelia and Jack Slade, and as long as we didn't get too close to each other, things seemed to work out between us. We threw ourselves into our research, focusing our efforts there instead of upon each other.

There was too much snow this winter for any more paranormal investigations at the cemetery. We decided we'd wait until spring to resume that part of our research. In the meantime, I spent hours gazing out my cabin window with its view of the cemetery across the valley. I'd sit at my table with a cup of coffee, trying to pinpoint the location of Amelia's grave, trying to connect with her, and wondering why she disappeared if she really wanted my help.

Maybe she wasn't there in the cemetery…maybe she preferred roaming around the world she once knew. The world of Virginia City during the gold rush days of the 1860s.

Lucky and I still went on our early morning walks before I had to go to work. The mountains were dressed in fluffy gowns of white crystals that danced in the morning sunlight. I'd hike past the café, smelling fresh coffee and bacon frying in the pan. The regulars were already coming in for breakfast. But I had more important things to do these days. I was looking for Amelia in the nooks and crannies of the ghost town where she once lived—and died.

Trying to clear my mind to open myself to her presence, I walked in silence. Listening. Hoping my spirit guide, if there is such a thing, would lead me in the right direction. I whispered Amelia's name, over and over again.

I usually ended up on the bench outside the blacksmith shop that contained the old hurdy-gurdy house. I felt like I belonged there. Today snowflakes fell gently as I sat there, trying to go back in time, back to the days when Amelia—

Suddenly, it hit me. *This* was where Amelia spent her time. *This* was where she wore that low-cut red dress. Could it be? Could Amelia have been a hurdy-gurdy girl? I remembered Paul's story about the jealous man who loved this hurdy-gurdy girl so much that he had a clock made with her initials engraved on it.

A.J. The initials on that clock were "A.J." Amelia? Could it be that Amelia 1868 was the A.J. in this old legend? I could hardly wait to begin searching through old records for an Amelia with a last name beginning with a J. "Help me, Amelia," I whispered fiercely. "I'm trying, but I need your help."

Despite spending long hours on my research, obsessed with finding an Amelia with a last name beginning in J, I hit one dead end after another. I could find no records of this woman. Perhaps they had been destroyed in one of the great fires—or someone had conveniently destroyed them.

Weeks crawled by. No sign of Amelia anywhere. She didn't respond to my continual requests for her help. Sometimes I wondered why I should care if she didn't.

One day at the library, I asked Paul about connecting with spirits. I needed to find out how to get them to appear and communicate with us.

"Any ghost in particular?" he asked, a hint of annoyance spreading across his face. Of course, he thought I was thinking of Amelia or Jack Slade once again.

"No, just in general," I lied.

"Not that I believe you," he sighed, "but—in general—you can't. The spirit world does not march to our sense of time, Rose. A spirit may come through to you at a time when you are open to the contact, a time when they feel safe enough to come through or have some unfinished business to take care of. But you can't call them out or make them show up whenever you want them to."

A flicker of disappointment crossed my face. I'd been trying so hard to call Amelia out, and it hadn't worked. "Are there ways for me to be more open? I'd really like to make contact with some of the spirits around here, Paul."

He got up and began sorting through a pile of books on his bookshelf. "Here." He handed several to me. "Read these. Meditation may help you open up to them, but overall, you need to be patient and wait for them to decide to come through. Do you want to tell me more about the contacts you're trying to establish?"

"Not yet." I stared at the floor. No sense in setting him off again.

"But if you do connect, no matter whom you connect with, I want to know about it. In the name of the research we're doing."

"Okay." I grinned at him. Someday I'd love to talk with him about Amelia. But not today.

Chapter 18

Time marched on as Virginia City began to gear up for the Christmas holidays. Candles and twinkling lights began to light up the nights. Homemade wreaths hung on the doors of houses and cabins tucked into the snowy winter landscape. The Victorian houses were decorated beautifully. Downtown, evergreen garlands decorated the shops along the boardwalk, and Christmas carols rang out from the café, drug store, and the bar.

As much as I loved my new home, I missed Walnut at Christmas. I thought about the huge Christmas tree twinkling in the middle of the brick-lined street. Mama would bake dozens of Christmas cookies for the carolers gathered around the tree, singing their hearts out. People strolled past the century-old buildings eating cookies, drinking apple cider, and shopping in the antique stores.

This would be my very first Christmas away from home, away from Mama, Papa, and Walnut. Away from Bob. My heart lurched into my throat as a lonely tear slid down my cheek. Of course, I still cared for him, but I could not face him. I could not go home. I could not hurt him anymore.

I drove to Ennis one day to pick out a special Christmas card for him. It was not an easy task. None of the messages seemed to fit our unique situation. Finally, I settled on a blank card; I'd write my own message. I thought he'd like the picture on the front—a photo of one of Montana's famous grizzly bears. Bob was an avid hunter and lover of wildlife.

When Mama tried to coerce me into coming home, I stood my ground and finally convinced Papa that they should fly out to Virginia City for Christmas instead. Of course there was no airport in Walnut or Virginia City, so I booked their airline tickets for them, leaving from Des Moines, Iowa, and arriving at the Bozeman, Montana airport.

Neither of them had ever flown before. Hard to imagine how sheltered their lives had always been. The farm and little Walnut were pretty much the extent of their world, and that's the way they liked it. Mama loved her quilting bees and church social events. She was always baking her famous pies for various bake sales and benefits. Papa loved all things related to the history of Walnut. I knew he'd be intrigued with Virginia City and its rich history. I hadn't yet told him about the book I'd written for him, based on his stories. I wanted to surprise him with a copy of *Memories of a Country Boy* for Christmas.

My cabin would not be big enough for all of us. Mama would complain endlessly about the cramped quarters. I'd give them my bed and sleep on the sofa or up in the loft, but she'd never let me do that. They needed their own space, and frankly, I needed some space of my own. So I decided to put them up in one of the Victorian bed and breakfasts as a special treat. They'd never stayed in a bed and breakfast before and certainly not in a Victorian home. Karen's Gingerbread House was already booked, but I was able to book the Rose Room in the charming Bennett House across the street.

Busy preparing meals, shopping, wrapping presents, and scouring every inch of my cabin so it would meet Mama's white-glove test, I tucked Amelia away in the recesses of my mind. She'd have to wait for me now, the way I'd been waiting on her.

Paul was unusually quiet at work these days, almost wistful as he gazed into space, trying to block out the Christmas carols floating through the air. His eyes still followed me around at times when he seemed to be deep in thought.

I wondered what he'd do for Christmas. He had no family, he'd told me. Holidays could be lonely if you had nobody to celebrate with. Christmas was a time for sharing, for being together with loved ones. Who did Paul have?

Finally, several days before the holiday, I asked him about his plans. He had none.

"It's just another day, Rose," he sighed. "People today make too damn much of it, buying gifts they can't afford, eating too much. I've got a few good books I want to read. Maybe I'll take a nice, long walk in the snow."

"Paul, my parents are coming, you know."

"Yes, I remember you told me," he laughed. I guess I'd told him more than once.

"Well..." I hesitated. "I'm making dinner on Christmas Eve. Why don't you come on over? You'd like my father. He's a history nut just like you." I waited for a response. "Well?"

A slow smile spread across his face. "I'd be honored," he finally announced. "Guess I can fit it into my busy schedule," he added.

"It's not a good day to be alone. I'm glad you're coming." I suddenly realized that I meant it. While I'd been trying desperately to avoid him and block my conflicted feelings for him, I had to admit that I enjoyed his company. Too much perhaps. But I did not want him to be alone on this holiday.

Suddenly he came to life, almost animated. "Do you have a Christmas tree yet?"

"Well, no, not yet," I admitted.

"You probably don't have an ax to cut one down or a truck to haul it home, do you?" he teased. "But I do. Come on." He grabbed me by the arm. "You can't have Christmas without a tree, you know."

"I don't have much room in my cabin, Paul."

"I know just the place to find us a small one that we can set up in the corner. And I have boxes of old ornaments and lights that have been sitting in the cellar for years. We will get the tree right away and set it up. Tomorrow I'll bring in the ornaments so we can decorate."

We? He had suddenly become a part of our family Christmas. As pleased as I was about that, a part of me worried about what my parents would think. I certainly didn't want them to think that I was already involved with another man. I'd need to be clear that he was my boss and would be alone on Christmas. The problem was that Mama would still grill him endlessly about his life and his family, trying to figure out why he was alone. Hopefully, Papa would steer the conversation in other directions. If I could get him going on his stories about growing up in Walnut, that would do it.

Paul and I climbed into his pickup after work and drove up into the mountains. We stomped through the snow in our heavy boots and headed toward a grove of evergreens. Swinging his ax, he whistled a Christmas tune, happier than I'd seen him since the night we'd played in the snow together. We were, once again, together in a winter wonderland...this time searching for *our* Christmas tree.

"How about this one?" Paul brushed mounds of snow from the branches of a little tree, which looked tiny against the backdrop of the mountains and huge sky.

"It's rather small, isn't it?"

He laughed. "It won't look small when we bring it home and try to get it into your cabin." He found another one close by. "Or how about this one?"

"Yes, that's the one," I decided, helping him brush snow from the branches. Our gloved fingers touched accidently. We stopped, staring at each other, hearts beating in sync.

"Oh my God, Rose," was all he could say as I trembled with desire, remembering the kiss we shared. He put his arm around me gently, pulling me close. "You're cold."

"I'm just…just confused. I don't know what's happening here, but it doesn't make any sense."

"I know that. It's just that I feel like I've always known you. What do you want me to do, Rose?"

"I don't know. I still don't know." Tears filled my eyes. He took his glove off and gently wiped them away.

"I will never hurt you, Rose. You need to tell me what you want from me…whenever you figure out what that is." A hint of annoyance and frustration underscored his words.

Once again, that warning voice whispered in my ear. Do not trust him.

Reluctantly pulling myself from the heat of his arms, I regained my composure. "I feel it, too, Paul. You already know that. But we cannot give in to this. It's not the right thing to do. Not now."

"That's all I need to know, Rose," he sighed with relief, obviously picking up on the "not now." He was satisfied, apparently willing to wait. Picking up his ax, he cut down the tree and hauled it back to the truck.

The sun went down in a blaze of orange, pink, and lavender as we drove back down the mountain.

Paul did more trimming before he hauled the tree into my place and set it up by the window.

"It's perfect!" I exclaimed, putting the past behind us. "Thank you, Paul."

"Okay, if I come back tomorrow with the decorations, I promise to behave," he joked.

"Yes, I want you to come back. It will be fun decorating together. Maybe I'll make a kettle of chili for dinner."

"I'd love it. I'll bring the wine." He hiked back out into the snowy night, leaving puddles of snow and tiny pine needles on my floor. For some reason, it felt good to clean up after him. What would it be like, I wondered, to have someone around to clean up after on a regular basis?

The next night, we decorated the tree after unpacking boxes of ornaments and lights that were wrapped in newspapers dated January 1950. They had not seen the light of day for sixty-two years. Some were antiques by now—considerably older than we were.

"Look at this one!" we'd call out to the other with each new discovery. Finally, the tree was finished. We then strung twinkling lights outside along the railing of the porch and around the door, adding the finishing touch: a fresh evergreen wreath that Paul had picked up in Ennis.

By the time we finished decorating, it was dark. The stars were brilliant, twinkling through the depths of a cold winter's night. We stood side by side, gazing out into the Universe. The world was wrapped in a cloak of silence, illuminated by pinpoints of light that floated backward and forward throughout eternity.

"What are you thinking?" Paul finally whispered.

"Just how insignificant I am, how insignificant my life and my problems are in the big picture of the Universe. What about you?"

"I'm just thinking about life in general. Look at all the planets out there, Rose. Do you think there are other people out there somewhere?"

"I do. Someday we will discover life out there. We have so much to learn."

"Someday, we will live on some of those planets or on space stations way out there." He gestured toward the brilliant sky. "Of course, that probably won't happen in our lifetimes, but I think the future of mankind lies out there somewhere."

"That's an intriguing thought, Paul."

"All planets eventually die. People will need to relocate. Who knows? Maybe we will be born again someday on one of the planets orbiting the stars we're watching together tonight." He paused. "Maybe we will even be together in another lifetime, Rose. Here or out there somewhere."

"Maybe we've already shared a lifetime or two." The words rushed from my mouth, surprising both of us.

Paul's jaw dropped as his eyes lit up. "Maybe that explains the connection that we share, little one."

Little one? The oddly familiar words rang in my ears, shocking me.

"Would you prefer that I call you 'darlin'?" he teased. "Maybe we're getting too serious here, eh?"

I was still mesmerized, however, as I stared into the night. I found myself, once again, searching for Amelia's presence. Paul waited quietly, giving me the space I needed.

Finally, I turned to him. "Do you feel any spirits out there?"

"I don't feel them tonight, but of course, they're there. They're everywhere. They walk beside us, you know. We usually don't know they're here since they operate on a different energy frequency than we do. Remember what I told you—they appear to us when they want to. Not on our schedules."

"I want to feel them, to know them." My voice rose in urgency.

Paul spun me around so we were face-to-face. Tilting my head up to meet his eyes, he spoke slowly. "Despite my better judgment, I will tell you something. I am convinced that you do have a special connection with this Amelia, whoever she was. She will come to you when she is ready. For some reason, she has chosen you to complete her unfinished business."

"Oh, Paul, thank you for understanding," I sighed with relief.

A shadow of concern clouded his face as he turned away from me.

"What's wrong?"

He shook his head in frustration. "I just...I just worry about what will happen when you do connect with her. What is her unfinished business? Why you?"

"I don't know that, but I cannot understand why you dislike her when you don't even know anything about her."

"All I know," he replied almost icily, "is that I don't trust her. I pick up a strong sense of betrayal coming from her. She did someone wrong, Rose."

"How can you possibly know that? You have no proof, Paul, no documentation, no rationale behind these feelings of yours." I tried to be calm, knowing I was already upsetting him. He prided himself on scientific paranormal investigation. Yet he was certainly jumping to emotional conclusions in this case.

He began to pace the length of the porch, running his fingers through his thick, black hair. I waited, picking tiny snowflakes off my gloves. The moon dove behind a bank of clouds, hiding from the world rumbling far below.

"You have a point," he finally admitted. "There is nothing scientific about my intuition in this case. Nothing whatsoever." He threw his hands into the air, obviously frustrated with himself.

"Intuition or feelings? You seem to have a strong emotional response to this woman."

He stopped pacing to stare at me. "What?"

"I don't mean to discredit you in any way. I know how thorough you are with your research, Paul. But I'm wondering if there is sometimes a place for intuition or emotional reactions in your work?"

"Well stated. I've always thought I was above that level of investigation, but maybe I'm not. There are people, like psychics, who communicate with spirits. They rely on intuition and feelings to some extent."

"Is that all bad?"

"Not always. Sometimes it can help point you in the right direction at least."

"I need all the help I can get to point me in the right direction as far as Amelia goes," I sighed. "I'm running on feelings and intuition. Still, I'm stuck. Any leads you can give me will help, whether it's scientific documentation or your personal feelings. I do need your help."

"Maybe we're a good team after all," he decided. "What puzzles me, though, is that your feelings about her are so different from mine. You don't think she betrayed anyone, do you?"

"I know beyond a doubt that she did not. She is the one who was wronged, possibly murdered, Paul!" I blurted out the burden that I'd been carrying around for some time.

"What?"

"Let's go inside by the fire, and I'll tell you what I've seen."

He followed me inside, stomping more snow around the room. The smell of the chili simmering on the stove drifted through the rustic cabin as the lights on the Christmas tree twinkled. Sitting together on the sofa, I told him about Amelia, about the visions I had of her, and about the possible connection between Amelia and the "A. J." inscription on that old clock that had haunted him for so long.

He was very much interested in what I'd discovered. "You need to tell me anything more that you discover, Rose. But you also need to be aware that this spirit will tell you what she wants you to know. *Her* side of the story.

You will not always get the full truth in cases like this. Just don't jump to any conclusions before we talk it over."

"You don't trust her, do you?" Nor should I trust him or disclose so much information.

"No, I don't." He stared into the fire and abruptly changed the subject as he opened the bottle of wine. "I'm starving. How about some of that chili?"

When I returned with our bowls of chili and a loaf of French bread, he handed me a glass of red wine and lifted his glass in a toast.

"To us…whatever that means, wherever this goes or doesn't go…but friends always." His eyes met mine, trying to connect.

"To us," I whispered back.

Chapter 19

It was the day before Christmas. I waited at the Bozeman airport for the flight from Des Moines to finally land. There had been several delays due to snowstorms blanketing the Midwest. Thankfully, the weather in Montana was picture-perfect.

Peering out the windows of the airport, I saw their flight land. Roaring down the runway, the airplane came to a stop and then began to roll in toward the gate.

Dear God, please let this visit turn out well, I prayed as I headed to the gate. I waited anxiously as passengers piled off the plane into the arms of waiting friends and relatives. Where were my parents?

Finally, they emerged, slowly, as if dazed by all that they were experiencing. They had grown older, I realized. Their eyes anxiously searched for me.

I ran toward them, waving my arms. "I'm here!"

Mama was carefully toting a large box in her arms. It had to be some of her homemade Christmas cookies. Papa couldn't take his eyes off the mountains that surrounded the airport.

"Over here!" I continued to wave until they finally saw me, waves of relief washing over their wrinkled faces. It had to be scary, I realized, to fly for the first time when you were in your seventies.

Papa gave me a huge bear hug, beaming from ear to ear. Mama fussed as I hugged her, wanting to make sure I didn't crush the cookies she'd spent so much time baking and decorating for our Christmas dinner.

After gathering their baggage, I packed them into my SUV as the sun began its glorious descent over the mountains. Papa tried to take pictures out his window. Mama lamented about the long and tiring flight. They'd had to wait endless hours to be de-iced in the biggest storm of the century, according to her. They were lucky their plane didn't crash in flight. It would have been *so* much easier if I had come home for Christmas.

"Hush, woman," Papa finally reprimanded her. "Look around you. See the mountains? All my life, I've wanted to see the mountains. Well, we're here. Remember how Rose used to draw sketches of the mountains when she was just a young whippersnapper? Well, I tell you, her drawings looked just like this!" His eyes glowed with pride, bringing tears to my eyes. Papa had always been there for me, always proud of my accomplishments—although they may have been few and far between...

"And you ain't seen nothin' yet," I laughed. "We're going to spend the night in a condo at Big Sky Resort. It's located at the foot of Lone Peak, one of the most beautiful mountains you will ever see in your life."

I didn't tell them that the luxurious but rustic condo actually belonged to Paul. He'd insisted on letting us stay there, assuring me that it wasn't rented out. He figured that my parents' late arrival would make it difficult to get back to Virginia City that same night. He'd even made us dinner reservations at the Peaks Restaurant in the Summit Hotel.

Mama complained that all she'd had to eat in the last twenty-four hours was a package of peanuts and a glass of water on her flight from Des Moines. Papa rolled his eyes, disputing her claim to martyrdom. Had she forgotten about the huge breakfast they'd had at Perkins before they left?

It was almost dark as we wound our way through the valley toward Big Sky. I knew that Papa would love seeing the majestic mountain peaks and crystal clear mountain streams that meander along the winding road.

Finally we turned onto Lone Mountain Trail to begin climbing toward Big Sky Resort. But several mountain goats stood there, blocking the road. Papa was thrilled as he almost jumped out of the passenger seat, forgetting his aches and pains, and began shooting photos of the mountain goats in the darkening sky. His pictures probably wouldn't turn out—it was too dark— but his enthusiasm was gratifying.

"Silly old fool," Mama grumbled. "I'm hungry, ready to faint if I don't get some food soon."

"Here's a candy bar." I tossed a Snickers bar to her in the backseat. "It will tide you over until dinner time."

"But it's past dinner time, Prairie Rose. You know we always eat at five o'clock. Why, it's already dark out."

"Mama, I can't help it that you didn't land until after five o'clock. I'm doing the best I can." I tried not to bristle under the burden of her relentless complaints.

"But I hate Snickers!" she whined.

"Pay her no mind," Papa winked at me. "She will survive."

We drove up the mountain in silence, trying to see whatever we could in the dark. Suddenly, a full moon rose over a majestic mountain peak that seemed to fill the entire sky. The brilliant moon illuminated what I knew had to be Lone Peak. It took my breath away.

"Stop! I need to get a picture!" Papa cried out, grabbing his camera as he threw his car door open. I pulled off to the side. Thankfully, there were no cars behind us. I got out with Papa and began shooting photos. It was an incredible sight, a special blessing.

Even Mama was impressed. "Oh!" she exclaimed from the back seat, gazing out the window at the mountain peak and forgetting all about her hunger pangs.

Soon we checked into our condo, climbing the few stairs to our unit. The spacious living room was dominated by a rock fireplace with a wall of windows looking out over the mountains and valleys below. There were window seats where one could curl up and read a good book while watching skiers whiz by. Mama was anxious to try out the indoor hot tub after we had dinner, so we headed immediately to The Peaks Restaurant in the Summit Hotel.

I could see Papa frowning at the prices on the menu. This wasn't Walnut, Iowa. It was Big Sky, Montana. The food was incredible, and people expected to pay a little more for the food as well as the view overlooking the ski slopes.

"It's on me, Papa," I assured him. "I want you to have a nice meal, both of you. After this, you will need to put up with my cooking."

"Have you finally learned to cook?" Mama sighed. "I sure hope so. No way will you ever get yourself a man if you can't cook, you know."

We settled on a rib eye steak for Papa, walleye for Mama, and I went for the scallops. All excellent choices. I even ordered a bottle of wine, which seemed to calm Mama and gave Papa and me a little peace. I tried to remember if Mama always been so difficult or if it was her age.

They were ready for bed by the time we returned to the condo. Papa wanted me to wake him early enough to see the sunrise. Soon, they were both snoring, side by side.

After tucking them in, I grabbed my bathing suit and headed to the Huntley Lodge's swimming pool and hot tub. Paul had told me about sitting in the outdoor whirlpool immersed in the steam, surrounded by banks of snow. I watched the snow-grooming machines climbing Lone Peak as they groomed ski runs for the next day. Their headlights lit up the mountains. Lone Peak towered above the valley, dominating the endless sky.

I was alone in the hot tub tonight, wrapped in a starlit Universe. The heat and relentless pulsing action of the whirling waters wrapped me in a cocoon of warmth that contrasted sharply with the frigid temperatures.

Breathing deeply, I submerged my body into the water, dunking my head. I emerged to find crystals of ice immediately forming on the strands of my hair. I closed my eyes, resting my head on the side of the pool, trying to clear my mind, trying to let go. Meditate, I commanded myself. Nothing happened. Maybe this was just a time to be. Nothing more, nothing less.

But I soon drifted off into a surreal dream. I was here, yet not here. Wild winds and waves tossed me out of the boat. Something was sucking me down into a whirlpool filled with tangled branches of ancient trees. I was drowning, slipping beneath the pounding waves, screaming for help. But the man I loved with all my heart disappeared into the fog, leaving me alone. I was going down, sinking into unknown depths of nothingness.

"My baby! God please save my baby!" I cried out as I went down for the last time.

As I disappeared beneath the murky waters of the river, I saw Paul's frantic face, distorted with rage, love, and regret. Then Bob's face as he clawed at the waves, trying to free me from death.

Shuddering with fear, I suddenly came back to the present, still immersed in the hot tub. I had to get out of here. Away from these nightmares. Away from the terrors of Amelia's life—a life from the past that seemed to be taking over my own. Anxiously peering through layers of steam rising above the pool, I was relieved to find myself alone. No Paul, no Bob. Nobody. I cautiously pulled my sluggish body from the hot whirlpool into the shockingly cold air.

I ran barefoot through the snow into the dressing room, slamming the door behind me. As I passed the large mirror, I was shocked at my appearance. Pale as a ghost. Huge eyes streaked with fear. Icicles hanging from my hair, dripping onto the marble floor.

Breathe deeply, I reminded myself, as I sank down onto a bench, wrapped in a warm towel. One thought dominated all others. *My baby!* Did Amelia have a baby?

I don't know how long I sat there before I decided to get dressed and return to the condo. Emotionally exhausted, I was relieved to find Mama and Papa still asleep. Aside from an occasional "Quit your damn snoring!" hurled from one to the other, it was a peaceful night.

I set the alarm clock early enough to be up before sunrise as Papa had requested. Then I drifted off into a deep sleep, so deep that Paul, Bob, Amelia, and her mysterious lover were not able to penetrate my dreams.

Papa was already roaming around, fully dressed, by the time my alarm went off. I heard him rumbling through the kitchen in search of coffee. Cupboard doors slammed. Water ran. He clomped around the condo in his heavy boots, opening the glass door to the deck, closing it again. He was anxious to get on with his day, anxious for me to get up.

"No coffee?" he asked in disbelief as soon as I stumbled into the kitchen.

"No clue, Papa. We just got here, remember? Maybe they drink tea here."

"Tea? Real men don't drink tea. No, sir. I need my coffee, Rose."

"I know." I grinned at him. "Come on, we're going down to the Huntley Lodge for one of the best cups of coffee you've ever had and maybe even one of their famous huckleberry scones. Is Mama ready to go?"

"Are you kiddin' me? She will sleep in as late as we let her."

The sky was turning into soft shades of pink and purple as we grabbed our cameras and ventured out into the frosty predawn stillness. I thought about hiking down to the lodge but worried that Papa would slip and fall on patches of ice along the way. He used a cane these days and had slowed down. I could easily keep up with him now after all the years that I'd trotted behind, trying to catch up. I convinced him to drive down instead.

"I could have walked, you know," he grumbled. "This old man of yours still has lots of good miles on him, you know."

"I know, Papa. I just thought you were dying for your morning coffee," I teased him. "Besides, the sun will be coming up soon. Don't want to miss that."

As we parked beside the lodge, the sun was just breaking through the mist over the mountains. We grabbed our cameras and began shooting pictures.

"Oh, Rose." He beamed at me. "I ain't never seen such a sight in my life. What a sunrise! All that snow. The biggest and bluest sky I ever did see, and that huge mountain. Lone Peak, you say?"

"Yes, Lone Peak. You can go on back home and show everyone the photos you took. Bet you got some nice ones, Papa."

His eyes sparkled as he tucked his camera into the pocket of his parka and followed me into the fireside lounge in the Huntley Lodge. A fire burned in the massive stone fireplace. The room was constructed of huge logs from long ago. We sat on a leather sofa in front of the fire, warming up with steaming mugs of coffee and devouring our huckleberry scones. Christmas music played softly in the background.

Soon the skiers and snowboarders would file in on their way back out onto the slopes. Once Mama got up, we'd sit out on the deck for a while and watch them whiz past. For now, it was just the two of us, Papa and me, sharing precious moments we were not usually allowed to indulge in. When Mama was around, bless her heart, she always dominated the conversation.

"So...you like it out here in Montana?" Papa asked.

"I do. I love it here. Wait until you see my place—not that it's big or glamorous like Big Sky here. But it has a deep sense of history. The kind of place where you feel like you belong. And the mountains are incredible. I can't wait to show it all to you, Papa."

"Do you ever miss Walnut?"

"Of course I do. You know I miss you and Mama and my old friends. Lots of good memories there. I miss hearing your stories about how things were when you were growing up. I remember the nights we spent out on the porch talking and watching storms together. Do you remember?"

He began to chuckle. "Oh, yeah...some of the best times of my life, I reckon. Aren't you gonna tell me, one more time, that I need to write those stories down for history?"

Not about to divulge my secret about the book I'd written for him, I shrugged. "Your stories will live on, one way or another. Now tell me how things really are back home."

Clearing his throat, Papa became serious. "We're doin' okay, don't get me wrong. Movin' a little slower these days. A few aches and pains. But that's life, you know. It's just..."

"Just what? I want you to tell me everything you are hiding from me."

Staring into the fire, he hesitated. Then he began to spill his guts. "It's your mama, Rose. You know she's always been difficult, always mad as a wet hen about somethin' or another. But she's gettin' worse. Never saw a woman who could carry on so. I've learned to just tune her out."

"You know that at her age she's not going to change. Hasn't she always been like this? What do you mean it's worse?"

"Sometimes she don't make a lick of sense. Like she's not thinking straight. She forgets things, puts things in the wrong place. She was in a flap before we left for the airport to fly on out here. Her purse was missing, and she swore she could not get onto that damn plane without her purse. Well, do you know where I finally found it, Rose?"

"In the car?"

"No. In the refrigerator! Who the hell would put a purse in the refrigerator? I just happened to open the fridge to get a glass of cold milk before we left, and there was her purse."

I stiffened. This didn't sound good. Was Mama getting Alzheimer's? "Tell me more."

"Well, she says mean things sometimes, things that hurt other people. She twists facts and tells stories that aren't really true. When I take her to church, I'm always afraid what she might say to other folks or about them. Last Sunday, poor Judy came in. Remember her, the Olson's daughter who came back home after her divorce from that punk she married?"

"Oh, yes, I remember. Nice-looking lady. Blond hair. Always dressed well."

"Well, Judy has had a hard time. She's gained weight. Don't take such good care of herself anymore. Still a nice woman who is kind to everyone, though. Anyway, when Judy came down the aisle, your mama turned and said, 'Look how fat she is! What a shame! Why don't she quit eating like a pig?' I could have hidden under the pew, Rose. Everyone heard what your mama said."

"Oh, Papa, I had no idea. It's not your fault, you know. People won't blame you. But have you talked to her doctor about this? Maybe she needs some medication or some help."

"Have you ever tried gettin' your mama to do anything? She says she's fine, and she don't need no doctor. Of course, she tries to blame you...you need to know that. As if she'd be fine if you hadn't left, if you'd married Bob and stayed home in Walnut."

"Papa, that's not fair! What am I supposed to do?"

"Look." He put his shaking hands on my shoulders. "What she says ain't true. She'd be this way if you were there or not. We all know that. You just need to know what she's sayin' to others."

"What can I do? How can I help?" I clenched my fists, dreading his response. Was I supposed to give up the new life I'd just found, right in the middle of solving the mystery of Amelia? Was I supposed to terminate my soul journey into the unknown so I could focus on the demands of my mother?

"What you can do is stay put and do what you need to do out here. Don't even think about comin' home, you hear me? I want you to figure things out and find the life you are meant to live. You can't do that if you give in to your mama's way of thinkin'."

Breathing a sigh of relief, I hugged him. "But what about you, Papa?"

"I can handle this. If it gets worse, I'll haul her into the doctor myself, kickin' and screamin'. I'll let you know how things are goin', if it gets worse. I don't mean to worry you, but you need to know the truth."

"Speaking of the truth, I have a question for you." I bit my lower lip. "Why can't I ever do anything right in Mama's eyes? I can't seem to please her, no matter what I do." I felt like a wounded little girl. Maybe that's exactly what I was.

His eyes widened as he placed his big, wrinkled hand over mine. "Look at me, Rose," he said sternly. I met his eyes. "One thing you need to know about your mama—and never forget this—is that she loves you, baby."

Baby? How many years had it been since anyone had called me "Baby"? Once upon a time, it was Papa's pet nickname for me. Tears welled in my eyes. "That's a strange kind of love, isn't it? I can't do anything right. I never could."

"Neither can I," he sighed, years of frustration bubbling to the surface. "I'm sure you've seen that. But it's her kinda love. It's all she knows. That's the way she was raised. If she didn't love you, she wouldn't care enough to criticize you or complain about everything. If you think she's bad, you should have known her mother. Someday I'll tell you about the grandmother you never knew. "

"Does that mean I'm going to be like her? That I'll raise my daughter the same way? Maybe I shouldn't have children."

"It will be different with you. I know that."

"All I need to do is find the right man. I haven't done too well in that area."

"But you will—if that hasn't happened already." He grinned at me and then turned serious again. "Ya know, I'm not a man of words. Never been one to say how I feel. Not a romantic bone in my body, your mama once told me. But I want to tell you something." He stopped as if trying to find the courage to go on.

"Please tell me, Papa," I whispered.

"I'm proud of you, Rose, proud of the person you've become. You're gonna do great things with your life, and I'm proud to be your father. I love you, baby. Shoulda told you that before...sorry I never did. Just thought you always knew that."

"Oh, Papa." I fell into his arms, tears dripping down my cheeks. "I love you too. You're the best father in the world. Thanks for all you've done for me."

A tear slid slowly down his weathered face as my heart became whole once more.

Suddenly, there was a noise behind us. We were no longer alone in the lounge. Spinning around, we found Mama standing there, her arms crossed over her chest. How much had she seen or heard?

"Mama, I didn't think you were up yet," I rambled. "We've been taking pictures of the sunrise and having coffee here by the fire. Come on. Sit down. I'll get you a cup of coffee and one of their delicious huckleberry scones."

"I thought it must be lunch time by now as long as you've been gone. I'm starving. Do you know how hard it was for me to walk all the way down here by myself?" She put on her exhausted face as she slowly shuffled toward the sofa and plopped down between Papa and me.

As I walked to the counter to order her breakfast, her voice rang out loudly. "Did you say huckleberry? I hate huckleberries. Get me something else."

"I'm sorry," I apologized to the cashier, beginning to understand what Papa was talking about. "Mama, you've never tasted huckleberry, have you? It's delicious."

"No, I have not tasted it, but I know I would hate it. Absolutely hate it! How about blueberry?"

She devoured her blueberry scone and coffee after I'd gone back several times to add more sugar and cream to her coffee.

After breakfast, we walked out on the upper deck overlooking Lone Peak Mountain and the ski trails. Basking in the warmth of the sun, we watched skiers swishing down the mountainside and riding lifts to the top. I reveled in the warmth of my father's love, something he'd rarely expressed to me before. I watched Mama carefully as she stared blankly into the blinding snow. I wondered what she was thinking about. I wondered if she'd overheard any of our conversation in the fireside lounge. Probably not or we would have heard about it.

Soon it was time to pack up and head for Virginia City. It was a beautiful drive, and I wanted them to see it in the daylight. Papa sat in front, his camera on his lap. He was entranced with the mountains and kept rolling the window down to snap more photos.

And Mama complained every time he did. "Stop it! We will catch our death of cold!"

I pulled over a number of times so Papa could get out and take more pictures.

In between her complaints, Mama started in on the recent election and her political views. I was amazed. Despite the fact that she sometimes said and did odd things, there were times when she was totally on top of it. She'd always watched the news on television and followed current events faithfully. Even now at her age, she knew more about what was happening in the world than I did. My world seemed to be headed backward in time.

Once we got onto the interstate, they both fell asleep, which was probably good. We had plans this evening, another special treat for my aging parents. It felt good to finally be doing something nice, something special, for them. Seems I spent most of my life annoying my mother, unable to meet her expectations. She seemed to be enjoying her visit—so far. And Papa was lovin' it.

The look on Mama's face was worth every dime I'd spent when we arrived at the Bennett House Bed and Breakfast right across the street from my cabin.

"I feel like a queen," she giggled as she strolled through the antique-filled parlor. She explored every nook and cranny of the elegant Queen Anne mansion.

Finally, we walked up the elegant carved wood staircase and entered the Rose Room where they would stay. Yes, Rose Room! The irony of it suddenly hit me. Decorated in Victorian rose colors, it was spacious and furnished with antiques.

Mama's eyes lit up as she settled in a chair in the window alcove overlooking the valley and my cabin. Grinning from ear to ear, she held her arms out to me. "Come here. You know you're my little girl, my Victorian Rose, don't you?" Hugging me tight, tears in her eyes, she seemed to be trying to tell me something more. Finally, the words came to her. "You're a good girl, Rose. I want you to know that. What you've done for Papa and me...well, I will never forget it. I'm happy we came, so happy."

"Oh, Mama." I wiped a tear from my eye. "Thank you for coming. Thank you for...for what you said. It means a lot to me."

Suddenly, Mama pulled back stiffly, a brief flash of bewilderment clouding her fading eyes. "You're all grown up now, aren't you?" The moment had passed. It had been a day for sentimental moments that I'd never forget. Perhaps all the more precious since they were so rare in my family. But she was not yet done with me. Her eyes bore into mine, searching for something she desperately needed. "No babies yet? No grandbabies for me?"

Trying to retain my composure, I could only reply, "Not yet, Mama. Not yet."

"Well," she giggled, "I think it's about time that you and that young husband of yours—Bob—got down to business in bed."

"Okay." I changed the subject. "I'll be back to pick you up in two hours for the holiday feast at the Elling House. Don't forget to wear your pretty dress, Mama."

"She will be ready." Papa winked at me as I left.

But she wasn't ready. I arrived a half hour early, just in case. As I climbed the stairs to their room, I could hear Papa's booming voice. "For God's sake, woman, put on your dress. You can't wear your old jeans tonight."

"I need to gather the eggs, you old fool!" she snapped at him.

"We're not on the farm, old woman. We're in Montana, and Rose is taking us out to some special feast tonight. Food of all kinds. Get dressed now!"

"Food?" Mama's voice perked up. "I'm starving. Where's my dress?"

Shaking my head in disbelief, wrapped in the sorrow of this new reality that had somehow crept into our lives, I knocked on their door. Papa was relieved to let me in so I could help get Mama ready for the evening. She no longer protested. In fact, she seemed to be back in the real world. Vibrant and curious, she asked questions about the Elling House as I brushed her hair and clasped a string of family pearls around her neck.

"You look beautiful, Mama," I told her as Papa and I escorted her to my car. He beamed with pride. She still was the apple of his eye, as he'd told her for so many years. And Papa himself looked rather dapper, as he'd say, in his old-fashioned funeral suit. Funeral suit? Yes, Papa had decided some years ago to order this brown polyester suit from the Sears and Roebuck catalog. It was the suit he'd be buried in someday in Walnut, Iowa. In the meantime, he wore it on special occasions. This was one of those special occasions.

While we could have easily walked down Idaho Street to the Elling House, built in 1876 by millionaire banker Henry Elling, I thought it best to drive. Just in case. The parking lot was filling up as we turned the corner and paused to absorb the eerie beauty of this Gothic stone mansion. Encircled by ancient wrought iron picket fences and a crumbling stone wall that was barely visible beneath tangled snow-laden vines, it resembled a haunted mansion. Lights flickered into the night through an impressive arched window on the upper level of the mansion.

I'd already heard the ghost stories about this place but had never before entered the mansion. Tonight we would be entertained in the grand ballroom where Henry's deceased wife, Mary Elling, sometimes appeared, or so they say. Despite her late husband's wishes, Mary had added a grand ballroom onto the house shortly after his death. It was her time to celebrate life in her own way—without the husband whom some described as a domineering and philandering man. It was Mary's wish that her ballroom would be used for community events and that the public would always be welcome in her home.

Mary continued from beyond her grave, they say, to insist that all restoration and redecoration projects of her beloved home met with her approval. The last incident occurred when the new owners decided to replace the aging wallpaper in the grand ballroom. Mary was not happy with their choices. Her spirit rifled through the books of wallpaper samples they'd left in the room. She continually turned the pages back to the design she'd chosen many years ago. Finally, when the workers removed many layers of old wallpaper, they found Mary's original wallpaper, which was exactly like the sample she kept referring them to. The new owners of the mansion decided to comply with her wishes.

Mama, Papa, and I arrived at the traditional holiday Splendid Feast hosted by the Elling House. We were greeted by water ice luminaries, tiny bulbs of light that lit up the driveway and entrance to the mansion. This eerie mansion had been transformed into a winter wonderland. Christmas carols drifted from the house into the mountains, echoing throughout the valley.

As we entered the house, we were warmed by a fire roaring in the hearth of the front room. A grand Christmas tree decorated with glowing candles, strings of cranberries, popcorn, and ornaments made by local artisans filled the entrance hall. Music drifted throughout the house as a pianist in a black tuxedo brought the keys of his baby grand piano to life. We stopped to listen and drifted into the holiday spirit as waitresses circled through the rooms offering glasses of wine, mead, and cider.

"I'm starving," Mama reminded us. We headed to the buffet where we splurged on a feast of culinary delights representing Christmas dishes from many cultures. Then we sat together on a sofa in the semi-darkness of the candle-lit front room, sipped our cider, and listened to the Christmas carolers.

Closing my eyes for a moment, drifting off into the past after a very long day, I was startled to find a vision of a prominent-looking gentleman standing before me, tipping his top hat in my direction as he bowed low. He sported a well-greased handlebar mustache and was decked out in a black tailcoat that hung knee-length in the back. A gold pocket watch and fob hung from the pocket of his festive vest, which was color coordinated with a fine silk cravat. His elegant walking stick was adorned with a faceted glass handle that sparkled with reflections from the Christmas lights.

I pinched myself to be sure I wasn't dreaming. Nervously glancing around the room, I realized that I was the only one who was apparently able to see this vision that had mysteriously stepped out from the past century. I could not take my eyes off him. There was something achingly familiar about him, about the thin moon-shaped scar on his left cheek, about those piercing eyes and the way he looked at me.

"Who are you?" I gasped quietly.

"Who am I?" he replied in astonishment. "My, my, how soon though dost forget all that we once shared. I shall try not to take offense, my dear. I have been waiting a long time for you." He beamed down at me as I squirmed in my seat. Had he actually spoken or had he somehow infiltrated my mind with his unspoken words?

Who was this man? Why was he appearing to me?

"Why am I appearing to you?" Rising above my apparent rebuff, he smirked dangerously, flicking the wing of his mustache in a playful manner. Leaning in closer, he whispered in a familiar husky voice, "Because I've always loved you, little one. I once promised you that I shall return for you someday. How could you have forgotten? Or have you fallen to the unscrupulous whims of another suitor perhaps? I suspect I have been betrayed—again. Is that not so?"

His smile suddenly faded into a grimace. His eyes flashed in anger as he clutched his walking stick, striking it hard against the floor. A blast of cold air rushed through me as he disappeared.

My eyes searched the room, anxiously trying to find him, trying to convince myself that I was not going crazy. But he was gone—as if he'd never been there.

Troubling thoughts tumbled through my mind. Who was this man, and why did he think he knew me? Could he have been involved with Amelia? And had she betrayed him?

"Absolutely not!" an injured voice from within penetrated my consciousness.

Shaking my head, trying to clear my mind from this madness, I focused on Mama and Papa who were still seated beside me as if nothing had happened. They were having a wonderful time singing along with the carolers.

I gladly accepted another glass of homemade mead as my eyes searched the crowd milling around the room. I was looking for Paul, but he was nowhere to be found. Maybe that was good. Still, I would have felt better to see his face, to feel the connection we shared. He was probably the only person who would ever understand some of the things I was experiencing. Not that I dared to share everything with him. I toyed with the idea of telling him about the appearance of this strange man tonight, but feared it would set him off as much as my comments about Jack Slade and Amelia had.

It was late. Mama and Papa were winding down, yawning, ready for bed. I escorted them back to their room, listened to their endless praises about the wonderful evening we'd shared. That made me happy. Had I finally done something right? Or was there some mysterious force at work here in Virginia City that was restructuring long-misunderstood family relationships?

Chapter 20

Christmas Eve day dawned bright and clear. I was to join Mama and Papa for breakfast at The Bennett House, prepared by gourmet cook Nancy who owned the old Victorian mansion. The smell of coffee and Canadian bacon frying in the pan welcomed me as I entered its beautifully decorated parlor. John, the local historian I'd met earlier, was there assisting Nancy and her nephew Gary.

"Merry Christmas!" they called out in unison as John handed me a hot cup of coffee. The table was set beautifully with an evergreen candle display. A plate of homemade muffins was already on the table. Tea lights flickered beneath an elegant silver coffee carafe. Soft Christmas music drifted throughout the house. I admired the Victorian buffet and artwork reminiscent of the last century. Finally, Mama and Papa came down the stairs, holding hands.

As we dined on eggs Benedict, blueberry muffins, and fruit cocktail, John entertained us with stories about the history of Virginia City. Papa was entranced, asking questions and telling him about his own efforts to preserve the history of Walnut, Iowa. Mama took it all in graciously, adding a comment or two. She was having a good day. Papa and John were already planning a walking tour of Virginia City for tomorrow morning, on Christmas Day, of all days.

"But tomorrow is Christmas Day, Papa," I protested meekly. "I'm sure John has plans."

"Oh no," John assured me. "We celebrate tonight."

"So do we," I grinned, greatly relieved.

"Besides, just ask Nancy." John winked at her. "One of the greatest joys of my life is telling others about the history of this place. I'd love to take your father and your mother...you are also welcome to come along."

"Really?" I lit up, unable to resist such an invitation from the man who probably knew more about this place than any other living human being. "You're on! I have lots of questions for you."

"I figured you might," John smiled as he poured another cup of coffee. "I see you walking around town, trying to absorb it all. Got a feeling you're learning things you never expected to learn?"

He knew. My eyes met his, and I felt common ground. I was certainly not the only one in this place who'd encountered spirits and unexplainable events.

"You want to know more about that hurdy-gurdy house, don't you?" He took a long swig of his coffee. "I've thought about that clock you told me about, and I've done a little more research on my own. Let's talk about that later."

My heart began to beat wildly. "A. J.? Do you have any clue what those initials could mean?"

"Well—"

"Could there have been an Amelia who worked there, John?" I couldn't help interrupting him in my excitement. "An Amelia with a last name beginning with a J?"

"Hmm...I'll check out that possibility. All I can tell you now is that the unofficial story about the girl commemorated by that clock is that she committed suicide."

"I don't believe that!" The words escaped from my mouth.

He looked at me long and hard, intrigued with my strong emotional reaction to his comment. "As I said, let's talk more later, Rose. Your folks would probably rather hear about the gold rush days here in Virginia City, eh?"

"Oh yes," Papa broke back into the conversation. "Tell me, when was gold discovered here?"

John began spinning his tales of the discovery of gold here in Alder Gulch, taking us back with him into the past.

In May of 1863, a group of six gold miners from the Bannack fields decided to pull up stakes and head for more lucrative grounds around the Yellowstone country. These fellas tended to get restless when their diggings began to dwindle. Following their dreams, they were always off to the next place where gold had been discovered—or may be found. Always following that powerful smell of gold...

These crusty old miners traveled light, their provisions strapped over their donkeys or horses. Essential gear included a pick, gold pan, shovel, bedding, a rifle, and sometimes a fiddle to play around the campfire at night. Some pitched a makeshift tent at night while others slept out beneath the stars.

Well, Bill Fairweather, Henry Edgar, and their men never made it to Yellowstone. They were turned back by the Crow Indians. Discouraged, they set up camp along a small creek sheltered by a fringe of alder trees in the shadow of the foothills of the Tobacco Root Mountains. Just beyond what is now Virginia City.

After they'd cooked a hearty supper over the fire of beans, bread sopped in lard, and muddy coffee, they grabbed their picks and pans and spread out to do some prospecting along the banks of the creek.

They swung their picks to loosen the rocky soil. Sand and gravel were scooped into pie plate-shaped metal pans and mixed with water from the stream. The miners tipped the pans slightly, swirling water over the pan's edge to remove the lighter-weight sand. The heavier gold pieces remained in the bottom of the pan. Some miners shoveled the sand and gravel into a rocker or cradle or used sluice boxes, which trapped the gold as the water washed away the gravel.

As the steady clinking sounds of picks against rock echoed throughout the gulch that evening, one of Fairweather and Edgar's men hit gold, lots of gold. They found such rich diggings that they rushed back to Bannack to stake twelve gold mining claims here. They named the place "Alder Gulch," recorded water rights, and tried to sneak back, unnoticed, to mine their claims.

However, news of their big find spread like wildfire. Within several days, they were followed by several hundred miners. Within weeks, according to one of the old settlers, hundreds of tents, brush wakeups, dugouts, and crude log cabins dotted the gulch in a haphazard way. The string of makeshift homes soon spread out along the gulch for fourteen miles, providing shelter for an estimated ten thousand people by mid-1864.

The miners were soon followed by merchants moving into the camps, selling their wares from tents and wagons. Soon they began building log cabin stores clustered around what became Virginia City's main street. There was even a makeshift bakery by the summer of 1863, followed by a saloon and hurdy-gurdy house, a blacksmith's shop, brewery, hotel and eatery, and a livery stable.

As word of the gold rush spread, investors and speculators moved in. So did the outlaws, the so-called road agents. They slunk around the mining claims and saloons, anxious to learn who'd discovered the most gold. Then they watched carefully, waiting for the day these miners would leave on the stagecoach to haul their gold back home with them. That's when they struck, robbing and murdering along the way.

They say that some of those miners who struck it rich simply disappeared, never to be heard from again. Sometimes a covered wagon train or stagecoach would discover the remains of a missing person buried alone in the wilderness. Wasn't long before the Vigilantes organized, taking the law into their own hands and hanging these outlaws.

"But I digress," John brought us back to the breakfast table. "I could go on forever. But as for that first big gold rush, it didn't last many years. Gold was soon discovered elsewhere, and many miners moved on. Some stayed. By then, Virginia City had grown roots. Families had come west, turning it into the great social city of the west. By 1880, only about 634 people lived here, however."

"How much gold did they discover?" Papa wanted to know.

"The Montana Bureau of Mines and the United States Department of Interior's Bureau of Mines claim that from 1863 to 1935 a total of close to fifty-four million dollars of placer and lode gold came from these Alder Gulch mines."

"WOW!" we all exclaimed in unison.

"Wish I'd lived here in those days," I sighed wistfully.

"Why, child? So you could strike it rich?" Mama pondered my odd statement. "I don't think girls could be miners back then."

John chuckled, swirling the cold coffee in his cup. "No, ma'am, but they could be wives or schoolteachers—or they could work in one of the dance halls or hurdy-gurdy houses." He glanced at me briefly, aware of my obsession.

"The what? Hurdy girdles?" Mama puzzled out loud. We all burst out in laughter.

John went on to explain that these girls worked in dance halls, dancing with the miners who paid them with gold dust. "There weren't a lot of women out here in those early years. Lonely men were anxious to dance with these girls."

Papa winked at me. "Bet they made a pretty penny."

"Oh yes," John nodded. "They could afford to wear some of the finest fashions and jewelry you could find anywhere in this country. Some of it came all the way from Paris. Quite a contrast to see one of these gals hiking along the rutted dirt street in her long fancy dress, trying not to step in piles of horse manure."

Of course my thoughts turned to my vision of Amelia hiking through the streets in her long red satin dress, but they were soon interrupted by a loud knock on the door. Peering out through the window, I saw a man who could have stepped out of the 1860s. He looked like one of the gold miners we'd just been talking about.

The door swung open as he sauntered in, a huge grin spreading across his weathered face. He tipped his hat at us, nodding his head politely.

"Mornin' folks, and Merry Christmas to ya'll." He plopped his large frame down into a chair at the table, rocking back on the chair legs as if he were in a saloon of the Old West.

"Well, Merry Christmas to you, sir!" Nancy got up to pour him a cup of coffee and offer him one of her homemade muffins.

"Folks, this is Diamondback Dave, one of our Virginia City regulars. A guy whose heart lives here in Virginia City. Dave, this is Rose, the new assistant at the library, and her folks—all the way from Iowa."

"Pleased to meet you." Dave stretched out his lanky legs, hooking the heels of his worn cowboy boots over the rungs of the chair.

"Your timing is perfect," John told him. "We were just talking about gold mining here. Dave can tell you everything you'd ever want to know about mining. In fact, he still mines here in his spare time."

"Oh, yes!" Dave came to life, passionate about one of his favorite subjects.

"Did you say diamondback, like a snake?" Mama's eyes were wide.

"Mama," I scolded her, embarrassed. But everyone else, including Dave, got a good chuckle out of her comment.

"That's right, ma'am," he replied. "A good old miner's name. You see, I'm proud of my handle, proud to be able to spend part of my life living in the past in the good old gold rush days."

I noticed a gold object glittering on a chain around his neck. Picking up on this, he took it off and showed me his good luck piece. "It's a gold nugget that I dug out of my claim, just up the road a ways. I wear it for good luck, and it hasn't let me down yet."

Dave went on to tell us about his old pack burro named Dusty. He and Dusty loved to ride up into the foothills and along the streambed with his pick, shovel, and pan. Alone in the early morning stillness, they'd rest a bit and he'd enjoy a cup of coffee from his thermos as the sun climbed above the mountains. Then he'd get to work, picking, sluicing, still finding nuggets of gold after all these years. One week he found ten ounces of gold—not bad these days when the price of gold had escalated far beyond anything that the old gold miners would have ever imagined.

While the thrill of discovering gold was always a high, it wasn't really about the monetary value, he assured us. It was about reconnecting with a part of himself buried deep within the past. Reconnecting with the world of those old miners.

One day as he dozed in the hot sun, alone with Dusty beneath the huge blue sky, his mind drifted back into a time warp from the past. He could hear the clanging of the picks and shovels and could see the dust-covered miners gathered around the stream swishing plates of gold or loading rockers. He swore he could hear their laughter, their cussing, their hoots and howls as they kicked up their heels when they got lucky. He could feel their exhaustion after endless hours and days of hard work and could almost smell the grimy banks of sweat wafting through the air. Then, suddenly, it all disappeared. He was alone once again, shaking his head in disbelief. Had he really seen and heard what he thought he had?

"I'll never know," Dave admitted. "It was an honor for a humble man like me to be allowed to tap into their world like that. Sometimes I wonder if that was once my world, my life."

Today, mining was a hobby that he loved, a drastic change from his high-pressured career. Someday he'd retire and come back to Virginia City, the place he felt he belonged more than any other.

I nodded eagerly. He was so much like me in some ways. Perhaps we were kindred spirits, gathering here by design or accident in this high-energy vortex that still belonged to the past.

Dave seemed to pick up on my thoughts. "Let's talk more someday, Rose. I could help you in your research. More importantly, I'm thinkin' we may share some common history here."

Then he was gone, and the rest of us went about our day preparing for Christmas Eve festivities. Mama and Papa took a nap and browsed through some of the books in the parlor while I rushed home to begin preparing Christmas dinner. Time had slipped away faster than I realized.

Thankfully, I already had the Christmas ham cooking slowly in the oven. I made my traditional green bean casserole, deviled eggs, cranberry sauce, a new wild rice dish with chunks of bacon and venison, and rolls. We'd have Mama's Christmas cookies for dessert. I made hot apple cider and opened a carton of eggnog. We could lace it with brandy if anyone wanted to.

Paul was bringing the wine. Paul! I'd almost forgotten about him. How I hoped things would go well and that Mama would behave. She seemed to be enjoying herself too much to complain or bicker with any of us. Maybe all she had needed was enough sleep and a change of setting now and then.

As I turned on the Christmas lights and began setting the table, I looked out the window to find snowflakes falling. It was going to be a White Christmas. I changed into a soft red dress that clung to my curves and reluctantly took off my green good-luck pendant. It just didn't go with the frilly dress. Instead, I wore my crystal snowflake pendant and earrings. Brushing and styling my hair, I glanced into the mirror and decided I looked better than I ever had since arriving out west. What would Paul think—and why should I even care what he thought?

Turning on the Christmas music, I began pulling on my boots and coat to cross the street and pick up my parents. But as I opened the door, there they were, standing on my doorstep. Their cheeks were rosy, their eyes glowing with excitement, and they were holding hands.

I seated them by the fireplace and offered them apple cider or eggnog. Papa wanted a swig of brandy in his eggnog. I had the same and handed Mama her apple cider. She wandered around my little place, admiring the way the table was set with her cookies prominently displayed.

Then she stopped, a puzzled look on her face. "Four places, Rose? Why, for heaven's sake, is Bob coming for dinner?" She seemed thrilled at this possibility.

I stopped in my tracks as Papa approached her slowly. "Mama, we're in Montana. Bob's not here...and you know, Bob and Rose—"

"Well, of course, I know that!" She snapped. "But who else is coming for dinner then?"

"Mama, remember I told you that my boss, Paul, was coming? He's alone without family. A nice man. You will like him. And Papa will love talking history with him."

As if on cue, there was a loud knock on the door. "Come in!" I called out as Paul entered, his arms full of wrapped packages. He juggled several bottles of wine.

"Here, let me help you." I gathered the gifts from his arms. As I approached, his eyes lit up in admiration. "You are beautiful," he whispered softly. "So lovely in red."

"Let me introduce you to my parents." I took his arm as we walked across the room where they were now seated beside the fireplace.

Paul broke the ice easily, I thought, casually engaging them in conversation as I put the finishing touches on our meal. I could hear Mama's laughter. She was happy. Maybe it helped that I sneaked a shot of brandy into her apple cider.

Soon we seated ourselves at the table. Paul held Mama's chair for her and then seated me. The perfect gentleman. He poured us each a glass of wine, complimenting me on the wonderful meal. Papa gave his traditional Christmas blessing, and we began dishing up our plates.

Amid praise for the holiday meal I'd prepared, all by myself for the first time in my life, we ate.

"It's nice you could come, Paul." Mama smiled at him. "How sad to be all alone during the holidays. What happened to your family?"

"Let's talk about history instead," Papa interrupted her, twisting his fork in his hand. "I want to know all about Virginia City, and I hear you're the man to ask."

"It's okay," Paul assured him. "I was an only child, and my folks, bless their hearts, are no longer here. Other relatives live too far away. I'm just grateful that your daughter invited me to celebrate with all of you. Don't know what I'd do without her. She's the best research assistant I ever had."

Mama carefully watched the warm looks passing between Paul and me. There was a shimmering, almost sizzling quality, I realized. She carefully folded her napkin in her lap and looked up as if she had an important announcement to make.

"Well, I'm honored you could come. It's nice to meet the man our daughter works for. Have you met Bob yet?"

Papa and I both tensed up.

Paul looked confused. "Bob? I'm afraid I haven't had the pleasure. Your son?"

"Oh no, we don't have a son. Just Rose. She's all we've got, but she's so far away. So is Bob. It's too bad he couldn't come for Christmas dinner too."

"Anna," Papa broke in. "Your food is getting cold." Then he turned toward Paul, a look of embarrassment on his face. " Bob's an old family friend from back home. I'm sure you've never met him."

"An old family friend?" Mama cried out. "For heaven's sake, you old fool, have you forgotten that he is Rose's fiancée, that she's going to marry him someday?"

Paul's face dropped as a flash of anger shot through his eyes. I don't think anyone else noticed it. He recovered immediately, although I could still see the tension in his jaw. He was trying hard to control his emotions.

"Wait a minute, Mama! You know that Bob and I broke up long ago. There's no need to talk about him. Let's pass the Christmas cookies you made for us. Paul, my mother bakes the best Christmas cookies you will ever taste. Try one."

Paul gratefully took several cookies from the plate and began to compliment her on the butterballs. He turned his gaze away from me.

"Well, you never know," Mama grinned at Paul. "Just because she left that nice young lad standing at the altar doesn't mean they won't make up someday. Why, he's loved her all his life—"

"It's over, Mama. You need to accept that. Now I do not want to hear anymore on this subject tonight. It's Christmas, and I think there are some packages under the tree that have our names on them." I took her arm and escorted her to a chair beside the tree. "Just sit here and look at the lights while I clean up the food." I found Paul and Papa clearing dishes, talking quietly.

"I'm sorry, Paul." Papa shook his head. "Sometimes when she gets tired, she gets a little confused and testy. She don't mean no harm."

Paul put his hand on Papa's shoulder. "I understand. No need to apologize."

"Is it time to open presents yet?" Mama sang out in a voice reminding me of a little girl.

Finally, we gathered around the tree, trying to recapture the initial magic of the evening. Trying to forget Mama's words. Paul and I avoided each other's eyes, focusing on my parents and the gifts instead. He'd bought them each a book about Virginia City—one about its history for Papa and a cookbook for Mama.

Papa was delighted beyond words, tears in his eyes, when he opened my gift to him. "The best gift anyone ever gave me, Rose." He hugged me close.

"I'd like to read it someday," Paul told him. "I'd like to know what it was like to grow up in your little town of Walnut, what your family was like." He seemed genuinely interested. Of course, he loved history and stories about the past. But was he also trying to pry into my past life? Was he looking for stories about Bob?

Mama was also thrilled when she opened the framed photo I'd taken of Virginia City, a view from my house looking out over the town below, surrounded by the mountains. Her mood seemed to change for the better as I had her look out the window at the same scene I'd captured on film.

Paul opened my gift—a rare book on the history of Alder Gulch. He was also pleased and couldn't resist paging through it, reading a line here or there. "It's perfect and a first edition, I see. Thank you, Rose." His eyes met mine once more.

I turned away to retrieve the two gifts remaining beneath the tree. They both had my name on them, both from Paul. Taking them from my hands, he put one gift back into his pocket as inconspicuously as possible while handing me a small box. Opening it carefully while all eyes watched, I lifted out a beautiful hand-painted Victorian ornament depicting Virginia City.

"It's beautiful, Paul. Thank you." I smiled at him as I hung it on the tree.

We made small talk for the rest of the evening, sipping our wine, until my parents began to yawn. It had been a long day, and they were ready for bed. At home, they rarely stayed up late enough these days to watch the ten o'clock news.

Paul and I walked them back across the street to their Rose Room. It was a beautiful snowy evening. The skies had cleared enough to show off a dazzling display of stars lighting up the night. We could hear a couple splashing about in an outdoor hot tub, enjoying each other beneath the stars on Christmas Eve.

After exchanging hugs and Christmas wishes, Paul and I left the house in silence. The snow squeaked beneath our feet. Christmas music floated into the night from the radio in my cabin. It was only nine o'clock. Was Christmas Eve already over?

When we arrived back at my cabin, Paul opened the door for me to enter and then stood on the doorstep, waiting.

"Aren't you coming in?" I asked, not sure if I wanted him to or not. I could sense a storm brewing within him.

"I'm not Bob! And I'm not sure I belong here, Rose. I thought I knew you...but now I'm not sure who the hell you are."

"Of course you're not Bob!" I snapped back. "But you can still come in for a nightcap. Where else do you have to go?"

Almost reluctantly, he stomped the snow from his boots and threw his jacket over a chair. He busied himself, furiously stoking the logs in the fireplace with a long red-hot poker and throwing a few more logs on. The fire blazed, the Christmas tree twinkled. We sat in silence, staring into the fire as we sipped hot apple cider.

Trying to break the silence, I blurted out the first words that came into my head. "So are your parents really dead?"

He looked at me, astonished by my blunt words. "No," he replied, "not as far as I know, but my grandparents are. They're the ones who raised me right on the Madison River in Ennis. But why should you care when you've lied to me?"

"I never lied to you, Paul DuBois!"

"Well you sure as hell omitted the truth, didn't you? You never mentioned another man, did you? You led me to believe you were unattached. That sure as hell is not the way your mother sees it. She thinks you're marrying him!"

"You know as well as I do that Mama is not entirely rational these days. And for your information, I am unattached. I'm thinking I need to stay that way forever. Have you forgotten our professional relationship? What about that?"

"You know as well as I do that we're in love with each other!" He almost spit the words in my face. "For good or bad, for downright ugly, there's something between us. Whether you like it or not, and I can't say I'm thrilled about it either, Rose. Why do I always end up with cheating women?"

"What?" I gasped. "Cheating? How could I have cheated on you if I knew Bob before I ever met you?"

Paul didn't answer.

"And you never told me about any cheating women from your past either, for that matter. Does that mean you were lying to me?"

Suddenly, we both realized the absurdity of this conversation and broke into laughter. The harder we laughed, the faster the anger melted away.

"This is crazy." He shook his head when he finally came up for air.

"So maybe we should just quit talking about it—"

"And go with the flow?"

"Maybe," I whispered, "maybe not," as his lips found mine once again.

Nervously glancing back through the windows facing Mama and Papa's room across the street, I could almost imagine them peering out and into my house. Surely they were aware that Paul's truck was still parked beside my cabin.

He flipped off the lamp and hungrily pulled me into his arms. We sank deeply into the softness of the sofa and into each other as the real world began to slip further and further away. Bob's shadow faded into the background of my mind.

The urgency pulsating through our bodies was suddenly disrupted when Lucky jealousy decided to leap up onto the davenport, settling his big furry body squarely between us. He would not budge as he laid his big head on my lap, daring Paul to try to interfere.

"Maybe that dog is right," Paul sighed as he stood and began to pace around the room. "We don't know what the hell we're doing, do we? We can't even decide if we love or hate each other."

I had to admit he had a point. Lucky had perhaps saved us from the passion of the night and from a future of heartache. Still, I wanted Paul to stay. "I have an idea," I told him. "Have you ever watched the Christmas classic, *It's A Wonderful Life?*"

"Of course. It's one of my favorite movies," he confessed, brushing his hands through his unkempt hair. Why did that simple gesture always stir my soul in strange ways?

"You're kidding me, right? Because that's *my* favorite movie. I've watched it every Christmas Eve since I was a child. I was planning to watch it tonight after you all left. Do you want to stay?" My voice sounded hopeful, more so than I wanted it to.

"Where's the popcorn? It's movie night," he proclaimed as he headed to my little kitchen to microwave a bowl of kettle corn.

"Do you think your folks would mind?" he teased as he planted himself on the other side of Lucky, his arm casually draped over the back of the sofa. One hand rested lightly on my shoulder as he balanced the bowl of popcorn with the other one. I playfully tossed kernels of corn into his open mouth.

The lights went off, and the show began. He got tears in his eyes at the end, the exact place where I cried every time I watched this movie. I couldn't believe we were crying together, tears of hope and happiness, by the time the old black-and-white movie wound down.

It was late, time for Paul to leave. As he bent down to grab his jacket from the floor, something fell out of his pocket. A small present wrapped in shiny red paper. The gift he'd hidden from me earlier.

He stared at the package for a minute as if trying to decide what to do with it. Finally, he pulled me closer, took my hand, and gently placed the present in my hand. "It's for you. You can open it now," he whispered.

Carefully, I removed the paper and opened the box. A beautiful antique cameo broach was nestled in a bed of soft white fluff. The face of an elegant Victorian lady, etched in ivory, was framed in a delicate oval of gold filigree. It hung on a fine antique gold chain.

I was stunned. "Why?" I whispered. "Why are you giving this to me?"

"I know it seems strange. I know we haven't known each other long, but...for some strange reason, I feel compelled to give it to you. I don't understand it, but it's important to me that you have it."

Touched, I carefully removed the necklace from the box, tears welling in my eyes. "I don't know what to say. It's beautiful, almost spiritual. I can feel it. Wherever did you find something like this?"

"Here, turn around. I'll help you." He spun me around and fastened the necklace around my neck. "Now, look in the mirror. How does it look? How do you feel?"

Gazing into the mirror, I felt like I'd stepped into a looking glass from long ago. "I feel like it belongs to me...or I belong to it. I love it, Paul."

His eyes glowed with happiness as he pulled me into his arms. "It *is* you. You are the one! I knew it. I just knew it."

"Where did you get it?" I had to know.

"It belonged to my grandmother, and I think she got it from her grand-father, or so they say. A family heirloom thing."

"And you're giving it to me? I still don't understand why."

"Because it belongs to you. After all these years, I've finally found the woman it belongs to. I've dreamed of placing this necklace around your neck—as if it were something important that I was supposed to do. I know it's strange, but maybe my grandmother is at peace tonight."

"You loved her, didn't you?" I had to change the subject.

"She was the only good thing in my life as I was growing up. She was the one who loved me, the one who believed in me. The one who made up for my parents not wanting me."

"I'm sorry, Paul." I reached for his hands and held them tightly in my own.

"It's okay," he grinned down at me. "Merry Christmas, Rose. Merry Christmas, Grandma. May you rest in peace."

Chapter 21

Sometimes it's good, I decided, to be too busy to think. It helps one to hold onto some semblance of reality instead of slipping down that treacherous slope into the past. My parents provided all the diversion I needed during their visit. It was a memorable visit, but it finally came to an end. I packed them in my SUV, and we headed for the airport.

Papa couldn't quit chattering about all he'd seen and learned about the history of Montana. He was anxious to share his new stories with his friends back in Walnut, and he couldn't wait to show them the book I'd written for him about his life. He wanted copies for the library and the historical society.

Mama kept thanking me, over and over again, for "the best Christmas ever." After all her complaining about having to spend Christmas out here, she actually had a good time.

All went well until we arrived at the airport. I helped them check their baggage and walked them to the waiting area where we sat watching people come and go until their flight was called.

We stood. I hugged them good-bye, tears in my eyes.

"What? Why are you telling us good-bye, Prairie Rose? You're coming with us, of course!" Mama seemed bewildered as she snapped at me, squaring her shoulders.

"Mama, you know I can't. I have a job here. This is where I live."

"That doesn't make a lick of sense, young lady. You belong home in Walnut!"

Papa put his arm around her waist protectively. "Now, Anna, we will see her again soon. You know she has to stay here for now. It's time for us to go."

She jerked away from him. "Well, I'm not going without her, and that's that!"

Papa and I exchanged a worried look. What was she thinking? How should we handle this situation? It was time to board the plane.

Mama was already walking away from us, shaking her head in frustration. Papa and I flanked her, gently holding her arms.

"If you don't come home with me, Anna, what am I supposed to do all alone? You know I can't hardly boil water by myself," he pleaded with her.

"Hmmm..." She stopped, deep in thought. "Well, you could stay here too. With me. In that lovely Rose Room."

"I think it's already booked by other guests, Mama," I said. "But you can come back another time, real soon."

"But I want to stay *this* time!" She protested like a little girl, stomping her foot on the ground for emphasis.

Papa shook his head. "What am I supposed to tell your Ladies Aid Society when you aren't there to host the next meeting and bake your cookies? You know nobody can bake like you can. You promised them...you can't let them down."

Mama perked up finally, sighing dramatically. "Well, all right then. I guess I have to go."

Breathing a sigh of relief, I walked them as far as I could and hugged them both good-bye. I waited until their plane took off, roared down the runway and lifted into the brilliant blue sky. I worried, wondering what was happening to Mama, what the future held for them, and how long I'd be able to follow my dream. For now, Papa seemed to know how to handle her, but how long would that last? I may need to go home someday to help out, I realized. The thought filled me with dread.

Arriving back at my cabin just before dusk, I felt restless and almost lonely after all the activity of the previous week. It was New Year's Eve, and I had no plans, aside from making my usual New Year's resolutions. Heading out for a brisk walk with Lucky, I hiked down the alley toward the library. The lights were on although it was a holiday. Paul's truck was parked in its usual place. He apparently had no plans either.

I couldn't decide if I should walk on by or stop in. As I stood there trying to make a decision, Paul peeked out his window and rushed out to join me.

"What a pleasant surprise!" he grinned, stooping to pat Lucky on the head. "So are the two of you spending New Year's Eve alone?"

"Guess so," I sighed. "How about you?"

"Not anymore. Look, there's a gathering down at the Pioneer Bar if you'd like to go. I hear there's even music and snacks. I don't usually do that kind of thing, but it is New Year's Eve."

"You're on." I perked up. His offer sounded more appealing than sitting home alone worrying about my parents and an unknown future. More appealing than dealing with Amelia and that man in the boat whom I was becoming convinced was probably her lover, maybe even her murderer. Of course, I had no proof or anything, just wild hunches. I needed to clear my head before I tackled these spirits of the past once again.

"Just one thing," I added, "let's not talk about ghosts tonight, all right?"

He raised his eyebrows sharply. "So I take it you've had another encounter, perhaps a troubling one that you're not ready to share with me yet?"

"Yes, you're right. And no, I'm not ready, Paul."

His eyes clouded over, the old sparkle gone, as if I'd just slapped him in the face.

"I'm sorry, but sometimes these visits wear me down. I need to get away from it all or I fear I'll lose my mind. Why me? Why won't they just leave me alone?"

After a long pause, he touched my arm gently. "*They?* Now there's more than one?"

I nodded, averting my eyes from his.

"Anything to do with Amelia?"

"I'm afraid so, and I seem to be caught right in the middle of it all. I don't want to talk about it."

"All right," he reluctantly agreed. "Just tell me this. Are you afraid? Are you feeling threatened in any way? Because if you are, you need to tell me. You cannot be alone."

"No, I'm not feeling threatened. Just overwhelmed, I guess. I'll tell you if I'm afraid or need your help. I'll tell you more later once I figure a few things out."

"Look, Rose. I can help you figure these things out," he shook his head as if exasperated with my secrecy.

"Then tell me why they're flitting in and out of my mind as if they're trying to take over my life. Sometimes I feel like I'm becoming her, becoming Amelia. Why me?"

"I don't know...my guess is that they have some unfinished business here on earth. This Amelia, whoever she was, seems to have chosen you to straighten it all out. Maybe there were other parties involved in whatever happened to her."

I sighed, finally looking into his steady eyes. "I guess. Maybe I need to set the record straight after I figure out who she was. Everyone seems to think she was a prostitute, that she betrayed and hurt someone. That she committed suicide. But that's just not true! She's the one who was betrayed, Paul!"

"Everyone?" He put his hands on my shoulders, holding me firmly in place. "Who else, except for me, has made accusations like that, Rose?"

"Well...I've...I've heard a few things from others, even John, the local historian."

"He didn't tell you all of that, Rose," Paul reprimanded me sternly. "I know him too well for that. What about the others you mention?"

Wiggling away from him, I took a few steps backward. "There is one other, an apparition of a gentleman who recently appeared to me. That's all I'm going to say about this matter. For now. I need to go home and feed the dog."

"Wait! No more questions, I promise. I'll pick you up at eight, all right?"

❧⚬❦

I'd never been in the Pioneer Bar before but was intrigued by the old town watering hole the moment we entered. A massive mahogany bar with carved wood pillars and an expanse of mirrors dominated one wall. An antique cash register was still in use behind the bar where regulars sat on old swivel stools munching on snacks. The ceiling was composed of scrolled tin tiles from well over one hundred years ago. Wagon wheel lighting fixtures cast reflections on an assortment of mounted animal heads covering the walls. There were buffalo and elk heads with huge racks of horns and antlers. A pool table filled one corner of the room.

Tables had been pushed aside to create a dance floor for this special occasion. A small band comprised of a guitar, fiddle, and banjo accompanied by a keyboard was already playing music that floated out into the street. Dancers were beginning to assemble on the floor, rocking to the music of the band.

Paul and I found a table in the corner. He made his way to the bar and came back with two glasses of beer that had been sloshed around by the crowd. Froth dripped from the glasses onto the table.

I recognized many of the locals including Maria, the waitress at the Outlaw, who stopped to visit with us. Paul seemed to know almost everyone in the place. They seemed surprised to see him at the bar.

After a few beers, we decided to join the others on the dance floor. He pulled me into his arms, holding me so close I could feel his heart beating against mine.

"Have I told you how lovely you look this evening, my dear?" he whispered in my ear.

"I'm just wearing jeans and a red silk blouse," I replied, surprised at his compliment.

"Red is your color, Rose, and you are wearing my grandmother's brooch. I can't tell you how happy I am to see you wearing it after all these years."

"After all these years?"

"After all these years." He immediately changed the subject, reminiscing about the way the old-timers would have celebrated this holiday. Sleigh rides. Oyster feeds. Fiddlers playing. People dancing.

At the stroke of midnight, the band broke into "Auld Lang Syne." I floated into Paul's arms without invitation, our lips meeting anxiously, clinging to each other for as long as we dared. Breathless, we finally parted, hearts pounding.

"Whew! I think we need some fresh air. Are you ready to walk home?"

Nodding, I stood as he wrapped my coat and scarf around me, took my hand, and led me out into the stillness of a new year. The music drifted into the background as we hiked down the boardwalk of the deserted ghost town. We seemed to be drifting into a world of the past.

Words were not necessary. Being together was all that mattered. Just living the moment without any thoughts of yesterday or tomorrow was more than enough. A moment forever frozen in time, I thought to myself.

When we reached the door of my cabin, Paul shoved it open for me. Taking off my coat, I turned around to find him still standing in the doorway. "Come on in," I smiled at him.

"Better not," he sighed. "I want to do it the proper way this time, the old-fashioned way. Tonight I do not trust myself to wait until...well...until you are my wife."

"What??" *His wife?* Hold on, this was moving way too fast.

"You have no idea how long I've been waiting for you," he sighed, a faraway look in his eyes.

"I don't understand you sometimes, Paul. We haven't known each other long enough to even think about a future together. But in the meantime, I'd love to get to know you better. Come on in for a while?" Even as my words spilled out, I wasn't sure exactly what I meant, exactly what my intentions were.

"We must learn not to give into temptation," he lamented in a proper tone of voice. "I must go. Happy New Year, darlin'." He bent to give me a quick kiss. Then he was gone.

I locked the door and leaned heavily against it. He was a strange man indeed. Maybe it was good that he'd left me alone tonight, alone with the crazy feelings he'd stirred up within my heart and soul. I needed some sleep.

Drifting off into a restless sleep, tossing and turning, I finally slipped away into the world of my dreams. Oddly enough, it wasn't Amelia who haunted me tonight. It wasn't even Paul. Instead, I found myself curled up in Bob's arms, wrapped in the warmth and security of his love.

Chapter 22

New Year's Day dawned bright and clear but very cold. A good day to stay inside by the fire, make my annual resolutions, and plot out my plan of attack. It was time to get back to work. Time to solve the mystery of Amelia. That was my number one New Year's resolution.

Dawn was creeping lazily over the snow-covered Tobacco Root Mountains when I stumbled out of bed and padded to the kitchen in my furry slippers. After throwing a few more logs on the fire, I settled at my little table by the window. I loved watching the sun rise, energized by the promise of a brand new day, perhaps a fresh start in life.

Gazing out through the frosty windowpanes, my mind drifted back to the gentleman who had appeared to me at the Elling House. His face was etched firmly in my mind. I was obsessed with finding out who he was, and how he was connected to Amelia. A leap of logic perhaps, but I felt strongly that there once was a relationship between the two of them. A tumultuous relationship at that. He, whoever he was, apparently felt she had betrayed him. But I felt he was absolutely wrong about that.

After a breakfast of Mama's leftover Christmas cookies, I bundled up and took Lucky out for a walk. Virginia City was perfectly still on this cold winter morning. I did not see a living soul, not even a ghost, as we hiked along our usual path through town. All stores were closed for the holiday. As cold as it was, even Lucky was happy to make it a short walk.

On a whim, I decided to climb the ladder up into the loft of my cabin. It was so cozy with its warm log walls and low ceiling dropping down to meet the floor at the far end. One small octagon-shaped window provided a bird's-eye view of the valley below and surrounding mountains. A perfect hiding place for children to escape into their make-believe worlds, I thought to myself. A refuge, perhaps, where I could try to connect with Amelia. It would be nice if I could somehow confine my work with the spirit world to the loft and have a normal life downstairs.

I decided to redecorate the loft to suit my purposes. First, I lugged a few big pillows up the ladder and arranged them on the little window seat beneath the window. I found my battery-operated camping lantern to provide light while I worked. I'd still need a warm rug. I decided I should be able to pick one up in Sheridan the next time I went in for groceries and my usual errands. Maybe I'd frame and hang some of my photos on the wall—photos of Virginia City. Hopefully they would inspire me to tap into the mysteries that surrounded Amelia and her life.

Feeling like a child building a secret fort, I climbed up again with my laptop, several books on the history of Virginia City, and my sketchbook and pencils. Settling into my soft window seat, I was content to gaze out the window, trying to let go and tap into the past. Trying to find Amelia—and her gentleman friend or lover—once again.

As I closed my eyes, the gentleman's face leaped into in my mind. The image was so vivid, so lifelike, that I felt compelled to sketch his portrait. Grabbing my old sketchbook and pencils, I began to draw furiously as if under a spell. I was hardly aware of what I was doing. My pencil seemed to have a mind of its own. Something guided my hand. I did not, could not, stop to evaluate my work or make any changes. Finally, exhausted, I felt the pencil drop from my hand.

I was astonished to see the exquisite sketch I'd drawn. It highlighted every detail of the man I'd seen at the Elling House, right down to the moon-shaped scar on his face. And it was more than his face staring back at me. It was a full body sketch. He wore the same vintage clothing I'd seen him in, even carried the walking stick with the glass handle. The look on his face, his arrogant posture...it was him, exactly as he'd appeared to me.

The sketch was so far beyond my abilities as an artist. There's no way I could have drawn it. When I looked at it, I could almost feel this man's eyes gazing into mine, following me around the loft. Unnerved, I flipped the drawing over, trying to get out from under his spell.

I stumbled down the ladder and out onto the porch to get some fresh air. A blast of frigid air tore through me, almost taking my breath away. It was stupid to be standing out here on my porch in a sweatshirt and jeans. What was I thinking? Shivering, teeth chattering, I went back inside.

Pouring myself a glass of wine, I plopped down beside Lucky who was sprawled out on the sofa by the fireplace. He licked my face, trying to comfort me. That dog of mine always knew when I was upset. He was always there for me, his human-like brown eyes staring into mine as if trying to assure me that it would be okay.

"I love you, Lucky." I cuddled up beside him as he plopped his furry head onto my lap.

The wind howled and rattled the windowpanes. I gathered flashlights and matches to light the kerosene lamp and candles in case the electricity went out. Assessing my woodpile beside the fireplace, I was thankful that it was adequate. I wouldn't have to venture out into the cold to replenish it. Paul had hauled in a huge pile of logs the last time he was here.

Paul...I wondered what he was doing today. I didn't know what to think about his strange words and behavior last night. Although I feared that I was falling in love with him, God help me, I was still reluctant to share some of my discoveries with him. Lingering suspicions still prevented me from fully trusting him.

I thought about showing him the sketch upstairs in my loft. Then, I began to question whether it really existed—or if it was just a figment of my imagination. I was beginning to doubt my perceptions. After another glass of wine, I grabbed a flashlight and climbed back up into the loft. I needed to make sure there was, in fact, a sketch of this gentleman.

I'd thrown it face down on the window seat when I'd scampered down the ladder. Shining my flashlight in that direction, I was shocked to discover that it was not there.

I cautiously swung my flashlight around the darkened room, searching for that sketch. I covered every inch of the floor. Nothing. Remembering the lantern, I reached up to flip the switch on. Suddenly, in the glow of the light, I found the sketch—hanging on the wall beside the window, staring down at me!

Shocked, I began edging my way back toward the ladder. I knew beyond a doubt that I had not hung that sketch on the wall. And nobody else had been in the house.

I remembered Paul's words, "Are you feeling threatened? Are you afraid?" As I pondered my feelings, wondering if I should call Paul, something caught my eye in the corner of the loft. I felt a distinct chill in the air as a semi-transparent image swooped through the loft. Looking closer, I recognized the Amelia of my dreams. I could even see the radiant and reassuring smile on her face. She was showing me through the sketch she'd drawn for me a piece of the missing puzzle of her life. Then she disappeared.

I needed to find out who the gentleman on my wall was and how he fit into Amelia's life. Of course, it would be helpful to know her full name and who she really was.

❧❧

The next few weeks of winter flew by as I worked on my research at the library. I was also beginning to edit some of Paul's chapters. Every spare moment I had was dedicated to searching through the archives, old newspapers, family histories, and the Internet for photos of men who had lived in Virginia City prior to 1868 when Amelia died. Granted, most of these photos would be of prominent gentlemen, not of the miners who lived here. But the man I was seeking was obviously prominent, based upon his clothing and demeanor.

If Amelia had really been a hurdy-gurdy girl, however, it seemed strange that her lover would have been a prominent citizen of this town. Or maybe not...

Frustrated, I ran into one dead end after another. While I occasionally came across photos that bore some resemblance to my sketch, nothing matched perfectly. Nothing felt right. Maybe I was wasting my time on a wild goose chase, as Papa would say. Maybe I needed to leave it alone for now and concentrate my efforts on Amelia.

I had not spent much time with Paul. One day he confronted me in my office. "Rose?" his voice broke through my reverie as he settled his large frame in the chair on the opposite side of my desk. "Working late again?"

I startled, unaware until now that it was already dark outside. Looking up, I saw a puzzled expression on his face.

"When are you going to level with me?" he asked sternly.

"About what?"

"About whatever it is that you've been obsessing over for the past few weeks. We've hardly talked, after all we shared together. You're too preoccupied to know that I exist."

"I'm sorry, Paul. I have been busy editing your work, you know."

"And I thank you for doing a great job. But..."

"But what?"

"You're hiding things from me, things that I should probably know about. Have you had any more contacts from Amelia or anyone else?" He sounded genuinely interested and almost hurt that I was not confiding in him.

"I have," I began warily. "I have a sketch of the man who appeared to me. Amelia was there, helping me to complete the sketch, confirming that this man was once a part of her life."

Paul perked up, sitting on the edge of his chair. "That's wonderful news...I guess. So I suppose you're trying to figure out who he was. That's why you've been pouring over all those old records?"

I couldn't seem to get away with anything when Paul was around. "You don't miss much, do you?" I grinned at him. "I cannot find a photo anyplace that matches the man I saw in the vision. I'm dead in the water right now and really frustrated."

"Dead in the water? Interesting expression."

"Well, you know what I mean. If you have any ideas as to where else I can look for information, I'd love to hear them."

"It's possible there are no photos, Rose, none that survived. Or maybe they're buried in an old trunk someplace in someone's attic. Come to think of it, I have an old trunk packed with historical photos. It belonged to my grandfather. Of course he lived in Ennis, not Virginia City. Still, maybe you'd like to come over and go through it with me?"

While my first reaction was to jump at his offer, a warning light flashed through my mind. I recalled the way he'd described the spooky mansion he lived in on the banks of the Madison River. I didn't want to go there, not even if there was a possibility of finding a match in that old trunk of photos. Maybe there wasn't a trunk there after all...maybe no photos at all.

"Well? I'll take you out for dinner at one of the restaurants in Ennis first. Or if you'd rather come over Saturday afternoon, in the daylight, we could make a day out of it." His eyes were filled with hope.

While my heart began to respond, my mind shut it down. "I'd love a rain check, Paul. This just isn't the time, not yet."

Frustrated, he sat back, shaking his head. "You are one mysterious lady. Sometimes I think I know you so well. Other times, you turn into a stranger, hiding things from me—as if you don't trust me. To be honest, you frustrate the hell out of me. In more ways than one."

"I'm sorry, but my gut feeling is that I've been trusted by Amelia to help her resolve her issues. She does not want me sharing some of this with anyone, not yet, not even you. If I do, I'm afraid she may disappear and I'll never learn the truth."

"So what? What if you never learn the truth about her life? Is that the end of the world?"

My Irish eyes began to blaze, furious at his insensitivity, but I soon regained my composure. "I need to know the truth, Paul. Somehow I know that my future depends on solving the mystery of her life. If she leaves me, I may be jeopardizing my own life. Does that make any sense to you?" As my words spilled out, I recognized the unmistakable ring of truth. *My* truth. I was not simply making excuses to keep Paul out of the loop.

"You win." He got up to leave. "Just remember I'm here for you."

"Good night, Paul. Thanks for understanding." I touched his arm gently, almost wishing I could ask him over for dinner. But I couldn't. I needed space to accomplish the work I was destined to do. This was not the time for us.

"No wonder she chose you to complete her mission." he tipped his hat and hiked out of the library.

As I walked home in the dark, I felt Amelia's presence smiling down on me as if she was pleased with the position I'd taken. Perhaps she was learning to trust me with her secrets from the past.

Chapter 23

Amelia seemed to be making herself at home in my place. She frequently hovered around the loft while I was up there researching and making notes, trying to figure out the mystery of her life. I no longer startled when she appeared. I'd just try to open my mind to any thoughts or images that she cared to share with me.

Sometimes when I was writing freely in long hand, letting my thoughts flow without censoring them, she seemed to interject her own ideas into my mind. When I'd read my notes later, I'd be surprised at some of the things I'd written. Amelia was helping me to find the truth, her truth.

The scariest part was the feeling that I was losing my own identity. I was losing myself in Amelia's life, almost becoming Amelia at times. Where did I end, and where did she begin? I could feel her emotions. I shared her sorrows although I did not fully understand her pain. I had to figure out what happened to her and what she needed me to do for her. I knew it had something to do with the mysterious man whose sketch hung on the wall of our loft. I suspected she had drowned in a river—and that this man may have played a role in her death. Exasperated after one exhausting but nonproductive Saturday morning in the loft, I climbed down the ladder to make myself a cup of tea. Lucky patiently waited by the door, eager for a walk. I tugged my boots on, grabbed my jacket, and headed out for our walk.

The fresh air was invigorating, and the sunshine brightened my mood. The cobwebs cluttering my mind began to clear. It was time to come back to the real world instead of burying myself in the past. I vowed to forget about Amelia for the rest of the day.

Maybe I'd drive over to Ennis for a late lunch. I hadn't seen Sally at the Ennis Cafe for some time. Paul could even be there. I'd been too preoccupied to think of him much less spend any time with him. Truth be told, I missed him. He had backed off, letting me have the space I needed. I wasn't sure if this was a professional decision or a personal one. Was he giving me space so I could complete my research and contribute to his book? Or did he genuinely care enough to respect my wishes?

The teapot was whistling, almost shrieking, by the time Lucky and I returned from our walk. I'd forgotten all about it. Shutting it off, I made myself a cup of green tea with honey and sat down at the table by the window. I could never get enough of this view.

A loud knock on the door interrupted my thoughts and plans for the day. Swinging the door open, I found John, the historian, standing on my doorstep. He had a huge grin on his face and an air of excitement about him.

Surprised by his visit, I invited him in. He clutched a package in his hands as if it contained something extremely valuable.

"Please sit down." I gestured to the table. "Can I get you a cup of tea?"

"Sure, that sounds good. I have some potentially good news for you, perhaps, if you're still looking for Amelia."

"Oh yes, I'm still looking for her," I replied as I handed him a cup of tea and sat down across the table from him. I waited anxiously as he carefully opened his package and withdrew a packet of letters tied together with a dainty yellow ribbon. They looked very old and fragile.

His eyes gleamed with excitement as he untied the ribbon and carefully placed the letters in front of me. He did not speak, allowing me to absorb what was in front of me without distraction.

The letters were addressed, in an old-fashioned script that had faded with time, to Miss Amelia O'Brien Johnston, Virginia City, Montana. "My Amelia?"

"It's possible. You were looking for an Amelia with a last name beginning in J, right?"

"Yes." I gently touched the handwriting on the envelope, trying to absorb the past into the present. "Where did you find these?"

"In an old box of historical documents, odds and ends that various people have contributed to the historical society over the years. Things we hadn't been able to connect with any of the pioneers that we knew of. I remembered that old box and decided to go through it, just in case I found anything interesting for you."

There were two letters, the first one postmarked September 1863 in a place called Galena, Illinois. I struggled to make out the return address until

John pulled out his magnifying glass. It read Mrs. Rosa Peterson, Galena, Illinois.

"Can I read them?" I whispered, almost in shock. If this Amelia Johnston was my Amelia, these letters could shed some light on her life.

"Of course. I've already made copies since they are so fragile. Just take good care of them."

"Thank you so much, so very much," I gushed. I had a strong feeling that this was in fact my Amelia. I could feel her presence looking down from her perch in the loft, delighted at this discovery, confirming that I was on the right track. I wondered if she had led John to finding these old letters.

He watched me silently for a few moments, knowing I was itching to open the letters. "I'm going to leave you alone so you can read them in peace, Rose. I hope you will let me know if you solve this mystery?"

"I certainly will...once I've put all the pieces together," I promised.

"I suspect you've already made some progress, perhaps even had a few visits from her or other spirits from the past?" John grinned knowingly.

"What? How do you know?"

"Because that's what happens here in Virginia City sometimes. There's a very high level of spiritual energy that some of us are able to tap into. I suspect that you were drawn here for a reason, Rose, am I right?"

"How...how did you know that?"

"I knew it the first day I met you at the hurdy-gurdy house. Guess I have a way of tuning into things like that. I'm a part of the past, just like you are."

"So I'm not the only one?"

"Of course not," he assured me. "It can be frightening at first—until we learn that most of these spirits are friendly. Until we learn to walk in and balance both worlds. If you ever want to talk about it, I'm more than happy to listen and share."

"I'd like that," I replied, "but I need to figure out a few things first."

"I understand. That's the way it is sometimes once you've developed a relationship with a spirit. You form a bond that you need to nourish, sometimes exclusively, until the time is right to share what you've learned."

"You have no idea how relieved I am to hear what you're saying, John. You have truly made my day. I cannot thank you enough."

"My pleasure, ma'am." He stood to take his leave, noticing my trembling hands hovering over the letters.

∽✥

My heart was racing as I carefully extracted the first letter from the envelope addressed to Miss Amelia O'Brien Johnston and opened it. The paper consisted of thin parchment. The handwriting was elegant and, thankfully, legible. I took a deep breath and began to read:

My dearest Amelia,

It gave me the greatest of pleasures to receive your post after many months of worry as to your fate. You must be aware that there have been wagon trains ambushed on their travels to the far west. Thank the Lord you arrived safely at your destination.

Your post arrived three weeks after the date stamped on the envelope. Nevertheless, I am so pleased to hear that you are safe and that living conditions are not as terrible as I have imagined. You know you still are my little sister, dear Amelia, and I shall always worry about you until you come home again someday.

You inquired about Anders and his new mining business. He is doing well, transporting many loads of lead ore up the Mississippi River to Saint Paul or downstream to Saint Louis by steamboat. We enjoy an evening promenade along the riverfront where we watch the steamboats coming and going.

Galena continues to thrive although some of our citizens are pulling up stakes and going west, following the trail of recent gold discoveries. General Ulysses Grant has built a lovely home here and is one of our most prominent citizens.

My garden produced many bushels of tomatoes, beans, cabbage, and potatoes this year. I've put up many jars of vegetables for the coming winter. Church socials and quilting bees keep me occupied when I'm not caring for my growing family.

I am in the family way once again, still longing for a little girl someday. Her name will be Rosa, of course. Her brothers need a little sister to keep them in line.

As for your little Jonathan, he has been such a blessing for us all. He is a happy and delightful little boy although he misses his mother. I tell him that you will be returning or sending for him as soon as you are able to do so. We keep your memory alive for him and pray for you together every night. I cannot imagine how difficult it must be for you to be apart from him.

My heart grieves for all that you endured at the hands of your despicable husband. I am so relieved that you are finally free. I am saddened, however, that you had to leave to make your way in the world, Amelia. You could have stayed with us and are still welcome to do so. However, I understand your strong sense of pride and independence. It's that Irish streak in you, the O'Brien curse that I'm afraid we all grew up with—all ten of us children.

I'm sorry to hear that it has been difficult for you to find employment as a schoolteacher. Hopefully, you will still find such a position once more families with children have settled in the West. You did not divulge the nature of the temporary work you have found.

Do not worry about sending money for Jonathan. Anders is doing well enough that we do not need assistance.

I shall be getting a portrait tintype made of your little boy to send to you soon. I would welcome one of you also to help Jonathan remember the mother who loves him enough to have made such a difficult decision. Someday soon you will be together again.

We miss you very much and wish you life's greatest blessings. May God surround you with his love and protection all the days of your life.

Your loving sister,

Rosa

I reread the letter several times, trying to absorb as much information as I could. Trying to read between the lines. At last I knew her name, even her maiden name.

So Amelia had a baby, one that she left behind so she could find a way to support him in the future. Tears welled in my eyes as I thought of Jonathan. I felt Amelia's pain as well as Jonathan's. Was there no other way? Perhaps not in those days, I realized.

"My baby, God, please save my baby!" The words of the drowning woman in my dream suddenly came back to me. I cringed at the thought that Jonathan might have drowned in the river with his mother. I needed to find out what happened to them both.

What I did know was that Amelia had a sister named Rosa O'Brien Peterson. That certainly gave me something to go on. I could hardly wait to get to the library and onto the Ancestry.com database.

Rosa O'Brien Peterson. Rosa Peterson? That was my great-grandmother's maiden name, the one I was named after, the one who'd settled in Prairie Rose, Iowa. A strange coincidence perhaps. Nevertheless, I decided to give Papa a call to find out as much as I could about my great-grandmother.

Mama answered the phone.

"Mama, how are you?"

"Who is this?" she asked, puzzled.

"It's Rose, Mama," I spoke slowly.

"Oh, of course. It's been so long since I've heard your voice, Prairie Rose, that I almost didn't recognize it," she zapped me.

"We just talked last week, remember?"

"Of course I remember. Do you think I can't remember anything anymore?" Her voice climbed a notch or two.

"Not at all. Anyway, how are you and Papa doing? I miss you and just wanted to give you a call."

"We're getting along one day at a time. It's not as easy anymore, and Lord knows we don't have nobody to help us out. Too busy with their own lives. Whatever happened to families living close by and helping each other? This world is going to hell in a handbasket, I tell you."

I was surprised at Mama's choice of words. I'd never heard her say the word "hell" before.

I soon heard Papa coming to the phone. "Who is it, Anna?"

"Nobody special. I've got it. You just go on back to that stupid television that you sit in front of twenty-four hours a day," she snapped at him.

Instead, Papa grabbed the phone. I could hear Mama whining in the background.

"Rose, so good to hear your voice!"

"Oh, Papa, is it getting worse with Mama?"

"Some days are better than others. But I swear she puts on her pity act and is worse when you call. That's how I knew it was you. You know your mama."

"What can I do?" I grit my teeth.

"Nothing any of us can do. It wouldn't do her one bit of good even if you were here. That's what her doctor told us."

"Thank God you got her into the doctor."

"Not an easy feat, I must say," he chuckled. "She went kickin' and snortin' like a mule, but she went. Afterward, she said she was glad she went. She likes the doctor and wants to go back and see him."

"What did he say about her, about..."

"Well, they say it's probably early Alzheimer's, Rose. Doc is watching her and giving her some pills so she's not so anxious. She gets upset sometimes when she forgets things or says something stupid."

"God, I'm sorry, Papa. I wish I was there to help. Just tell me what I should do. Please."

"You don't think your old man can handle it? I can—for now. If that changes, I will let you know. For now, just be patient with her and don't let her get you down. Call her when you can. But I want you to stay put and do what you need to do out there. I know it's important to you, Rose."

For a man of few words, Papa packed a lot into that small speech, I thought with relief.

We chatted awhile about how things were in Walnut. He'd shared the book I wrote for him with all his friends and had become a celebrity overnight. "They all want copies, Rose," he chuckled. I promised to send him more.

I told him I was doing research about some of the pioneers out here and had come across a woman named Rosa Peterson.

"Why that was your great-grandmother's name, you know, before she married Johanssen."

"Do you know where she came from before she moved to Prairie Rose? I know you've told me Illinois, but where in Illinois?"

"Hmmm...someplace on the river, a busy port in northern Illinois..."

"Could it possibly be Galena?" I held my breath.

"Why, now that you mention it, you just may be right. Galena. I'll dig back into my old family records and see what I can find. Anything else you want to know?"

"Anything you can find out about her."

"I don't think she ever went west, Rose. She lived and died right here in Walnut after Prairie Rose disappeared. Born in 1877, I remember that. Can't recall the year she died, but she's there in the cemetery. I'll let you know."

"You have an incredible memory, Papa."

"Good that one of us does, what with your mama and all."

After I hung up, I thought about it. If Rosa was born in 1877, that was fourteen years after Amelia died, so they could not have been sisters. It had just been a crazy idea of mine, I decided. Still, I had gathered other valuable information that I would use to search for Amelia and her family members.

It had been a very long and eventful day. I could no longer think straight. After dinner I turned on the television—something I rarely did—and tried to think about anything else. But my thoughts kept drifting back to Mama and Papa. I was losing my mother, little by little, to the horrors of Alzheimer disease. Although we'd always had some differences and I could rarely seem to please her, it still hurt. I wondered what the future would be like for her, for all of us, and how it would feel to gradually lose your ability to think and to function.

Chapter 24

Amelia, are you up yet? This was the first thought that drifted into my mind early the next morning. Throwing back the covers on my bed, I was anxious to climb up into the loft to find her. She seemed to enjoy hanging out up there these days.

I had to laugh at myself. Of course she was up. Spirits didn't sleep. They had no sense of time. At least that's what I'd been led to believe.

Amelia was becoming my invisible roommate. I just wished she would talk to me and answer my questions. Strange that I had an imaginary friend named Amelia when I was a little girl. Now I had a spirit named Amelia who shared my home.

Stuffing my feet into my fuzzy slippers, I carefully picked up her letters and climbed up to the loft where I settled into the window seat and wrapped a blanket around me. It was so quiet, so peaceful, as I gazed out the window. Where was Amelia?

It was time to open the second letter, also addressed to Miss Amelia O'Brien Johnston. This one was posted September 1, 1865, also from Mrs. Rosa Peterson of Galena, Illinois.

My dearest Amelia,

I fear the postal service is not as reliable as one would wish. I have written you many letters although you apparently have not received them all. I hope you receive this one so your fears are calmed and you know that your little Jonathan is doing well. It is hard to believe that he is almost five years old and already such an intelligent young lad.

I was pleased to have finally received another letter from you. The money you sent was much more than we ever anticipated. We will use some of it for Jonathan's birthday celebration next month. What he wants more than anything is a puppy. We plan to get one for him. He wants a "girl puppy" and plans to name her Mommy. He spends hours playing with his spinning top and his marbles and watching his cousins walking on their stilts. He is anxious to be old enough to try this feat himself.

I am also pleased that you are doing so well in Virginia City. I understand you cannot yet find a teaching job, but I must confess that I am concerned that you are working as a dancer. I understand that you are saving the money you earn to build a little home and a new life for you and your little boy. While I commend you for your noble efforts, I do hope your employment is safe and honorable. We hear stories about dance halls and saloons in the West, places no respectable woman would enter. But of course I trust that you are not dancing in such places. Surely there are other proper sources of employment for single women such as you. Your safety and timely return are all that matters to us.

Thank you for the tintype you sent of yourself. Thankfully that letter was received. It was lovely, your clothing so elegant and fashionable as if you had stepped out from the pages of a fashion advertisement from Paris. Jonathan looks at your image every day. He proudly tells me, "That's my mommy. She is pretty." He misses you.

I hope you received the tintype we sent you of Jonathan. He was so proud to graduate from his white nainsook gown into the sailor frock that he wore in his portrait.

We are doing well, although I am feeling poorly of late. It shall pass. I am once again in the family way, still longing for a daughter after birthing five sons.

Aside from that, little has changed in Galena since my last post. We and the other town folks were greatly saddened to hear of the assassination of the honorable President Abraham Lincoln in April. I shall always remember that warm summer evening in 1856 when he spoke to the crowds from the second-floor balcony of the DeSoto House Hotel here in Galena. Such a tragic loss for our country. He shall go down in history as one of the greatest leaders of our time.

Until we meet again, I remain your loving sister, Rosa

I carefully refolded the letter and slipped it back into its envelope. As much as I wanted to believe that these letters belonged to my Amelia, I had no proof. Paul would be the first to point that out to me. There could be more than one Amelia. I wasn't even sure that her last name began with a *J*. It was merely speculation based upon the initials on that old clock.

As I pondered the facts, I felt Amelia swoosh into the room in her long gown. I knew she was there although I could not see her this morning.

"Amelia, are these your letters? Is your name Amelia O'Brien Johnston? Please tell me," I begged out loud. "I can't help you if I don't know who you are."

Silence. I waited. More silence. Finally, I decided to read the letters to her, hoping she was listening.

As I finished, I heard the gut-wrenching sound of a woman weeping in the far corner of the loft. Nobody was there as far as I could see. Waves of grief flowed through the room like an endless river that could not be contained. I could feel her pain piercing my heart.

"I'm so sorry, Amelia, sorry you had to leave Jonathan behind," I whispered to her.

The sobbing stopped. She seemed to be listening.

"Is your name Amelia O'Brien Johnston?" I tried again.

Suddenly an unspoken message crept into my mind. "I am Amelia O'Brien Johnston," her silent words flashed through me. "Rosa is my dear sister," she continued, "the one who raised my beloved Jonathan."

"Oh, thank you, Amelia. Thank you for coming to me. I need to know all about your life. You've become an important part of my world, and I need to know the truth. Perhaps I can help to set you free."

"The truth shall be revealed to you in a timely fashion, Rose. I shall tell you the story of my life," she promised as I felt her presence slipping away. But before she disappeared, she sent me another thought wave. "You *are* a part of me, my dear, and you always shall be."

I pondered her strange words. I was a part of her? Well, yes, I was a part of her family now, wasn't I? She even called me by name. She'd confirmed her name, even the fact that she had a sister named Rosa. Could I believe the thoughts that she had planted in my mind? Or was I losing it?

"Believe. Have faith in me. Please..." Her words fluttered into my mind once again.

Stunned, I slipped down the ladder to go about my day. Coffee first. I needed a good strong cup of coffee.

Still in my bathrobe, hair flying in all directions, I sipped my coffee at the table. I was delighted over my breakthrough with Amelia. She was communicating with me, promising to tell me her story. I was thrilled but frightened.

The ringing of the phone finally broke through my troubled thoughts. It was Papa, and he was excited.

"Rose! I have information for you. Just got back from my walk in the cemetery."

"Well, good morning to you, Papa," I grinned into the phone.

"Do you have a pencil? You'll want to take this down."

"I'm ready."

"Okay, your great-grandma, Rosa Peterson Johansson, died here in Walnut in 1957 at eighty years of age. But wait till you hear what else I found!"

"I can't wait. Tell me, Papa."

"Okay, well I have some information about her birth and her parents. Rosa was born in Galena, Illinois, the place you talked about. Her father was Anders Peterson, a Swede. Her Irish mother was Rosa O'Brien Peterson, born in 1835. So maybe you can get onto that Ancestry site and find even more. What do you think, Rose?"

I almost dropped the phone. I could not speak. Rosa O'Brien Peterson, Amelia's sister, was my great-great-grandmother?? Did that mean that Amelia was my great-great-aunt?

"Rose, are you there? Did you hear what I said? Rose?"

"I'm here," I whispered into the phone. "I'm in shock, Papa. Two Rosas? Are you sure?"

"Yup, two of them, no doubt about it. What's so shocking about that? In those days, people named their kids after them quite often."

"What's shocking is that I've just discovered that not only am I related to Rosa O'Brien Peterson, but that the person I'm researching out here, Amelia, is her sister. Amelia is my great-great aunt!"

"Afraid you've lost me, but that name Amelia seems to follow you around, don't it? Remember that imaginary friend you had when you were little? Her name was Amelia, too," he chuckled.

"Papa, I can't thank you enough. You have solved a mystery for me, one that I've been working on ever since I arrived here. Now I can complete my work and do what needs to be done."

"Do what?" he was perplexed.

"I'm not sure yet…whatever is needed to set things right." I had no clue what that might be, just that I was on an important mission—one that I would accomplish no matter what it took. "Damn the torpedoes!" as Papa used to say.

"Well, good luck. Glad I could be of help. Mama's calling. Better go."

I could barely believe what I'd just heard. Apparently Amelia, my great-great-aunt, was the one who'd called me to Virginia City to set her affairs straight. Dying to share this news with someone, I was almost tempted to drive to Ennis and find Paul. He of all people loved discoveries like this. But a small voice within warned me not to go, not to divulge the exciting news I'd just discovered.

Besides, Amelia would not be pleased. Now that she was apparently trusting me with her life story and counting on me, I could not risk alienating her. She was my great-great-aunt after all! I'd need to live with the excitement, perhaps pour it all out in my personal journal. And that's exactly what I did that evening after Lucky and I took a long walk in the snow.

That night, I drifted off into a deep sleep, deeper than usual. Before long, I was lost in a strange dream that would not let me go. I wasn't sure if it was Amelia—or if it was me, but one of us was on the ground, frantically clawing at the earth, digging for something as if our life depended upon it. The ground was hard, still frozen. It didn't matter. We dug until our fingers were raw and bleeding, finally penetrating the earth, digging deeper. The wind blew, creating a small cyclone that swirled around us as we continued to dig for the buried treasure, whatever it was. It was critical that we find it now.

All night long I dug, floating between the pain and the cold, knowing I could not give up. I could not go back to my warm bed until I'd succeeded.

The shrill ringing of my alarm clock brought me back to my bedroom, exhausted after an endless night of digging. The dream had been so real that I inspected my hands. I was surprised to find they were not bleeding.

Shaking my head, I buried myself beneath the covers, trying to get some sleep before I had to get up and leave for work. But it was useless. I was too tired to sleep, and I had too much to do at the library today. I'd fallen behind on editing Paul's chapters, and I desperately needed to get back onto the genealogy data base to see what else I may learn about my newly found relatives.

Deep in thought, I stumbled into the kitchen to make breakfast. What was that earthy smell? Something smelled like old dirt. Glancing around the cabin, I noticed a musty old book sitting on the table. As I moved closer, I saw that it was frayed and faded, and covered in a coat of fresh earth. I picked it up carefully, dusted off the cover, and opened it. There on the first page in fancy bold script were the words "Journal of Amelia O'Brien Johnston."

I felt faint and collapsed on the sofa with the book in my hands. Amelia's journal? Was that what we'd been digging for all night long? She had delivered on her promise, I realized. She had given me her life story.

"You must not share this with Henry!" Amelia whispered into my mind.

"Who? Who is Henry?"

She did not reply, but I felt her looking at me in a way that implied I would find out soon—or as she would say, "in a timely fashion."

Lucky was whining at the door, needing to go out for his walk. I reluctantly threw on my old jeans and a jacket and headed out with him after hiding the journal under my bed. Just in case.

As I did so, something fell out of the book. It was a tintype photo of a darling little boy, probably about four years old. It had to be Jonathan, Amelia's son. I figured it must have been taken about 1864, based upon her sister's letters. My heart lurched as tears filled my eyes. I prayed that Amelia and Jonathan had been reunited before she died in 1868…and that little Jonathan had not drowned with her. A deep chill crept through my soul.

I could not peel my eyes away from the photo of this chubby little boy with a dimple in his chin. He wore a dark boyish frock with pleats. It was styled in a nautical theme with a large sailor collar falling broadly across the back. The front was V-shaped with an embroidered nautical shield insert and a row of buttons. He wore a loose belt with a buckle, leggings, and boots that laced up to his ankles.

Oh, Jonathan, my darling Jonathan. The words rushed through my mind. Amelia's words—or were they mine? I couldn't be sure. I was falling under his spell, as if I were his mother. I longed to hold him in my arms, to tell him that everything would be all right. But everything would not be all right. His mother had less than four years to live.

I wondered if little Jonathan ever saw his mother again and cringed to realize that he might not have. I'd find out soon enough, once I had time to begin wading through this thick book. It was going to be a long day at the library.

I worked furiously editing and organizing Paul's work all morning, trying not to think about what waited for me at home. But at noon, as soon as he left for his usual lunch at The Outlaw, I rushed to the computer in the genealogy room and logged on.

Now that I had a name, it did not take me long to find a match. Amelia O'Brien was born February 1, 1840 in Galena, Illinois. One of ten children, she did have a sister named Rosa, who married an Anders Peterson. Oh my God, I'd found her! Breathing hard, searching faster, I clicked on the links to discover more about her life, more proof that this was the Amelia I was searching for.

Amelia O'Brien married an Emil Johnston and had a son, Jonathan, born in 1860. I could find no records of a divorce. No additional children. Just an incomplete death record listing circa 1868 as Amelia's date of death. The place of death was simply Montana.

Holding my breath, I began searching for a death record for Jonathan, fearing he had died with his mother in 1868. I was greatly relieved to learn that he had died in 1922 in Galena, Illinois. It didn't make sense that Amelia's last words, in my dream, had been, "God, save my baby!"

My head was reeling as I stared at the screen in shock. I don't know how long I'd been sitting there when I felt a hand on my shoulder. Startled, I spun around to find Paul watching me intently. His eyes were clouded with worry.

"I found her! Oh my God, I've found her!" I blurted out the words without thinking, unable to contain my excitement.

"You what? You mean Amelia?" He leaned in over my shoulder to look at the computer screen, closer than he needed to be. I showed him her birth record and other information.

"O'Brien?" He puzzled out loud. "That's a leap, Rose. What makes you think your Amelia's maiden name was O'Brien? I'm sure more than one Amelia died in Montana in 1868. I know how much this means to you, but you need more proof. Just sayin'..." He gently stroked my back, trying to console me.

"Well, I have other information," I began to protest, defending my research. What was I doing? Betraying Amelia's confidences?

"Oh?" He seemed intrigued. "I suspected you were on to something. I've been waiting."

Shaking my head, I rose, breaking away from the sweet comfort of his closeness. I'd already said more than I should have. "I'm sorry, Paul. I can't tell you anymore, not yet."

Once again, that dark, gloomy look spread across his face. He had a dark side, and it scared me sometimes. I could not deny that I was attracted to him, but sometimes I felt I was dealing with two different personalities, walking on eggshells until I knew which one I was facing.

"When in the hell are you going to level with me, Rose? Why are you so damn secretive about all of this? Have you forgotten we are working together?" He paced the room, kicking a pencil out of his way.

Wanting to get away from him, I began to retreat to my office. He followed, spinning me around, his hands firmly positioned on my shoulders. His eyes blazed with a mixture of anger and pain. "What in the hell is going on with you, with us?" he demanded. "Have you found someone else?"

I almost laughed in his face. As if I had time to find another man. Was that what this was all about?

"I have no time in my life for anyone right now. There is no one else... I mean...no one," I stumbled on my words. Then my anger began to surge. Who did he think he was, holding me captive, demanding an explanation from me? My green Irish eyes began to spark. I could feel it, and Paul began to back off. "I will tell you what I know, Paul DuBois, when I am good and ready to do so. In the meantime, back off, will you?" I pushed his hands from my shoulders.

"Why?"

"Because I need space, and because I am not about to betray confidences bestowed upon me by Amelia. I have promised not to divulge some things. This is not the time. Do not ask me again, Paul."

"Well, I'm impressed that you've made a breakthrough, Rose. I guess you will have to do it your own way then. I'm dying to know what you've discovered, however. It could be important to our research."

"Someday you will know whatever is important for our research," I promised him. That day would not come, however, until I'd read Amelia's journal and completed her unfinished business on this earth. "Is that all?" I asked curtly.

Sighing, he shook his head, looking at me sadly. "Just one thing. You need to break away from all this secret research and your obsession with Amelia. For your own good. You need to live in the real world, to balance yourself."

"And what do you suggest?" I made the mistake of looking into his eyes. My heart fluttered just thinking of the kisses we'd shared.

Of course he didn't miss the look of longing in my eyes, the look he'd been waiting for. "Oh, Rose, let's be friends. I've missed you. How about dinner this weekend?"

Against my better judgment, I blurted out "Yes, I'd like that. Very much."

Squeezing my hand warmly, he left the room.

→←

Finally, the day was over. I hurried home, took Lucky for a faster-than-usual walk and then went into my bedroom to recover the journal beneath my bed. It wasn't there! I searched thoroughly, climbing under the bed, looking in the corners of my bedroom. But Amelia's journal was gone.

Frantic, I began to search the entire house, throwing books off my bookcase, rummaging through kitchen cupboards, looking under the sofa. I was close to tears. The proof of Amelia's existence had slipped through my fingers. I was doomed to fail at my mission.

Dear God, please help me find it, I prayed out loud as I climbed into the loft. Maybe Amelia could help me. But as soon as I turned on the lamp, I saw it. It was on my window seat, opened to the first page as if waiting for me to begin reading it.

Relieved, I sank down beside it, knowing very well who had moved it. "Amelia?" I inquired, a hint of exasperation in my voice.

"It belongs up here in the loft," she replied firmly. This time it was more than a thought implanted in my mind. I could hear a quaint Victorian voice. Amelia's voice.

Grinning from ear to ear, I looked around to find her. I could feel the familiar chill of a resident ghost, but she was not visible. It seemed that I could only see her in my dreams.

As my eyes searched the room, I noticed another change. Propped up on the windowsill was the tintype photo of little Jonathan. Amelia was making herself at home, rearranging the loft to suit her.

Chapter 25

August 10, 1863

Dear Diary,

I have decided to document my journey west to the little town of Virginia City where gold was recently discovered. I shall establish my new home there in the land of opportunity.

My purpose in writing is to leave behind a record for my beloved son, Jonathan, in the hope that he will someday understand the difficult decision I've had to make—and what my life was like. I write this first entry from the back of a covered wagon somewhere on the wild prairie west of Galena.

I find myself alone in life and in need of money to support the baby son I left behind with my dear sister, Rosa. Leaving Jonathan was the most difficult thing I've ever had to do. However, I had no choice. I am running from his father, the husband who abused me repeatedly and has threatened to kill me if I ever dared to leave him.

Little Jonathan is far too young to travel west. Babies frequently do not survive the strenuous journey. He will be safe at my sister's home until I am able to return for him. I need not worry about his father claiming him since he does not wish to be bothered with children, not even his own flesh and blood. I pray that my son shall not judge me too harshly for the difficult decision I have made.

Every day, this trail of tears takes me farther away from all that I love. My tears have flowed endlessly, quietly, in the wagon at night, but my dreams keep me going. Someday I will have enough money to build a modest home and bring Jonathan west with me. I live for that day.

Women do not travel alone, of course, aside from the soiled doves. I am most certainly not one of those. I was blessed, however, to have found a family who allowed me to accompany them west in exchange for serving as a nanny for their four children. They range in age from eight to thirteen years. Tonight, they are fast asleep. It has been a difficult journey for them so far. They have been quite ill at times and without access to any medical care. Watching them struggle, I am grateful that I did not subject my baby to this ordeal.

Tonight, the wagons are clustered in a circle for protection, they say, since we have now entered Indian country. While the scouts stand guard with their rifles, the women and children sleep. Except for me. I'm lying on my bedroll in the back of our wagon, flaps open so I can see the brilliant stars glittering in the black sky. A full moon stands guard, the same moon that my Jonathan may be watching back home in Galena. A gentle breeze drifts across the vast prairie, rustling the tall grass. 'Tis a welcome relief after the scorching heat of the day. The sun beat down upon us relentlessly as our wagon train crawled through the brush with the snakes.

I'm writing by the dim light of the lantern positioned precariously upon the mess box beside me. It is eerily quiet tonight. I enjoy the solitude after a strenuous day on the rutted dirt trail. The only sounds to be heard are the sweet breathing of the children sleeping beside me and the howling of a wolf in the distance. He calls for his mate. He is lonely, I think to myself, perhaps as lonely as I am.

ॐॐ

Closing my eyes, Amelia's diary propped open upon my lap, I gently touched the words she wrote, trying to absorb the essence of this woman, my great-great aunt, through the tip of my finger. Trying hard to slip back in time so I could accompany her on her journey. Suddenly, I found myself floating back with Amelia into the life she lived 148 years ago.

Amelia wakens to the smell of coffee and salt side pork frying over the campfire. Hopefully, there will also be thick slabs of sourdough bread with sorghum molasses. The rumor around camp is that we will need to begin rationing food before long to make it last another month. It's difficult to pack and haul enough food to last the three months it takes to cross the country. We rely on wild game and fish along the way.

The wagon trails follow the riverbeds and streams to ensure an adequate supply of water. We bathe occasionally in the cool waters of the river. We also wash our clothing and dishes in the rivers and streams, drying them on rocks in the hot sun.

It's going to be a hot day, Amelia realizes, as she pokes her head out through the canvas flap of the wagon. The cooks are already preparing breakfast over the fire in the circle as the scouts ride out on their horses to scope out the area.

She dons her long dress and boots before dressing the children and brushing their hair twenty strokes each. Grabbing her frayed sunbonnet, she climbs out of the wagon, bidding good day to the other travelers emerging from their wagons.

As she and the children dish their food up on tin plates and settle on one of the logs around the fire, a woman wearing a fancy satin dress and glittering jewelry strides over to join them. She is still trying to impress them all with the importance she once held back in Galena. She is the children's mother. She bends to peck each of her children on their cheeks, leaving a smudge of red lipstick behind.

"Good day, Mrs. Callahan," Amelia greets her, noticing the deep frown creasing her brow.

"I declare there is nothing good about it, my dear. I am not sure I can tolerate too many more of these dreadful days on the trail. Why, I have no earthly idea what my husband was thinking to pull up stakes and put us through this endless misery. I long for my lovely home and gardens back in Galena, and I fear that I shall never again lay eyes upon my grand piano, my crystal chandeliers, or my lovely gardens." Mrs. Callahan sighs dramatically as she arranges her full satin skirts and seats herself beside us. "Shall we all perish in this God-forsaken land?"

She is one of the few women on this wagon train who cannot seem to get over all that she has left behind. While the rest of us dress simply in practical clothing and do not fuss with our hair or toilet, she insists upon dressing "appropriately and fashionably rather than succumbing to the heathen ways of the West," as she likes to say.

Mr. Callahan seems to avoid his wife as much as possible. He's usually up front with his rifle, leading the train and scouting for bear, buffalo, and Indians. His eyes sparkle with excitement, unable to contain his enthusiasm. Of course, he plans to strike it rich in Virginia City.

Meanwhile, his wife spends her days doing fancy work in the back of the wagon as it lumbers along the trail in a cloud of dust. She cries out every time the wagon hits a rut in the trail and she pokes her fingers with a needle. Most of us walk a good part of the day, trying to alleviate the weight in the wagons that the poor oxen are pulling. We've already lost several of these beasts and have had to leave one crippled wagon behind. We loaded the family and their meager belongings into other wagons.

We've also buried two of our travelers so far after they succumbed to illness that spread through our camp like a wildfire. The men dug a grave beneath a giant willow on the riverbank. They erected a cross made from tree branches and whittled their names onto a plaque made from a log. After saying a prayer together, we all sang a hymn and trekked back to our wagons. What a lonely way to die out here on the windswept prairie so far from loved ones back home. So far from the land of opportunity that these brave men were seeking.

As we finish eating our grub this morning, we hear the sound of horses galloping toward us. The scouts have returned.

"Well?" our designated leader, Butch, calls out to them as they dismount. Butch, if that is actually his name, is a tough, surly-looking character that nobody dares to challenge. He hides behind his long beard. Nobody knows where he came from or what he's running from. All we know is that he is hell-bent on moving this train safely to what he calls "the land of milk and honey." And he's prepared to fight to the bitter end to make that happen.

The camp cook hustles to dish up two heaping plates of food that he hands to the scouts. Hard work is rewarded out here in the wilderness. Those who contribute the most eat the best.

"Looks clear, no sign of Injuns or bears," the head scout calls out for all to hear. "But the river widens down yonder. We must find a place to cross. It's not going to be an easy crossing no matter where we decide to cut over. I think we follow the river for another day or so. Bound to be a place farther downstream where other wagon trains have crossed. I say just follow the trail for now."

Having already devoured his food, he spits a wad of tobacco on the ground and clears his throat. "I need to tell ya all that we did come upon a makeshift grave out there on the banks of the river. Sign says, 'Harvey O'Conner 1863, killed by Injuns.' "

Silence falls upon the camp aside from several gasps from the womenfolk who are known to have fragile dispositions.

"All right, men, you heard the man," Butch roars. " I want more scouts out front and around the perimeter of the wagon train. Tonight we double up on watch. Curly, you handle the schedule." He nods at his right-hand man.

"We may need a few good women to assist," the leader takes a swig of his muddy coffee before dumping it onto the ground.

"Why, I do declare!" Mrs. Callahan exclaims dramatically. "Women? This is shocking!"

"Ain't nothing shocking about it, ma'am," Butch glares in her direction, blinded by the sunlight reflected against her sparkling diamonds. "Men need some sleep too. I've made my decision. Ladies, talk to Curly if you are willing to take a shift. You won't be alone. You'll have a good man at your side."

Amelia, who is dying of boredom and anxious to do her part, is the first to approach Curly. She offers to take her turn on watch. The other women turn their eyes away, afraid they will be called upon. Finally, several of them decide to offer their services as well.

Mr. Callahan grins at Amelia and comes over to pat her on the back. "Thank you, Miss Johnston. You are one brave woman, and I respect you for that." Mrs. Callahan bristles in her rustling skirts, glaring at the husband who has inflicted this torture upon her. He shrugs his shoulders and dismisses her.

What's going to happen to this marriage? Amelia worries that Mrs. Callahan won't like Virginia City any better than the journey to get there. Will she stay? Or will she go back to Galena with the children? Without this family to care for, Amelia won't have a job.

After a long day on the parched trail, we set up camp for the night. Covered in layers of grime and sweat, most of the travelers head down to the river to wash up. Some will come back to bathe after dark. With the Indian threats, however, there will probably be guards stationed there as well. Privacy will not be an option.

The men set out to catch fish for dinner, an easy chore along this wild river teeming with fish of all kinds. The Indians spear them with sticks.

The circle is enclosed, protected by guards sitting on the benches of the covered wagons, peering out into the wilderness with loaded rifles on their laps.

After a meal of beans, fish, and sourdough bread, everyone gathers around the fire. The men enjoy a few swigs of brandy or whiskey from their flasks. The designated fiddler begins to play as people sing along, clapping to the music. Some dance a jig or two. Laughter rings out across the windswept prairie. This is the time to celebrate having traveled another thirty miles today. We are that much closer to the river of gold waiting for us beyond the mountains.

Conversation frequently turns to gold, to staking claims and building shelters for our families. Truth be told, there aren't many women or children heading west these days. Most gold-seekers and merchants travel alone, leaving families behind until they have settled in. Or, until the Wild West becomes a little tamer.

Tonight as the moon rises in all her splendor, defying the blackness of the Universe, we stoke the fire silently. We pay our respects to the God out there somewhere who will hopefully guide us safely to our destination.

One old codger with a dirty gray beard sits in the shadows, propped up against his wagon as he empties the last drops from his flask. "I ain't scared of no Injuns," he boasts to the others. "They'll leave us alone if we leave them alone, I tell ya. They're just curious about the white men crossing their land, that's all."

"I hope you're right, Fritz," one of the scouts shouts back. "Time to get some shut-eye." He rises from his perch beside the fire, grabs his rifle, and heads for his wagon.

"Men," Butch shouts out, "and women too," he adds reluctantly. "Man your positions. Wake me if you see any activity. Until tomorrow..." Butch struts off into the shadows of the night, dual pistols dangling from his hips. He cautiously gazes around him, his beady eyes shifting from left to right, as he heads toward the light of the lantern in his wagon. As the leader, he has the privilege of a wagon of his own. A wagon loaded with God only knows what. His oxen struggle as they pull the heavy load he's packed within.

The others leave the warmth of the fire for their wagons or guard duty. Two men settle down by the fire, stoking it back to life. They will take turns keeping the fire going throughout the night. It's a good way to scare the bears and other predators away. After all, we are heading into grizzly bear country. Black bears are one force to contend with, but nothing compared to the grizzlies and mountain lions we will soon be meeting up with.

Amelia tucks her charges into their bedrolls in the wagon. As soon as they are asleep, she tiptoes out into the starry night. She climbs up onto the bench beside her assigned partner. He hands her a loaded rifle. This is her first shift as a watchman, the first time she's held a rifle in her hands. She is proud to be a part of something this important. Proud to be treated like a man in a world that discredits and sometimes abuses women. She swears silently that she will do whatever it takes to defend the camp.

Henry nods at her curtly, not at all pleased that he has been assigned duty with a woman. A woman! He will need to watch his back tonight. What in the Sam Hill would she know about shooting to kill? Women weren't meant for this kind of thing, he laments. They don't belong out here in the wilderness. What the hell was this young woman doing venturing out to a gold mining town that will eat her alive? Don't matter that she's mighty pretty. That was probably all the worse, a curse that will destroy her. She will be devoured by characters that pay no respect to the likes of women. Unscrupulous scoundrels who have forgotten the values their mothers once tried to instill in them.

He falls into a gloomy silence, staring intently into the hiding places of the night. She follows his lead. Watching his every move, she tries to mimic them. But she soon falls under the spell of the Universe, gazing up into the heavens above. The stars seem to twinkle messages amongst them, radiating beams of light and hope down to the earth below.

A tear trickles down her cheek as her thoughts turn to the son she left behind. She turns away from this man called Henry to conceal her weakness as a woman. But he sees. He feels. He seems to know. Dropping his gaze momentarily from the shadows of the night, he focuses upon his partner.

"Are you all right?" he whispers as he scans the horizon. It's been a long time since he's had a woman. This one seems to be distracting him. Hopefully, he will not be paired up with her again.

"But of course," Amelia replies, as she refocuses her energy on the task at hand.

As luck would have it, poor Henry finds himself paired with Amelia on a regular basis. He decides there could be worse fates. In fact, he begins to look forward to their night shifts together. The silence between them is comfortable and comforting, taking the edge off their loneliness. Sometimes they talk in whispers so as not to disturb the others.

"What are you going to do in Virginia City?" he asks her one night. He worries that she is too young and innocent to survive in this wild mining town. Somehow he feels the need to protect her from the evils she may encounter.

"I shall stay on as a nanny for the Callahans."

"Well, I hope that works out for you," he hesitates.

"What do you mean?"

"I've observed that the Callahans do not seem to be getting along. She hates the West and wants nothing more than to return to the home she continually talks about. I don't see her staying in Virginia City—or with him."

He's right, Amelia realizes. Mr. and Mrs. Callahan are no longer speaking to each other. What will she do? Suddenly, she perks up. "My dream is to become a teacher, to teach the children who will soon be arriving."

"A noble dream, one at which I believe you will excel. You are an intelligent and educated woman, very good with children. I have watched you with your charges."

Her face turns pink. Thankfully, it is too dark for him to notice.

Amelia and Henry become friends, frequently sitting together around the campfire. He also becomes her protector. Anytime one of the men gets rowdy around her or bothers her, Henry puts him in his place, fast.

Amelia notices that Henry displays a very jealous and intense nature at times, a dark side that erupts now and then. It puzzles her to watch his transformation from a devoted, kind friend into an angry man who seems to be driven by the forces of evil. She treads lightly in his presence. While his behavior can be unsettling, she still cherishes the good times. He is, after all, her only friend in the world.

"What will you do in the West?" she asks him one night by the fire, assuming he will be panning for gold like most of the others.

"I intend to stake a claim and become wealthy," he winks at her.

Somehow he doesn't seem like an ordinary miner, she thinks to herself. "And?"

"I also plan to establish the first bank in Virginia City, affiliated with my banks back in Illinois," he casually discloses his goal. "Of course, I prefer that this information not be shared with the others." A look of shock registers in his eyes as if he can't believe he has relayed this information to a virtual stranger.

"You have my word, sir. My lips are sealed."

"And I shall hold you to that," he promises, his eyes penetrating hers, emphasizing the seriousness of this matter.

෴

Day after day, the train of covered wagons lumbers along the trail, dodging potholes and boulders. Wagon wheels break and need to be fixed.

The relentless heat bears down upon us as we pray for rain, for clouds to block the rays of the sun. Tempers flare in the heat.

We lose one wagon crossing the raging river. Those who already made it across safely gasp in horror as the last wagon breaks an axle, tips over midstream, and the family and their possessions are thrown into the turbulent river. The men rush into the water to save the family and try to rescue some of their goods before the river carries them downstream. The poor oxen are yoked to the wagon, snorting, thrashing, unable to break free. The wagon slams against the rocks, breaks into pieces, and disappears into the river. The oxen go down with it.

Amelia tries to comfort the crying children who witnessed this horrific scene, hiding the tears in her own eyes. Mrs. Callahan is too busy shouting at her husband as if it were his fault.

One night, a hungry bear breaks into camp, trying to steal our dwindling supply of food. Gunfire blasts through the camp, waking us all. The men grab their rifles and rush out of their wagons, still in their long johns. Two watchmen are standing over the huge black bear they've just shot. There will be bear meat for dinner the rest of the week.

Another night, we are awakened by the warning sound of the horn. That means Indians have been spotted. The men crawl out of the wagons with their rifles, staying close to the wagons as they cautiously skirt around them toward the sound of the horn.

"Over there!" Curly hisses, pointing toward the hill on the opposite side of the stream. There, illuminated in the moonlight, stands a row of horses mounted by Indians in full feather dress. They do not move. They make no sound. They watch us in silence.

The men begin to raise their rifles, focusing on the Indian braves.

"Hold your fire! Do not shoot!" Butch barks at them. "Put those damn guns down!"

"But—" one man protests.

"But nothing. They're just watching us. They may be friendly. You want to start a war, you fools?" Butch snarls.

It seems to be a standoff. Nobody is moving. Finally, one brave cautiously rides toward us, waving his hand in the air as if in greeting. He rides slowly beneath the light of the moon and wades across the shallow waters of the stream to our side. There he dismounts, takes a bundle off his horse, and places it carefully on the ground. Again, he waves at us, gets back on his horse, and returns to the other braves. Then they disappear into the woods.

At daybreak the next morning, the scouts ride out to the clearing where the brave had left his bundle. It contains a deerskin pouch filled with wild blueberries and an assortment of Indian trinkets.

Amazed, we realize that these are friendly but curious Indians. They are making a peace offering, welcoming us. The old man, Fritz, is right. He decides to put together a welcome bundle and peace offering for the Indians. Before we begin our day's journey, he collects items and treks out to the clearing to leave his bundle.

Day after day, the endless prairie land rolls by until one early September day when we catch our first glimpse of mountains on the horizon. The camp comes to life, energized by the surreal beauty of the towering giants looming before us. Waves of relief wash over the camp, knowing that we are coming close to the end of this difficult journey.

Days later, we finally reach the mountains and find that maneuvering our wagons and animals through the steep mountain passes is not easy. We are relieved, however, to discover that nights in these higher elevations are cool, sometimes marked with snow flurries. The sweltering days of summer are over. The fresh, cool mountain air is invigorating, and the beauty of the mountains stunning.

Finally, one late September day, our journey along the Bozeman Trail ends. We have arrived in Virginia City with our wagons packed full of all the belongings we have left in this world.

Chapter 26

I am abruptly torn from Amelia's world, spiraling ahead through time to the year 2011. I felt as if I had actually been transported back into her world. I was there in that covered wagon with her. Or had I *become* her for a moment in time?

Trying to reorient myself to the present day, I glanced around the semi-darkness of the loft. Night had fallen while I'd been away, lost in the past. A silver moon beamed through the window above me, illuminating Amelia's diary on my lap. It was still open, but the pages had been flipped forward.

I sat in the dark, marveling at all I'd learned about Amelia's life. I'd even met Henry—probably the same man she cautioned me about. Do not tell Henry, she had whispered into my mind after I'd discovered her journal. As if I'd be able to travel back in time to find this man and tell him anything. Still, I *had* been transported back in time, hadn't I? My experience seemed so real. It had to be more than a dream.

Henry…I pondered the name for a while. I wanted to learn more about this man, but I realized that Henry had been a popular name in those days. Based upon the research I'd done, there had been a number of men named Henry in these parts.

My gaze fell upon the sketch of the man hanging on the wall, the one of the vision that had appeared to me at the Christmas party at the Elling House. Amelia and I had drawn that sketch together. Maybe that's Henry, I thought to myself. But maybe not, I reprimanded myself. This was not the time to jump to conclusions. The truth will come "in a timely fashion." I grinned to myself, thinking of Amelia and her quaint vocabulary. I could feel her gentle smile warming my heart.

No sense, I decided, in pursuing the Henry thread of my research until I'd finished reading Amelia's diary. The answers may all lie within the pages she had so carefully written so many years ago. I wondered where that diary had been buried all these years.

Finally, I turned on the light and climbed down from the loft. I needed a diversion. I needed to escape from the past for a while, from that diary that kept calling me back. I sensed that Amelia was anxious for me to read it, but I had enough to think about for one day.

"I'll be back, Amelia," I called out casually as Lucky and I headed out for the evening. "And thanks for an incredible trip today. I can hardly wait to get back to your diary."

I loaded Lucky into my SUV. It was too late and too cold for a walk. We'd take a drive instead, maybe find a place to get a hamburger for dinner. The only place open in Virginia City was the Pioneer Bar. That's where the locals hung out during the winter, whether they imbibed or not. Maybe we could get a hamburger there.

I parked the car and went in, somewhat anxiously. I wasn't used to going into bars alone. I'd only been here once before—on New Year's Eve with Paul. I would never forget that special night. It would be nice to see him again this Saturday—as long as he didn't pry for information about Amelia.

Glancing around, I saw a few familiar faces that I'd seen at the library or around town. I stepped up to the bar and ordered two hamburgers to go.

"Rose, good to see you!" a familiar voice rang out from a table in the far corner. It was Maria from the Outlaw Café. She was having a beer with another woman. "Come on over and join us."

I pulled a chair up to their table and was introduced to Carla, a good friend of Maria's who was visiting. Carla's teenage daughter was babysitting for Maria's little girl, Mia, while the two women were enjoying a rare night out on the town.

"Not a lot to do here in the winter, is there?" Carla yawned.

"Not unless you like solitude or are a writer like Rose here," Maria boasted. "She's writing a book on the history of our town."

"You need to come on back in the summer," I chimed in before the conversation turned to my research. "There are vaudeville shows, ghost tours, living history days, Victorian balls. Everything is open—all the shops, museums, and restaurants. I'm anxious to see it all next summer."

We chatted until my hamburgers were ready, and then I excused myself. "My poor dog is in the car waiting for dinner," I told them.

"You could have brought him in," the bartender told me. "No rules here, especially in the winter, to keep pets out."

"I'll remember that in the future," I laughed.

"Rose, we need to get together again," Maria touched my arm. "It's been too long. I know you're busy with your work, but you need to get out once in a while, you know. Unless you're too busy with Paul."

"Paul?"

"Don't forget I saw you together on New Year's. You make a wonderful couple."

"Well, I don't know about that. He's a good friend."

"Could have fooled me!" she teased as my face turned pink.

"But, yes, we will get together sometime soon," I promised.

Lucky was happy to see me, sniffing at the bag of hamburgers on the seat between us. I didn't feel like going back to my haunted house, not yet. Maybe we'd have a picnic someplace. The roads were good enough to drive up toward the cemetery, so that's what we did.

I parked the car but left it running to keep warm. What a spectacular view of the lights in the valley below. More lights cascaded across the lower levels of the surrounding mountains. I often wondered what the people in these houses were doing, what their lives were like...if they also had resident ghosts to keep them company.

Lucky had already devoured his hamburger while I, lost in my thoughts, nibbled on mine. His eyes pleaded with me to give him a bite of mine. This was a special treat for my big dumb dog. His diet was usually restricted to dog food and an occasional table scrap. I finally gave in, handing him the last bite of my hamburger. He laid his big head in my lap to show his appreciation.

We drove around for a while, all the way to Sheridan and back. I played classical music on my CD player as we drove, relaxing to the strains of the music. Finally, we went back home.

Lucky plopped down in his favorite spot by the fireplace and fell asleep. After going through my mail and paying a few bills, I turned off the lights and went into my bedroom. I needed some sleep if I was going to keep up with Amelia.

Turning on the light in my bedroom, I saw something waiting for me on my bed. Amelia's journal! She had opened it to the page where I was to resume my reading.

"I thought it belonged in the loft, Amelia." I smiled to myself.

"It belongs wherever you are, my dear," Amelia whispered into my mind. "Most of the answers you seek are waiting in the pages of our diary. Most…not all."

Our diary? The boundaries between our very different worlds seemed to be blurring, merging into one. It made no sense.

"Good night, Amelia," I carefully moved the diary to my bedside table, turned down the covers, and crawled into bed. I could feel her displeasure. She wanted me to continue reading. Had she forgotten that mere mortals need to sleep now and then?

Chapter 27

Exhausted, I soon fell into a deep sleep. But it did not last long. I found myself drifting back into Amelia's world.

She is walking into Virginia City beside a rambling train of covered wagons as the sun sets behind the mountains on a cool September evening. Some of the wagons are limping into town on three wheels. They are tattered and torn after the long and sometimes brutal journey.

The turbulent mining town lies in a valley surrounded by towering mountains. Fields of daisies and goldenrod shimmer in the breeze in the shadows of the mountains. The sheer beauty takes Amelia's breath away. The town, however, is rough and tough.

Peering through the clouds of dust and grime, trying to avoid stepping in piles of manure or muddy water holes in the rutted dirt road, she lifts the skirts of her long dress. Probably doesn't matter, she thinks to herself, embarrassed to be seen in such a state. After three months on the trail, the travelers look like a sorry lot. Tattered clothes. In need of a real bath and real food.

They have finally arrived. Now what? The land of their dreams stands before them, shocking them with sensory overload. After a relatively quiet and monotonous journey, they are overwhelmed with the hordes of characters rushing about. Miners sporting red and blue flannel shirts, cumbersome boots, long beards and mustaches plod along on their loaded-down burros. Cowboys with pistols on their hips race through town on their horses, kicking up clouds of dust. Painted ladies swish down the boardwalk in their fancy dresses, trying to entice men into the saloons and dance halls. Gamblers, outlaws, and merchants swarm through town, in and out of the saloons and crude log stores.

Loud talk, music, and whiskey flow through the French doors of the log buildings on the main road. The occasional crack of a pistol can be heard as cowboys tumble out of the saloons and into the street to settle their differences.

Wagons begin to split off from the train, bidding their fellow travelers good-bye. They are all anxious to stake their claims and begin building shelters before winter sets in. Many will continue to live in their wagons until they find shelter. Others will camp out in their bedrolls in one of the establishments.

Virginia City is a confusing maze of hundreds of wagons, tents, and a few crude shacks built of hand-cut logs. Some of the miners sleep in brush wakeups or beneath the stars near their claims.

As for Amelia and the Callahans, they set their wagon up on the edge of town in a makeshift settlement of other wagons from their train. Amelia continues to care for the children while Mr. Callahan busies himself with building a shelter for his family. Mrs. Callahan falls oddly silent, no longer complaining, barely speaking to any of them. She stares into the distance, her mind many miles away. Her heart still lives in Galena, Illinois.

Mr. Callahan finds the land he plans to build upon. He claims it by felling four large trees and arranging them around the perimeter of the house he plans to build. The men work together cutting logs, hauling them back from the nearby mountains with their ox teams, and gathering for house-raising parties.

Amelia takes the children to watch their house-raising party. They hike through fields of wildflowers, stopping to pick bouquets for their new house and braiding clover into a necklace for their silent mother.

From a safe distance, they watch the roof being constructed of log poles. It is then covered with a plaster made of mud. Once it dries, layers of earth are thrown over it to make a warm, and hopefully waterproof, roof. The floor is made of dirt. It is leveled, moistened, and tamped with a flat board until it is so hard that it can be swept without raising dust.

Mr. Callahan spends long days hauling rocks from the creek bed to build the fireplace. Finally, the house is ready to move into. It's very small, but it will provide shelter for the winter. He takes pride in the fact that he has built a home for his family with his own hands and a little help from his neighbors.

While Amelia and the children are appreciative, looking forward to a new life in their own home, Mrs. Callahan is not pleased. Having refused to visit her new home until moving day, she is aghast at its simplicity and the lack of amenities she enjoyed back home.

On moving day, they arrive in the wagon, ready to unload all of their possessions and settle into the house. The children scramble into the house, exploring every nook and cranny, finding the big wood bed their father has constructed for them. Curtains will be hung later to separate living and sleeping areas in the one-room dwelling.

Amelia wishes for a bit more privacy but is not in a position to do anything about it. Someday, she will find a better job and a place of her own. And someday beyond that, she will have enough money to build her own home and bring her own little boy west to live with her. The very thought makes her smile.

Meanwhile, she overhears Mr. and Mrs. Callahan having an escalating discussion back by the wagon.

"What the devil do you mean, leave your things in the wagon? We're moving into our new home!" He raises his voice to her.

"I shall not be staying in this God-forsaken land, Mr. Callahan!" She stomps her foot on the ground, eyes blazing.

Amelia moves closer, hiding behind a cluster of trees, straining to hear the rest of their heated conversation. Her worst fears are coming to pass.

"What about the children?" he finally asks his angry wife, his voice deflated in disbelief.

She bristles. "They will return to Galena with me, of course. Have you forgotten that our home awaits us? *My* home, sir! The one I inherited from my beloved parents. I shall raise my children there by myself. I have nothing more to say to you."

Stunned, he shakes his head. "They are my children too," he reminds her.

"And have you ever heard of a man getting custody of his children?" she scoffs, slinging around legal terms she learned at the knee of her lawyer father. Of course, she was right. That never happened. Courts always felt that children belonged with their mother, regardless of the circumstances.

"And what about me, Johanna?" Mr. Callahan sounds crushed as if she'd kicked him in the gut.

"You are free to do whatever you choose. Live your foolish dream. Dig for gold. Start a business so you can become a proper wealthy man instead of relying on me for support."

Oh, that must hurt, Amelia thinks to herself, her heart going out to poor Mr. Callahan. After all his work to bring his family west and provide shelter for them, she was not only leaving him but insulting his manhood as well. For a man with any amount of pride, that would be the final blow to their marriage, Amelia realizes.

Yet, Mrs. Callahan did have a legitimate concern. Her husband had not taken her feelings into account before uprooting his family from their privileged lifestyle back home. He had insisted they accompany him on a difficult journey that most men did not subject their loved ones to.

Regardless of whose fault it was, this marriage is over. Amelia soon learns that Mrs. Callahan and the children will be leaving on the stagecoach for Salt Lake City tomorrow morning. From there, they will take the first train or coach back east. While the others had been busy at the new house, the bitter wife had apparently used her time to arrange transportation back home.

It is a strange final evening. While Mr. Callahan unloads his belongings into his empty new house, his wife sorts through things, throwing unwanted items into a heap on the ground. She packs small carpetbags for herself and the children since space will be limited on the coach.

Amelia takes the children for a walk to keep them occupied and finally brings them back to the house in time for dinner. Nobody is making dinner. The children are hungry. Amelia drags out the pots and pans while Mr. Callahan builds a fire for her to cook on. She cooks a simple meal. Their last supper together, she thinks to herself, as they all sit quietly around the fire.

Mr. Callahan finally announces that his wife and children will be returning to their home in Galena the next day. He is, after all, still the head of the household—until tomorrow. A stunned silence follows before the children climb onto his lap with questions. Will he be coming with them? Why not? Why do they have to leave? Questions that he is unable to answer.

"Ask your mother," he replies icily. "I will miss you all and long to see you again as soon as I can."

"But you have to stay behind to find gold before you come home?" their little son inquires, looking into his father's eyes for assurance. Wanting to be sure his father comes home again.

Amelia watches Mr. Callahan dab at his eyes as he turns away to stoke the fire. He tucks the sleepy children into the covered wagon with their mother before finding his flask of whiskey. He slumps down beside the fire, his dreams crushed, his family about to leave him.

Amelia is not sure what to do or where to go. She sits beside the fire across from her employer, wanting to say something, anything, to comfort the poor man. He remains lost in thought, drowning his sorrows in drink.

"I'm very sorry, sir," she finally blurts the words out. "If there's anything I can do to help..."

Bleary-eyed, Mr. Callahan tries to focus upon the young woman who has been so good to his children on this difficult journey. "Much appreciated," he finally nods at her. "Not much anyone can do but get on with life. I'll stay here in my home, do some mining, build a business of some sort."

Amelia listens, wondering what will happen to her in this foreign land.

Finally, the same thought seems to register in his mind. "What about you? What will you do?"

"I...I don't know what I'll do or where I'll go," she whispers the scary thought out loud for the first time.

He leans in closer to her, the smell of whiskey on his breath. "Will you stay?"

She sighs. While she'd love nothing more than going home to Jonathan, she knows she cannot do so without risking her life at the hands of the husband from whom she fled. She also needed money to make her own way in the world. She has no choice but to stay.

Mr. Callahan watches her closely, shadows from the flames flickering across his dark face. "I will stay, but I need a job," she confesses.

"Where will you stay? Ya know, I have room here for a pretty gal like you." He points at his new house, the one he constructed with his blood, sweat, and tears. His drunken eyes sweep slowly up and down her body.

She startles. Of course she cannot stay with this man. It would be totally improper, and if he continues to drink like this, she could find herself in a less than desirable situation.

"Thank you, sir, but I shall need to find my own living quarters. It would not be proper to live with a man," she replies curtly. "I will be on my way tomorrow if you will kindly give me my wages."

He stumbles into his house and back out with a pouch of gold coins for her. "As promised, Miss Amelia. Don't forget my offer..." He looks at her sadly, hopelessly, before turning his back and retreating to his lonesome house.

Amelia climbs quietly into the wagon, trying not to wake the others. Settled into her bedroll, she tosses and turns, wondering what tomorrow will bring.

A voice pierces her thoughts. "Are you returning with us?" Mrs. Callahan calls out from her bed in the front of the wagon.

"No, I'm staying. I'm sorry to see you all go, however."

"Just stay away from that old fool! You're too nice of a young lady to get involved with something the likes of him."

"Of course, ma'am."

"Thank you, Amelia, for your kindness to the children. They shall miss you, and so shall I. Sleep well."

৵৵

Loneliness engulfs Amelia the next afternoon as she stands beside the stagecoach waving good-bye to the family she's spent the past four months with. Her carpetbag, stuffed with all the belongings she has left in this world, sits beside her.

She is terrified to find herself all alone in this wild western town. She must find a place to stay before the miners get off work and come into town to raise hell. She can still hear the distant sound of picks and shovels clanging against rock as the miners pan for gold along Alder Gulch.

Trying to act much more confident than she really is, as if she knows where she is going and what she is doing, she hikes down the boardwalk. Finally, she finds a crude hotel with a sign, "Room for Rent," and enters. While the desk clerk looks surprised to see a young woman alone, he rents the room to her. She pays him with gold coins.

"It's room and board, miss. Meals served down that-a-way." The whiskered, gray-bearded man gives her a toothless smile.

Her room is tiny. It is sparsely furnished with a thin, lumpy mattress filled with horse hair and a single chair. She will shove that chair against the door at night to keep out any possible intruders.

She has a hot meal at the hotel, the only woman there, trying to ignore the stares from the hungry men. They nod politely at her, showing respect for her as a woman. Afterward, she fills her water pitcher and takes a sponge bath in her room. Tomorrow she will begin her job search.

Finding a decent job in old Virginia City, she soon discovers, will be a formidable task. With few families here yet, there does not seem to be any need for nannies. The few families affluent enough to afford one already have one. Her heart set on becoming a schoolmistress, Amelia inquires around town only to discover that the one available position was filled last week. It wasn't even a real school, just a room in the house of the one of the prominent families in town.

Every day she walks the street during the safe hours, stopping at the various businesses to ask about a job. Every day she returns to her tiny, suffocating room, fighting tears. Is there no work for a decent woman in this town?

As her gold coins begin to disappear, she becomes frantic, frantic enough to hesitantly pry open the door of a dance hall just down the street from her hotel.

Chapter 28

The shrill ring of the alarm clock penetrated the world of my dreams. But I was not ready to leave Amelia's world, not yet. I had to find out what happened to her. Burying my head beneath my pillow, I tried to fall back to sleep, to continue where I'd left off. Poor Amelia. Perhaps she had no choice but to work in a dance hall.

"A hurdy-gurdy house, my dear," Amelia corrected the thought flowing through my mind.

"Take me there, Amelia. Please take me back with you," I pleaded.

"It is not yet time for that. You are not ready, and you shall not be ready until you've advanced farther in reading our memoirs. It shall happen—in a timely fashion," she assured me.

At work that day, my thoughts kept drifting back to Amelia. She was becoming so real to me, such an important part of my life.

After work, I took Lucky for his walk, still deep in thought. I barely noticed the glorious sunset streaking across the sky. All I wanted to do was climb up into the loft and return to Amelia's world. After making myself a tuna sandwich for a quick dinner, I did just that.

Sitting there in my window seat in the dark, I waited for her to arrive. Where was she? I finally turned on my lantern and picked up her diary. A dainty ribbon had been inserted in the pages of the book, as if Amelia had marked the place for me. Opening the book to that page, I began to read:

December 15, 1863
I am greatly saddened this day. While I have finally found employment, this is not the position that I desire. I cringe to think of it. I pray that my family back east shall never know that I work as a dancer, a hurdy-gurdy girl, in a saloon. It is what I must do to support myself and make enough money to support my beloved son someday. May God forgive me if he finds my behavior sinful.

Wiping tears from my eyes, I could feel her pain. Women in those days certainly did not have the choices or the power we do today. I wondered what Amelia thought of my lifestyle in the year 2011. Was she shocked by the freedom I enjoyed, by the choices I was able to make?

As I stared out the window, she began to nag me to get back to reading her diary. I read on, becoming more and more fascinated with the colorful snapshots she created through her words, glimpses of her life in the 1860s.

かめ

January 1, 1864

I suffered through the Christmas season, my first one away from home. I sent a small package to Jonathan and am hopeful that he received it by Christmas. The stagecoach has not come through for weeks—too much snow—so I am feeling totally cut off from the world. No letters from home.

Nevertheless, it was a festive season. I attended church on Christmas Eve, dressed in my most conservative clothing and hiding my face beneath the brim of a large hat. I recognized some of my regular dance partners sitting beside their wives and children. I watched them squirm in their seats when I walked by.

I prayed to God for his understanding and forgiveness. I begged Him to show me another way to support my son and myself.

*A bit of excitement swept through the town on Christmas Day. A newspaperman by the name of Mark Twain arrived in Virginia City. He is a writer for **The Territorial Enterprise**. An avid reader myself, I am impressed with his style and way with words. I believe he will establish himself as a prominent writer in time.*

かめ

February 1, 1864
Dear Diary,

It has been a difficult winter in Virginia City, one plagued by stage robberies and murders. It is not safe to travel. The outlaws, also known as road agents, strike fear in the heart of every man and woman. They ride fast, well-trained horses and disguise themselves with masks and blankets before plundering or ambushing stagecoaches traveling through the wilderness. This group of outlaws hangs out at the Rattlesnake Ranch or Robbers Roost. They have killed about 102 men, it has been said. Other miners who have left Virginia City with their gold have never been heard from again. Their families try in vain to find these missing men.

Finally, the pillars of our community banded together and took the law into their own hands. The Vigilantes, as they are called, have hung many of these outlaws. Once again, Virginia City is relatively safe.

I shall never forget that dreary day in January when I witnessed five limp bodies swinging from the gallows. It pained me dreadfully since one of these young men had been one of my regulars at the hurdy-gurdy house. Always a gentleman around me, he was just a boy who had gotten himself involved with these heartless bandits. I wondered if his mother would ever know the cruel fate of her son who had gone west to strike it rich. He had talked to me about his dream of bringing gold home to provide a better life for his poor parents. Now that shall never come to pass.

It is a hard life out here in the west. There are no doctors, so we must doctor ourselves. One of the best ways to cure most ills—everything from a stomachache to a broken leg—is by drinking bitters.

I am making very good wages now that I've learned to smile and entertain the gentlemen who come in to dance and drink with me. I live in a small log cabin with three of the other dancers. Aside from buying myself lovely dresses, hats, and jewelry to ensure that my looks will appeal to the men who pay to dance with me, I save my money for the day my little boy will once again live with me.

かめ

June 8, 1864

Dear Diary,

We have had several Indian scares and must always be on the lookout for warring tribes. The Indians resent the white men for invading their territory. Virginia City is equipped with an arsenal that includes muskets, cannons, and ammunition.

We're fortunate to have a friendly tribe living nearby. The Bannocks, led by Chief Tendoy, sometimes camp just east of town. They are a sight to behold. The Indian bucks wear leggings and moccasins made of animal hides and embroidered with beads. Around their heads they wear bands of red and blue cloth decorated with the feathers of native birds. They also wear colorful beaded necklaces over their bare brown chests. Animal teeth and eagle's claws hang from the necklaces. In the winter, they wrap bright blankets around themselves to keep warm.

Chief Tendoy has become a friend. After drinking whiskey with some of our town fathers, he allows himself to be dressed up in a good suit of clothes and a stovepipe hat. He struts up and down the streets in his white man's clothing, grinning his toothless grin.

かめ

July 4, 1864

Dear Diary,

The Fourth of July is perhaps the most festive and important day in Virginia City. The day always begins at dawn with the firing of the town's cannon across Daylight Gulch. The whistle at the printing press office blows as the church bells ring out across the valley. Once the town folks have gathered, there's a festive parade followed by the reading of the Declaration of Independence, an oration, and music by a chorus. There are horse races and rock drilling contests in the afternoon, fireworks in the evening, and a grand ball at the courthouse.

Of course, I, as a hurdy-gurdy girl, do not participate in many of these activities. I watch from afar, longing someday to be acknowledged as a respectable citizen who will be welcomed at celebrations such as this. Perhaps I shall even go to a ball someday...

༺♥༻

April 5, 1865

Dear Diary,

My world is quite narrow in comparison with all that happens in this town. The rough edges of the Wild West are being polished into a more refined culture. Virginia City is rapidly becoming the social city of the West now that more families and businessmen are locating here. It is a melting pot of diverse nationalities, including French, Irish, Russian, Polish, German, and Chinese.

We also have our share of Civil War deserters. Fights between those who support the north and those who support the south frequently spill out from the saloons into the streets.

We depend upon stagecoaches from Salt Lake City to deliver everything from turkeys to wine, eggs and luxury goods. Billiard tables and grand pianos are transported by ox-drawn wagons. The arrival of the stagecoach is a special event, greatly anticipated by all. We anxiously await letters from home, letters that usually take a good month or two to arrive.

*There are churches and church socials, theatrical productions, spelling bees, poetry recitations, and respectable dances. Piano, singing, dancing, and French lessons are available. We even have our own newspaper, **The Montana Post**, which was founded here this past August.*

In the winter, there are sleigh rides followed by oyster feeds. The children race down the hills on bobsleds.

The upper-class men now have a literary society. They spend time at the Gem Reading Room on the second floor of the Stonewall Building. Here they read the latest newspapers, periodicals, and books. They discuss events of the day and play dominos, chess, or checkers.

Women play croquet, attend quilting bees, and do needlework. They call on each other during the day, leaving a calling card if the lady of the house is not home. They also enjoy horseback riding and picking berries. They stroll along the boardwalk in their long, full dresses, carrying umbrellas, on the way to Mrs. Frank's Millinery and Ladies Clothing Store for dress fittings or to purchase a new hat.

These God-fearing women also look suspiciously upon the likes of the hurdy-gurdies and prostitutes who continue to do a brisk business. We are not one and the same—at least most of us are not. But these righteous women are now attempting to impose a "sin tax" on establishments like the one I work in. They want to drive us out of business. Of course, they worry that their own husbands will stray and visit our establishments.

Truth be told, many of them do visit us. I have acquired many more male friends than female ones—aside from the other dancers like myself. My partners include bankers, merchants, miners, cowboys, gamblers, and outlaws.

ও◌ৎ

March 11, 1867
Dear Diary,

Tonight we experienced a spectacular sight as a meteor, a luminous body traveling across the sky, produced two separate explosions. A blinding flash lit up the heavens like sun at noonday as particles fell to the earth. People rushed out of their homes to see what had happened.

This spectacle reminds me of what is happening in my personal life. While I have been seriously remiss as far as confiding in you, my dear diary, I shall try to make up for this slight. I shall attempt to reconstruct what has happened. Perhaps I shall, through my writing, learn to understand why it happened and what course of action I should take to resolve issues that have come to pass.

For now, I will simply tell you that I am in love, deeply in love, with a prominent gentleman. I pray for a future with him. His name is Henry.

Chapter 29

Henry again. I ran my index finger over the words Amelia had scribbled in her diary so many years ago: *His name is Henry.* Was that not also the name of the watchman/banker she met on her journey west?

Bleary-eyed, I closed my eyes for a moment. When I opened them, I was surprised to find the sun already creeping up over the horizon. I'd been so engrossed in Amelia's life that I'd read most of the night.

I was tempted to call in to work, telling Paul that I was sick. I could take a quick nap and then get back to her journal. But he was counting on me that day. We were wrapping up several important chapters of our book and had a deadline to meet. I should not let him down. But...

As I pondered my decision, the open journal on my lap abruptly snapped shut. "That is enough for now. It is time to go to work!" Amelia shouted in my ear. Shaking my head, I followed her orders.

My morning walk with Lucky woke me up. The chill of the frosty morning was invigorating. The trees were blanketed in a glistening coat of thin ice that sparkled like diamonds in the sunlight.

Retrieving my camera from my pocket, I took a few shots. I'd e-mail copies to Mama and Papa. They always seemed to enjoy my photos. Perhaps it gave them a diversion from the everyday issues they were now dealing with together. I worried about them and called frequently to check in.

Paul was waiting for me when I arrived at work. He already had the table in his office stacked with the chapters we needed to finalize. A pot of coffee and a plate of Danish rolls were also waiting for us.

"Good morning, Rose," he welcomed me with a warm smile. My heart smiled back at him. It had been too long since we'd spent any time together.

He pulled a chair up close beside his own, gesturing me to join him. I slipped into the chair, very much aware of his closeness. I could smell his musk-scented cologne, a familiar scent for some unknown reason.

"You're looking chipper today, sir," I teased him.

"But, of course, my lady," he bowed his head. "How could I not be chipper, as you say, when we are finally going out together tomorrow evening?"

I'd forgotten, as busy as I'd been with Amelia. That's right—tomorrow was Saturday, the night I'd promised to have dinner with him. Of course that meant a delay in my plans to complete Amelia's diary.

He shot me a sharp, puzzled look. "Have you forgotten our plans?" There was a touch of hurt in his eyes.

"Of course not," I touched his arm. "I had just forgotten that it's Friday already. That's all. Where are we going?"

"You like poetry, don't you?"

"I love it. Why do you ask?"

"Because there's a poetry reading at a quaint little café in Bozeman where all the writers and poets hang out. They will be reading some of the classics—Elizabeth Barrett Browning, Emily Dickinson, Shelley, and Yeats. The weather is supposed to be perfect for a drive to Bozeman. I thought we could drive over and take a look around. There's a fantastic museum—the Museum of the Rockies. After that, we can even do a little shopping, have dinner at the restaurant of your choice, and then take in the poetry reading."

It sounded wonderful to me, aside from the fact that he was tearing me away from Amelia's life. But perhaps that was what I needed. How long had it been since I'd been away from Virginia City? While I loved it here, in fact belonged here, I'd always loved to see and explore new places.

"You're on, sir," I grinned at him. His eyes glowed with relief. I'd been putting him off for so long that the poor man didn't know what to think. Neither did I.

We had a productive day together, working very well as a team. He was pleased and gave me a hug when I left. "Until tomorrow. I'll pick you up about ten o'clock, all right?"

"Perfect." I danced my way down the alley to my cabin, a smile on my face.

☜☞

Saturday dawned bright and clear. The sky was a brilliant blue, contrasting sharply against the snow-covered mountains. The drive to Bozeman along the back roads was filled with photo opportunities. We stopped to take pictures of the scenery and of each other. Sometimes we posed together, arms around each other, as the camera went off.

Laughing, joking, and enjoying each other's company, I felt like I had known and loved this man forever. So why did I keep him at a distance? Maybe it was time to change my habits.

Paul, always the perfect gentleman, opened the doors for me and escorted me with his hand on my arm. Together we explored the fabulous Museum of the Rockies, which has one of the largest collections of dinosaur fossils in the world, including a number that were unearthed here in Montana. Obviously history buffs, we lost ourselves in the regional historical artifacts and the photo archives.

Of special interest to both of us were the photos dating back to the 1860s. We found several of life in Virginia City that neither of us had previously seen. Paul jotted information in his pocket notebook. Maybe we could get permission to use several of these photos in our book.

Time was flying. There was so much to see here that we'd need to come back again. For now, we decided to take in a show in the planetarium. Once we were seated in our chairs, the lights went out, throwing us into pitch darkness. Paul reached over for my hand and held it firmly as the dome lit up and turned into the night sky. We were alone in the Universe, basking in the endless mysteries of the stars, planets, and black holes that continue to intrigue mankind.

Sitting closely beside this man, a feeling of utter contentment and peace washed over me. When he squeezed my hand, the feelings flowed between us, expressing all that needed to be said.

Still holding hands, we hiked through the historic district of Bozeman for a while, stopping to browse in several shops along the way. We were both getting hungry by the time we came upon a quaint restaurant located in an old brick building that was designated as an historical landmark. The sign informed us that it had been built in 1905.

"Shall we?" Paul beamed down at me, sensing that I was also excited about dining in an historical building.

"Oh, yes!" I followed him into John Bozeman's Bistro, anxious to absorb the essence of the history that had once unfolded in this building. That's what I loved about old buildings. It was fun just trying to imagine the people who frequented these places and the events that once took place here.

Old cowboy photos and murals lined the walls. A mounted longhorn cattle head stood guard over the majestic wood-carved and mirrored bar.

Despite the Wild West flavor, there was a distinctive feeling of historical elegance that permeated the little restaurant.

Seated at a table in the corner, we were trying to make a selection from their extensive list of fine wines when we noticed a list of beer selections. "Big Sky Trout Slayer Ale?" Paul laughed.

"Let's do it," I grinned at him.

It was difficult to make a selection from the extensive menu. Paul settled on the Wild West Buffalo Medallions, and I chose a steak. We chatted over our dinners, discussing the history of Bozeman and all that we'd learned at the museum. Soon it was time to leave for the poetry reading.

The café was illuminated with candles flickering in the dark. A makeshift stage filled one corner of the large room. Several violins and a golden harp played softly in the background. A high stool stood center stage beside a podium.

Once our eyes adjusted to the darkness, we found ourselves a cozy table in the back and waited for the reading to begin. Before long, the place was packed and a man with a goatee, dressed in black, seated himself on the stool.

The house fell silent as we all sipped our wine, listening intently. The poet's voice was rich, quaint, with a distinguished English accent reminiscent of what one might expect Yeats or Shelley to have sounded like. He held us spellbound as he read. The atmosphere was charged with emotion and deep philosophical insights. Several women also read the poetry of Emily Dickinson and Elizabeth Barrett Browning, charming the crowd.

After thunderous applause, the poets left the stage. The soft romantic music resumed. While some of the guests began leaving, Paul was in no hurry. Neither was I. The magic of the night had bound us together. Why let it end?

"I have a poem for you," he announced quietly as he retrieved a large, old book with a well-worn cover from his satchel.

I leaned close to read the faded inscription. "The Poetical Works of Percy Bysshe Shelley?" My eyes grew huge in disbelief.

"Yes, it's a rare first edition that has come down through my family. Shelley has always been my favorite. He is, I think, the greatest lyrical romantic poet ever born. He speaks to the soul. Let me read for you. This is for you, Rose, from yours truly." He brushed my hand with his and began to read. Within moments, he turned his gaze from the book, looked deeply into my eyes and recited the verse by heart:

> The fountains mingle with the river,
> And the rivers with the ocean;
> The winds of heaven mix forever
> With a sweet emotion;
> Nothing in the world is single;
> All things by a law divine
> In another's being mingle—
> Why not I with thine?
> See, the mountains kiss high heaven,
> And the waves clasp one another;
> No sister flower could be forgiven
> If it disdained its brother;
> And the sunlight clasps the earth,
> And the moonbeams kiss the sea—
> What are all these kissings worth
> If thou kiss not me?

This poem was achingly familiar to me for some reason. I knew I'd heard these words before. As tears filled my eyes, Paul reached across the table, lifted my hand to his mouth, and kissed it gently.

" 'Love's Philosophy,' " I whispered the name of the poem he'd just read for me. My heart was overflowing with feelings for this man, the one I'd held at arm's length for far too long.

"Yes, 'Love's Philosophy,' little one."

"I cannot find the words to tell you how much this means to me, Paul. It's the most romantic thing anyone has ever done for me. You truly are a gentleman from the past."

With that, he stood, pulling me into his arms. We began to dance around the tables to the slow music of the violins. His mouth met mine, urgently, and held me until the end of the song. Dizzy with emotion, we left hand in hand.

We drove home silently, basking in the feelings that flowed between us. When we pulled up to my cabin, Paul brought out the book of poems once again and placed it in my hands.

"I want you to keep this, Rose," he said softly. "It is my gift to you, and I will be greatly pleased if you will read it and enjoy it as much as I have."

I was shocked. "That is so generous of you, but I cannot possibly accept something like this from you, Paul. This is a rare first edition, probably worth a fortune."

"Not nearly as valuable as you are to me, Rose. Please, I will be offended and forever hurt if you do not accept my gift."

"Why? Why are you doing all this for me?"

At first he did not answer. Had I offended him once again? I seemed to have a talent for doing that. Finally he made an odd comment. "Maybe I'm just trying to make things right with you, making up for the past."

I was confused. "But you've never done anything to make up for."

"Perhaps. Still, I cannot shake this feeling that lingers in my soul."

"You sound like a poet, you know. Like Shelley perhaps?" I teased him, changing the subject. Paul had a formal way of speech at times, as if he were lapsing back into the past. Maybe we both spent too many hours doing historical research at that old library.

"Let me walk you to your door." He swung his car door open and came around to open mine.

"Aren't you coming in?" I had to admit I did not want this magical night to end. Not yet.

"I've learned that a gentleman does not take advantage of the lady he loves. I will bid you good night at your door."

After a warm, lingering kiss, he was gone. Confused and frustrated, I took Lucky out for a quick walk and then settled beside the fire with Shelley's book before me.

Someone had obviously devoured the poems in this book, as it had been well used. I could almost picture Paul's grandfather or his great-grandfather paging through the book, marking their favorite poems. The book seemed to open naturally to a poem entitled "Bereavement." Several verses had been underlined in shaky handwriting. They read:

How stern are the woes of the desolate mourner
As he bends in still grief o'er the hallowed bier,
When floods of despair down his pale cheeks are streaming
When no blissful hope on his bosom is beaming.

I recalled the vision that I'd seen hovering beside Amelia's grave the night that Paul and I spent doing paranormal research in the cemetery. This verse reminded me of that devastated spirit, of the horrific pain that I'd felt emanating from him. Or her.

Putting the book aside, I stared into the fire for a while, thinking of Paul and the wonderful day we'd shared together. I was falling in love with him, helplessly in love, I feared.

"Beware! Things and people are not always what they seem," Amelia's silent voice shouted at me. I felt as if she were trying to shake some common sense into me.

What was she talking about? She knew nothing about Paul DuBois. Just because she'd fallen in love with the wrong man, at least once, it did not mean I was about to repeat her mistakes.

Amelia was silent, sulking, as if she had read and was reacting to my thoughts.

"I'm sorry, Amelia. I did not mean to hurt your feelings. Perhaps I'll learn from your mistakes. We all make them, you know. Myself included. If you only knew," I sighed.

"Of course I know. The truth will set us both free, my dear. It will be revealed to you in a timely fashion."

"Good night, Amelia." I locked the doors and retreated into my bedroom. I still glowed with memories of the day I'd just shared with a man whom I suspected was my long lost soul mate. Pulling the covers up close, I knew I would soon be dreaming of Paul DuBois.

☙❧

Before long, I drifted into a fantasy world in which Paul and I lie entangled in each other's arms in a sleepy cove on the banks of the Madison River. We nibble on crackers and cheese and sip on wine while watching the rapids rushing past our secret hiding place. An occasional canoe shoots the rapids, sometimes spilling its occupants into the churning waves. I am surprised to see that we are dressed in the Victorian fashions of the 1860s.

As the sun slips into the wild river and darkness descends upon the earth, Paul's unrelenting passion and promises of a future together arouse me to the point of consent once again. His skilled hands unlace my corset and toss my bloomers into the brush. I swoon as his lips move up and down the growing contours of my body. His manhood, in all its extended glory, slips forcefully into that place he's long since claimed as his own. I shudder as waves of passion reverberate throughout my body, surrendering once again to the love of my life.

Gripping the growth in my stomach, I find the courage to boldly announce to my beloved that I am with child. I wait for him to enfold me within his arms, telling me once again how much he loves me and cannot live without me. I can only imagine how thrilled he will be to learn that I shall soon deliver his child. Of course, I expect that this revelation will also be enough to convince him to divorce his wife and establish a home with me, the woman he has loved for the past five years.

"What the hell?" Paul hisses at me, pulling up his trousers. "How do you know I'm the father of this bastard child? For Christ's sake, Amelia. You cannot have this child. Do something about it, do you hear me?"

Amelia?? Why does he call me Amelia? What happened to Paul and me?

As I toss and turn, the dream plunges once again into the depths of the swirling river. Amelia is drowning, her frantic cries echoing through the stormy night.

"I can't swim!" she sobs, as waves crash over her head.

"I know," a man with a deep voice replies icily as he and his boat disappear into the fog.

Escaping from the dream, I struggle to see the man's face. But I cannot. All I can see is Bob's face as he holds his arms out to me. As if he is trying to save me from Amelia's fate.

Chapter 30

I spent the next few weeks interviewing local residents who had fascinating stories to tell about the history of Virginia City as well as the nearby ghost town of Nevada City. I took a tour of the old historical buildings which had been preserved through the generosity of Charles and Sue Bovey beginning in the mid-1940s. While their efforts had already been well documented and would not be a focus of our historical book, it was still fascinating to learn all that this couple did to restore and re-energize these old mining towns that they loved.

Although many of the buildings and attractions were not open during the winter, I loved the peace and solitude of winter in Virginia City. It was a time to absorb it all, to connect with restless spirits who probably preferred spending time here when their old haunts were not crowded with tourists.

As devoted as I was to solving the mystery of Amelia's life, I was also learning to balance the worlds I walked between. I'd finally learned that timing truly was everything. I could not force communication with the spirit world. I had to wait until Amelia was ready to reveal information to me. I could not coerce her in any way. Sometimes she seemed to have completely disappeared from my life. Sometimes, she even hid her diary from me.

With Saint Patrick's Day approaching, I decided to take a break from my work and make it a special day in honor of Amelia and Rose O'Brien and their Irish heritage. *My* Irish heritage.

As I decorated my house for Saint Patrick's Day, I hoped Amelia would show up to see what I'd done in her honor. I strung green shamrock-shaped lights around my porch and found a six-pack of green beer.

One day, I drove to a gift shop in Ennis where I found the most delightful little Irish trolls and bought an entire family of them. I left one in Paul's office and perched another on my desk. Every time I looked at them, I grinned. I thought of Amelia and all she'd gone through to come west. She was a true Irish pioneer at heart. So was Rosa, my great-great grandmother and Amelia's sister.

The other trolls were arranged on my table at home around one of my African violet plants. I took a picture of them and e-mailed it to Mama and Papa, who got a kick out of it. Papa had mastered the art of e-mail. Although Mama didn't have a clue, she still liked to look at the pictures I sent and was always asking Papa to find them for her on that "newfangled gadget" of his.

Mama planned to make her traditional corned beef and cabbage for Saint Patrick Day's dinner. She was pleased when I asked her for the recipe. "Are you making it just for yourself? Or is Bob coming over for dinner?"

Poor Mama. Why could she not remember that Bob and I were no longer together? Or did she not want to remember? Did she need to keep rubbing my failures in my face?

"Mama," I began patiently, "Bob's not here in Montana. He's back in Walnut, isn't he?"

"Well, of course, I know that," she bristled. "But if he's not coming for dinner, who is?"

"My boss, Paul. Remember, he came over for Christmas Eve when you and Papa were here?"

"Oh, yes, the one who didn't have a family. He gave me that nice book for Christmas. But the way he looked at you, Prairie Rose...I'm not blind, deaf, and dumb, you know. Have you told Bob you're having company for dinner? Maybe he'd like to come, too."

"Thanks for the recipe, Mama. You know you always made the best corned beef and cabbage I ever had."

She was content to change the subject after that and finally handed the phone back to Papa who assured me that things were going as well as could be expected. Thank God.

❧

I wore green on Saint Patrick's Day, including the prized malachite pendant Little Bird in Seeley Lake gave me. Someday I planned to make a trip back to see my old coworkers again. I missed them.

It was a warm day that felt almost like spring. Heavy chunks of snow occasionally slipped down the rugged face of the mountains. The snow-covered streets were beginning to transform themselves into pockets of slush. I breathed deeply of the almost spring-like air as I walked to work that morning. I longed to see the wildflowers poking through the dwindling patches of dirty snow. Of course, I realized there would still be winter storms ahead. But for today, spring filled my heart.

At noon, I walked home to start the corned beef in my slow cooker. After work, I'd add the cabbage and little red potatoes.

"I'll help with dinner," Paul volunteered as we were closing up the library for the night. "What an incredible day," he exclaimed as we walked out into the warmth of the sunlight and the chatter of the birds. They were also anxious for spring and, perhaps, for the wintering birds to return.

"You're on," I grinned up at him as I walked closely beside him. "And yes, it's almost too nice to stay inside. Maybe we should eat out on the porch so we can enjoy the weather."

Paul chopped cabbage while I washed the potatoes and arranged everything in the Crock-Pot. "Let's go for a walk while it cooks, before it gets dark," he suggested. We strolled around the town, noticing early signs of spring, sharing stories about the various buildings and their pioneer residents. I'd learned so much from my recent interviews, so much that I was anxious to share with him. We could talk forever about the history of this town, one with which we both felt a strong connection.

Paul swore he could never leave. His roots, he said, ran so deep here that he would be a lost soul if anyone ever dragged him away. "I hope you feel the same way, Rose. I know you haven't been here long, but I feel strongly that you belong here—with me.

My heart beat faster as we reached out for each other, embracing outside the old Sauerbier Blacksmith Shop, home of the old hurdy-gurdy house. A car of Saint Patrick's Day revelers drove past on their way to the Pioneer Bar, blaring the horn.

"Is that a yes?" Paul's voice was husky and heavy as we broke away from each other.

"A yes to what?" I took a step backward as déjà vu flooded my soul. This exchange had happened before. I could feel it.

"Rose? Are you all right?"

"Just thinking. For a moment, it seemed like this had already happened to me, to us."

"Maybe it did," he watched my face, fear clouding his eyes.

"What are you afraid of, Paul?" I whispered.

"Don't leave me, darlin'. For God's sake, don't leave me again. I shall not be able to tolerate it." Another side of Paul emerged, pleading with me.

Bewildered, I took another step backward. What was happening here, and why had he suddenly lapsed into another persona? But before I could speak, the old Paul was back, grinning in embarrassment.

"Hey, this is getting a little heavy." He grabbed my arm. "Let's stop at the Pioneer for a green beer. I think we need to celebrate the day."

Still confused, I decided to let it go. A band was playing in the bar as revelers drank green beer. Shamrocks hung from the ceiling and around the mirror over the bar. We each had a beer, joked around with the other patrons, and then headed back home for dinner.

The sun was setting as we settled ourselves on the porch with our plates loaded with corned beef and cabbage. Afterward, as the chill of the night seeped into the air and chased away the illusion of spring, we settled by the fireplace.

Paul played with my Irish trolls, moving them around the table as if they were puppets interacting with each other. He was a complex man with many sides to his personality, including a very funny one. Before long, we were laughing together until tears ran down our faces.

"Stop! I am about to die from laughter!" I cried.

"Okay, but only if you tell me a story about these crazy trolls or leprechauns or whatever they are. Where did they come from?"

"From Ireland, of course." I winked at him. "Just like my Irish ancestors. They were pioneers who came west in the 1800s."

"So did they bring trolls with them for good luck or what?" His eyes twinkled with mischief, like a naughty little boy.

"I don't know, but what I do know is this…" I leaned in closer to him, ready to divulge the legend of the leprechauns in the same dramatic fashion that I was certain my great-grandmother would have used.

"Once upon a time," I began in traditional folklore style, "far across the sea on the emerald island of Ireland, in a tiny little village, there lived tiny fairy creatures called leprechauns. They looked like miniature, wrinkled old men with beards and pointed noses, and they wore pointed hats. They were as green as the emerald island and they loved playing tricks on each other.

"Shoemakers by trade, they made tiny green shoes for their villagers. They were paid with gold coins, which they hid in a pot of gold at the end of the rainbow." I paused to be sure he was still with me.

"Somewhere over the rainbow, way up high," he began to sing in a silly voice. Then he stopped. "So tell me more. What happened to all that gold?"

"Nobody knows," I glanced around the room with wide eyes as I leaned in closer to Paul and lowered my voice to barely a whisper. "What we do know is that these pots of gold hold magical powers. If they are ever captured by a human being, he or she will be granted three wishes in exchange for the release of the gold. End of story."

"Three wishes...hmmm. If you had three wishes, Rose, what would they be?" Paul slipped his arm around me casually.

I had to think as he stared at me intently. "Well, I'd wish for good health and freedom from diseases like Alzheimer's. You know my mother is in the beginning stages." I wiped a tear from my eye.

"I'm sorry, Rose." He rubbed my back gently.

"My second wish—to solve the mystery of Amelia and find myself in the process. My third wish is for love and happiness. Now, what about you, Paul?"

"Well, I'm glad that love entered into the equation for you," he smiled gently. "All I can think of right now is a relationship with you for the rest of my life."

I cuddled up in the warmth of his arms as we watched the flames in the fireplace dancing like two lovers coming together in passion, parting in frustration, and finally resuming the dance—or disintegrating into smoldering ashes.

Lucky reminded us that it was time for his nightly walk. Looking at his watch, Paul also decided it was time for him to head home to Ennis.

As we untangled ourselves from each other's arms and stood up, he looked back at the Irish troll family on the table. "That's strange," he puzzled out loud.

"What's strange?"

"One of your trolls is missing. The old grandma troll, I believe."

We searched around the table and under the sofa. But I wasn't worried. I had a good idea where I'd find the troll.

"It can't just disappear, Rose. Don't you find it a little odd?" Turning toward me, he noticed the grin on my face. "You're not the least bit concerned, are you? Why not?"

Against my better judgment, I led him up into the loft and turned on the light. Sure enough, the troll sat on the window seat.

"What the hell?" Paul shook his head. "Do you have a resident ghost here or something?"

"I think I do, Paul. Her name is Amelia." I was thrilled, expecting the paranormal researcher in him to also be excited about this news.

But he was quiet, very quiet. Finally, he spoke in a tight, restrained voice. "That's good news then. I guess. It can be exciting to make contact, and I hope you learn what you need to learn. Just be careful—that's all I'm going to say. There are two sides to every story."

We climbed back down the ladder, and he kissed me good-bye at the door. It was a fiercely possessive kiss, as if he were laying claim to my soul.

Why was he so afraid of losing me? Sometimes he seemed jealous of Amelia; perhaps jealous of the time I spent obsessing over her. Now that the spirit of Amelia had taken up residence in my home, he didn't seem to like that.

Lucky and I took a quick walk as I pondered Paul's strange behavior. When we returned, I climbed back up into the loft, looking for Amelia.

"Happy Saint Patrick's Day, Amelia," I sang out, hoping she was there somewhere. "This day is for you, you know, to celebrate your Irish ways. To celebrate your life and that of your sister, Rosa, my great-great-grandmother."

No response. I tried again. "I hope you liked the Irish trolls. I see you picked one out for yourself. It was precisely the one I wanted you to have."

Then I felt the warmth of her smile as I heard a rustle in the background. But within seconds her smile was replaced with a chill and a frown. I could feel her emotions swirling around me.

"What is it?" I asked.

"It appears that you have become so preoccupied with your gentleman friend that you no longer have time for me. Have you forgotten our journey into the past? Do you still strive to discover the truth about my life?"

I was stunned. First of all, there seemed to be competition and animosity brewing between my resident ghost and my boyfriend. How strange was that? Secondly, how could Amelia possibly think I'd abandoned my mission?

I assured her that I had not replaced her in my heart or soul, and that I wanted nothing more than to find the truth about her life. "I've been waiting for you, Amelia, for the right time. You always tell me that things will happen 'in a timely fashion,' so I've been waiting for that time. I will be ready whenever you are."

I actually heard her long sigh of relief. Then I watched her tiny troll dancing an Irish jig upon the window seat.

"Perhaps we shall journey back in time tomorrow," she hinted as she continued to play with her troll.

"I'll be here, waiting for you in my window seat, tomorrow evening."

Chapter 31

I could hardly wait for the workday to pass. After taking Lucky for his walk after work and gulping down a plate of leftover corned beef and cabbage, I climbed up into the loft and waited for Amelia to arrive. Hours passed. Soon I was engulfed in darkness. No Amelia. She'd promised to take me back in time with her this evening. Finally, I closed my eyes and began to breathe deeply, trying to clear my mind and open myself to the past.

As I flashed back to 1868, I realized that something was different this time. Very different. I was on my own. I was no longer a spectator watching Amelia's life unfold. Instead, I had *become* Amelia!

I find myself on a boardwalk at dusk on an early spring evening. I'm surrounded by loud noise, laughter, and music flowing out into the streets from the saloons and dance halls. Horses gallop through the rutted dirt road, kicking up clouds of dust.

I'm jostled by an assortment of rough characters as I walk to work—miners, gamblers, road agents, and cowboys—all out on the town for a good time after a day's work. Averting my eyes away from their lustful looks, I carefully raise my long satin skirts just above my ankle, hold my head high, and proceed across the muddy road toward the hurdy-gurdy house where I work.

A gunshot and wild whoops ring out as Mr. Fairweather, one of the first men to discover gold here at Alder Gulch, races through the street on his stallion. He tosses gold nuggets into the crowds, flinging a handful directly at me as he whistles loudly. He is known, after consuming too much whiskey, to ride his spirited horse through the French doors of one of the saloons or dance halls.

I ignore the gold nuggets at my feet and the commotion, even the drunken slurs and bold propositions from some of the bystanders leaning up against the hitching posts. "How much?" one shaggy rascal grabs at the hem of my fancy dress as I walk past. I shake loose, slapping his hand away. But I do not respond to his crude comment. I do not bother to tell him that I am *not* a prostitute. I am a hurdy-gurdy girl, one who hopes she never has to dance with the likes of him.

I think of Jonathan at times like this. I am doing this for my son so that I will be able to support him someday soon. Once I've saved enough money, nobody will ever again treat me this way.

I keep my eyes focused straight ahead at the establishment where I am employed, one of the thirteen hurdy-gurdy houses doing a brisk business in Virginia City. It's a wood frame building with a western-style false front. Two pairs of double French doors are topped by a row of windows and a wooden cornice that is decorated with dentils.

Slipping through the doors, I find the smoke-filled room packed as always. The clink of whiskey glasses and Faro chips mingles with loud laughter. Soon the music will start. I make my way to the elegant Queen Anne chairs along the wall where I seat myself beside the other dancing girls.

We are all wearing our finest highly fashionable dresses. Mine is ruby red, tightly cinched at the waist, full-skirted, has a low-cut bodice, and is trimmed with white lace. I am jeweled in a heavy crystal brooch and long matching earrings that sparkle as I dance. And, as always, I wear a red rose in my hair, which has become my trademark. Men come in requesting dances with the girl with the red rose in her hair. Some just call me Rose. That is all right with me. I prefer they do not know that my real name is Amelia.

Beautiful chandeliers sparkle overhead. They, along with the ornate piano, were hauled 450 miles by Overland Freight from Salt Lake City.

I peer discreetly at the beautifully carved and polished bar that runs the entire length of the back wall. Looking into the huge mirrors behind the bar, I can see the faces of the gentlemen waiting to purchase dances with us. Some are leering at the paintings of voluptuous women scantily draped with filmy veils. As they gulp down their whiskey, they toss gold nuggets and gold dust onto the bar to pay for their drinks and the dances they wish to purchase. I do not see the particular gentleman I am seeking, the one I anxiously await each evening.

The fiddlers begin to play, and I am immediately swooped out onto the dance floor by my first partner of the evening. Although this miner with his unkempt beard reeks of whiskey, he behaves like a gentleman, and he dances rather well. I assume he has taken lessons in fine dancing at the new studio in town.

Lonely miners and merchants, many having left their womenfolk behind, crave the companionship of a woman out here in the untamed West. They are willing to learn to dance and to clean up enough to make themselves presentable to the few women in these parts. They flock to the hurdy-gurdy houses to dance, drink, and converse with a pretty woman.

After each dance, be it a schottische, waltz, polka, or the Virginia reel, my partner escorts me to the bar where he is required to purchase a drink for each of us. I sip slowly on mine, not liking the taste of whiskey nor the effect it has on me. Sometimes I offer my drink to my partner or leave it on the bar.

We converse as we drink. I am required to be friendly so the men come back. That is not always easy for me. If a man becomes too unruly, he is thrown out into the street by the owners of the establishment.

The nights fly by, I must admit, since I dance every dance. Despite the fact that I refuse to offer the extra favors that some of the other dancers do, I find myself in demand.

I circle through the room, my skirts swirling high into the air, to the strains of loud polka music. The music is punctuated with the sounds of clapping hands, stomping boots, hoots, and howls from the appreciative men. My partner is a fine dancer, perhaps the best one in Virginia City. He twirls me through the air, scoops me into his arms, and dips me low to the floor as the dance ends in a burst of applause.

Some of the men who'd been watching us dance are now scrambling to the bar, emptying gold dust from their pokes as payment for a dance with me. At one dollar in gold dust per dance, less the house commission, I will make good money tonight. I'm one night closer to the home I'll soon be able to provide for my son.

As my partner bows low, offers his arm, and leads me to the bar for the customary drink, I cannot help but think of the legendary Jack Slade. This gentleman is the spittin' image of poor Mr. Slade. He looks like him, carries himself like him, and dances with the same skill and wild abandon that Mr. Slade always did.

I miss that poor soul. He always was my favorite dancing partner—when he was sober. When he was drunk, he was a terror and not welcome in our establishment or anyplace else. His drinking had been his undoing.

My long-time gentleman friend had disliked Mr. Slade intensely, sometimes accusing me of improper behavior with him. He had not shared my remorse when Mr. Slade was hung from the gallows in 1864. I shall never forget the last dance I shared with Mr. Slade just one week before his streak of luck ran out.

I shudder even now to think of the cruel fate bestowed upon this gentleman, one who possessed two vastly different sides to his nature. He was both good and evil wrapped together in one irresistible package that was difficult for most women to resist. Yet he was a man who had deeply loved his eccentric wife. While I revered him as a dance partner, almost as a friend, I never succumbed to his charms. My heart always belonged only to my beloved gentleman friend. It still does.

Tonight as I dance, my eyes search the room. I'm waiting for my gentleman friend to appear. A part of me is well aware that he would not appreciate the liveliness of this dance with my advanced dancing partner. He does not, in fact, appreciate my dancing with any man but him.

"Last dance," the man calls out. My partner propositions me as he bows at the end of the dance. I refuse him, of course. There are some things I will never do for money. Several of the other dancers leave on the arms of one man or another.

I gather my cape, draping it carefully over my bare shoulders, and walk past the pendulum clock hanging on the wall. The one with my initials prominently displayed on its face. My wealthy gentleman friend had the clock made for me. It was his wish that it be hung here in the dance hall in my honor. I feel like the face of the clock follows me around the dance floor, watching my every move.

Tonight I slip through the back door in the company of another dancer as I usually do. It's easier to dismiss advances from drunken men lurking in the streets when you are not alone.

However, as soon as I step out into the late night, a man steps out from the shadows. Frightened at first, I soon recognize the handsome, bearded face of my beloved. Impeccably dressed as always and wearing his top hat, he impatiently taps his crystal-headed walking stick on the ground. My lover is waiting for me, wrapped in an uncharacteristic cloak of gloom and melancholy that surprises me.

"Henry," I gasp. "You gave me quite a fright!"

He wraps his arm around me protectively and proceeds to walk with us, swinging his lantern into the night to light our way home. Always the gentleman, he escorts my dancer friend to her cabin, removes his hat, and bows to her as he bids her good night.

"I was waiting for you, my darling," I purr into his ear once we are alone.

"Hmmm…it did not look as though you missed me," he sulks. I realize he's been watching me dance again from afar. Had he been peering through the doorway while I danced with that young Jack Slade look-alike? I dare not ask the question of him.

"Have you no idea how much I would have preferred waltzing in your arms, sir?" I sigh, turning to him. My heart beats against his. All he has to do to end my dancing career is to ask for my hand in marriage, I think to myself. I would be his forever. Or does he actually find me to be a soiled dove, despite the undying love he has declared for me?

Henry takes me home with him to the elegant Queen Anne Victorian mansion that had just been completed for him. It is one of the nicest dwellings in Virginia City, and he is quite proud of it. It is an appropriate home for a prominent banker and large enough for a family someday. Our family.

As he settles me on the loveseat beside the fire in the drawing room and departs to fetch me a glass of fancy wine, my mind drifts back to the day I met him almost four years ago. We'd traveled together on a wagon train bound for Alder Gulch where gold had just been discovered. We often share a laugh about how we'd been thrown together as night watchmen and how humiliated he was at first to stand guard with a lady. But we'd grown to value our time together. We became friends, and he became my protector. Perhaps he still saw that as his role in life.

However, not long after I'd settled into my duties as a hurdy-gurdy girl, Henry showed up at the establishment. Shocked at first to see me there, he began coming in on a regular basis, buying most of my dances. We fell in love, and our relationship moved out from the confines of the dance hall into the real world.

"Penny for your thoughts?" he inquires as he settles beside me on the loveseat, handing me a cordial of port.

"My thoughts are of you, always, and how much I love you. I cannot bear to think of ever living without you," my words spill from my heart uncensored.

Henry raises his glass to propose a toast. "To Amelia, the most beautiful lady in Virginia City, the woman I shall always love." He clinks his glass against mine, his eyes penetrating mine. But he abruptly shifts his glance away from me and stares into the flames of the fire.

"Always?"

He does not reply. Instead, he downs his wine in one long swig and pulls me roughly into his arms. His passion is more urgent than usual. Instead of reading to me from his collection of poems as he normally does, he plucks my glass from my hands, splashing drops of wine onto the table beside his cherished book of poems by Percy Shelley.

He carries me into his elegant bedroom, deposits me on the down-filled quilt, and almost rips off my clothing in his desperation. I shudder as he takes me forcefully. There is something different about his lovemaking tonight, almost as if he fears it shall be the last time we will be united like this. Yet, he's just told me that he will always love me…

Something does not feel right when he walks me home. He is quiet, gloomy, as though his thoughts are elsewhere. Perhaps he has business-related concerns on his mind. Of course, he does not discuss such things with me. While I would enjoy listening, men do not share these things with the women they love.

"Until tomorrow?" I inquire outside my cabin door.

"Hopefully," he hesitates, "but I shall be rather busy the next few weeks. Business, of course. I have guests arriving on the next stagecoach—business associates and some of their family members."

My chin begins to tremble as I am consumed with a sense of impending doom.

He tips my face up to his, gently touching my cheek. "Do not fear, I will never leave you, regardless of other commitments in my life. You are mine. You shall always be mine."

True to his word, I do not see him for several endless weeks. Sometimes I stroll past his bank during the day, hoping to catch a glimpse of him. Hoping he will be stepping out at noon to take lunch at one of the local establishments.

One day, word spreads throughout town that the long-awaited stagecoach is finally arriving. It is the first one this spring after a long winter that has curtailed travel. I am dying for letters from home, for news of my child.

As I run down the street in my day dress and sunbonnet, following the coach to its arrival destination, I remember that Henry is expecting guests. He may be there to greet them.

As I approach, I see that passengers are already spilling out of the coach into the rutted dirt road. And there is Henry, waving his hand at the newly arrived passengers, a large smile plastered across his face. He does not see me. He is too busy watching a beautiful woman in an elegant dress stepping down from the coach. Two young children hold on to her skirts.

"Father! Father!" the children cry out as they rush toward Henry, jumping into his open arms. He ruffles their hair and hugs them close before looking up at the woman. I long to see the expression on his face, but I cannot. Is he looking at her the way he looks at me?

My heart shatters as he takes her into his arms, holding her close. She clings to him as though she has not seen her husband in years. Of course, she hasn't. He spent the last four years of his life loving me, never acknowledging that he had a family back East.

"Let's go see our new house!" Henry's little son shouts. He looks so much like his father. He must be about Jonathan's age, I figure, as a stinging pang of loneliness rips through what is left of my heart.

I stumble into the shadows behind the nearest building as waves of nausea surge through my body. I'm going to vomit.

Chapter 32

I'm spiraling forward in time, back to the year 2011, back to the loft of my cabin.

Totally disoriented at first, I needed to remind myself that I am Rose, not Amelia. The year was 2011, not 1868. Breathing deeply, counting slowly, I soon emerged from the sea of fog that separated our respective worlds.

But I was still weeping for Amelia, longing to comfort her, and to find out what happened after Henry betrayed her and broke her heart. What a scoundrel, I thought to myself. How could he have treated the woman he supposedly loved so cruelly? Yet how could he leave his children behind? His behavior was despicable, juggling the love of two women. I'd love to give him a piece of my mind, I decided, realizing that I was sounding more like Amelia than Rose. Our lives were blurring into one that breached the century between us.

As I fumed over Henry's treatment of Amelia, I happened to glance up—and into the face of Amelia's Henry hanging on my wall. It was illuminated eerily by the moonlight that streamed in through my window. I knew beyond a doubt that this was the man who had deserted by great-great Aunt Amelia. Every detail was exactly as he had appeared to me when I'd traveled back in time, right down to the unusual glass handle of his walking stick.

I began to pace around the loft, trying to make some sense out of these strange events that were taking over my life. At the moment, the only tangible thing seemed to be Amelia's diary. I carried it downstairs with me and settled beside the fireplace. Restless, I soon got up to fetch a glass of ice water and step outside into the fresh air, trying to ground myself in reality.

When I returned, I found that the diary had mysteriously opened. Instead of directing me into the future, Amelia apparently wanted me to read her entries about the things I'd just experienced in my regression. As I did so, I was amazed to discover how accurate they were. I was able to confirm the validity of all that I'd just experienced.

But I was anxious to find out what happened after Henry's wife and children had arrived in Virginia City. I tried to turn the page, but I could not. An invisible hand reached out to grab mine, holding it firmly.

"Amelia?" I whispered as tingling vibrations ran up and down my arm.

"Fear not," her words floated into my mind. "This is not time to proceed. It is time for you to retire to your chambers, my dear."

As I stared down at my hand, still firmly clasped in hers, she let go. I watched in amazement as the diary closed by itself and floated up into the loft.

"Good night," Amelia called down to me. This time I heard her soft voice.

Unnerved by all I'd experienced, I woke Lucky. Although he was in no mood to get up and go for a walk, I bribed him with a dog biscuit. The city slept on this starlit night as we walked silently. I swung my lantern from side to side, lighting our way through the deserted streets of Virginia City. I thought about Henry swinging his lantern as he escorted Amelia down these same streets so many years ago.

We stopped outside the hurdy-gurdy house where Amelia once worked. I thought about the clock that once hung on the wall here, the same clock that led me to Virginia City last fall, and to Paul. Perhaps things happened for a reason.

Finally, I obeyed Amelia's orders and retired to my chambers. I'd barely closed my eyes when *the* dream returned. Once again, Amelia was drowning in the river. Just before her head disappeared beneath the waves for the last time, her piercing cry echoed through the Madison River valley. "Henry!" she screamed hysterically, her flailing arms reaching toward the boat disappearing into the fog. Then she was gone.

Bolting upright in my bed, heart pounding, I felt my fears had been confirmed. Henry had indeed been responsible for Amelia's death after all. He had murdered her, and he must be brought to justice. I felt compelled to set history straight, to make sure that Henry would go down in history as a murderer instead of as a prestigious banker and honorable man.

Doubts soon drifted into my mind, however. I could hear Paul's words of warning, "There are two sides to every story, Rose." But what of my recurring dreams, my regressions, Amelia's journal? How could I know what was real and what was not?

Instinctively, however, I knew that Henry was responsible for Amelia's death. Nothing could convince me otherwise. And I felt responsible for avenging the murder of my great-great Aunt Amelia.

Slipping out of bed and into my slippers, I climbed into the loft. Standing before Henry's sketch on the wall, I stared into the eyes of the man I'd loved while I'd lived Amelia's life. "You will pay, Henry. You will pay for what you did to Amelia," I hissed at him.

A sigh of relief floated through the air as I felt a smile spreading across Amelia's invisible face.

Chapter 33

Paul's place was everything he had claimed and more. Perched on a knoll overlooking the rumbling Madison River, it was concealed by a wild maze of gnarled, ancient trees. The old mansion was made of stone that his great-grandfather had hauled in to the remote property many years ago. It loomed three stories high and was punctuated with turrets and spires. The walls were now covered with weeping trails of ivy and patches of moss.

The mansion had a ghostly feel to it, just as Paul had warned me. I stood in awe in his driveway, picnic basket in hand. Looking around, I realized that there were no neighbors in this remote area. We were alone with any ghosts haunted this place. Surely there had to be some.

Seeing my reaction, Paul put his arm around my shoulders. "Surely you aren't afraid of ghosts when you live with one?" he teased.

"Is it haunted, Paul?"

"Perhaps, but they're family and friendly." His eyes sparkled with mischief. "Come on, I'm starving. Let's have that picnic."

Relieved, I followed him down the trail to the banks of the river. I was delighted to postpone the tour of his house.

This was one of the first warm, sun-drenched Saturdays of spring. The woods were carpeted with delicate pink and white wild moss and an occasional bluebell. The birds sang out in unison, thrilled to return after their winter retreat. Squirrels chattered as they scampered into the woods, climbing high as they swung into the trees.

Finally, the trail ended in a secluded cove on the banks of the river. I noticed that Paul had already spread a blanket on the ground and stashed a few bottles of wine. I set the picnic basket on the blanket, kicked off my shoes, and walked to the edge of the river. Diamonds of sunlight bounced across the waves as I savored the feel of the swirling water rushing over my bare feet. There was something magical and soothing about a river, despite the fact that I'd always had a love/hate relationship with water. Today I craved its healing powers, hoping they would restore some badly needed balance into my life.

Paul came up behind me, put his arms around me, and held me close against him. "Just what the doctor ordered?"

"What do you mean?"

"You need a break, Rose, from whatever you are struggling with. I imagine it has something to do with your resident ghost." He waited, but I did not reply. "Nevertheless, I thought a picnic in this special place would be good for you. Good for us..." He searched my eyes for a hint of my love for him.

I'm sure I constantly frustrated him. We'd share intimate moments that felt so right, so lasting. Then I would suddenly retreat back into my shell like a frightened turtle.

"So this isn't just about going through that old trunk of photos and papers in your house?" I grinned at him, noticing once again how ruggedly handsome he was as he stood beside the river, hands on his hips, his hair blowing in the breeze. I wanted to take his picture—so I did.

"If you don't feed me first, I may not have the energy to show you my family's treasure trove of historical artifacts." Paul plopped down on the blanket beside me and opened the picnic basket, which was filled with fried chicken, potato salad, and chocolate cake.

As we ate our picnic lunch and sipped our wine, we watched a mother duck swim past with her baby ducklings. She squawked at them relentlessly, nudging them along. She had to watch them closely because the eagles that nested nearby ate baby ducklings. It was the sad reality of the food chain, Paul explained.

Finally full, Paul lay down on the blanket, watching me intently as I finished my last chicken wing and licked my fingers.

"What?" I asked as he smiled at me.

" 'How do I love thee? Let me count the ways.' " His eyes turned serious as he began to quote from Elizabeth Barrett Browning. " 'I love thee to the depth and breadth and height my soul can reach—' "

Easing myself down beside him, I leaned into him as my mouth impulsively covered his, drowning out the rest of the poem. His arms held me fast as he devoured me with kisses until we were both breathless.

Suddenly, he pulled away from me, shaking his head, trying to regain his composure. "I think we need a glass of wine. Time out, all right?" He stood up, paced back and forth along the shore before refilling our glasses.

"Paul," I whispered, "I think we need more than a glass of wine." I opened my arms to him as he turned his back on me and walked down to the river where he sat drinking his wine. I'd never had a man reject me the way Paul just did. After all, shouldn't I be the one to turn him away—assuming I wanted to turn him away? And I did not. In that moment, I most certainly did not. Picking up my wine glass, I sat down beside him as he stared out into the waves. "What is it, Paul?"

His face was tense, his eyes full of agony, as he finally looked at me. "I shall never again take advantage of the woman I love," he announced firmly.

"I don't understand."

"Nor do I. Just let it be and trust that I am doing the right thing for your sake."

We sat in silence, lost in our thoughts as we enjoyed the warmth of the sun and the sound of the river rushing by. Paul was a strange man indeed, full of secrets that he was not about to disclose to me. Sometimes I wondered if he even understood why he did and said the things he did.

Noticing that the sun was slipping lower into the sky, I finally interrupted his silence. "Paul, if we're still going to go through that trunk, perhaps we'd better do it before the day gets away from us."

The old Paul returned. "Of course, you probably don't want to be in that haunted house after dark, do you?"

"Preferably not."

He laughed as he gathered up the remains of our picnic lunch and led me up to the house on the hill as if everything was perfectly fine between us.

Paul's family home was both elegant and formidable, filled with ornate hand-carved furniture that his great-grandfather had imported from Europe many years ago. When we entered the great room, a large oval portrait hanging on the wall beside the massive rock fireplace greeted us. The stern elderly man in the portrait seemed to stare right through me as if he was displeased that I had invaded his fortress.

I stopped abruptly. "Who is that?"

"Grandfather, please meet Rose." Paul nodded toward the portrait, a gleam in his eye. He seemed to be enjoying my discomfort. "Rose, my grandfather welcomes you to his castle, the one which he still rules from afar."

"It certainly looks that way. Has anything changed here since he died?"

"Not much, I must admit, but I rather enjoy it the way it is. It's the only home I've ever known. Sure, it's a tad gloomy at times, but I also have many fond memories here...mostly of my beloved grandmother."

I touched the pendant Paul had given me, remembering the grandmother who had meant so much to him. "I'd like to see a picture of her, Paul."

"You will." He pointed to a large immigrant's trunk sitting on the Oriental rug before the fireplace. "First, I'm going to light a fire to take the chill out of the air."

"What about your grandfather?" I inquired as I watched him start the fire.

"What about him?"

"Do you have the same feelings for him that you do for your grandmother?"

"Look at his picture, Rose. Does he look like the kind of man who would show any love to anyone?" He tensed up, stabbing a log with the poker. "No, Grandfather was a harsh man who cared little for anyone or anything aside from making money. That he was very good at. I can't say that I really knew him, despite having grown up in his house. I feared him, however."

"I'm sorry, Paul."

"Don't be sorry for me," he scoffed. "My grandmother is the one to feel sorry for. She didn't have much of a marriage or any companionship to speak of."

"But she stayed with him."

"Of course. Women in those days didn't have many options. Besides, she had me to raise." His mood brightened. "Grandma and I were good friends, right until the day she died."

I liked this side of Paul, that he was so deeply attached to his grandmother. "Well, I'm glad she had you in her life." I touched his shoulder gently. "Did she ever tell you how she felt about your grandfather?"

"She accepted what was, that's all. Said he was just like his father, a mean old coot," Paul laughed. "Come on, let's open this trunk." He knelt down to pry open the lid. "It's been many years since anyone has seen any of this. I was never allowed to open the trunk. Guess it's mine now."

I still didn't understand why he'd asked me to be here with him for this occasion. "You're sure you don't want to be alone for this?"

"Absolutely not. I want you here with me." He looked intently into my eyes. "At first, I was only thinking of finding some interesting historical documents and photos for our book—and I still expect that will be the case. But..."

"But?"

"I grew to realize that I just plain wanted to share this experience with you. You love history, and I just wanted you here with me. That's all."

"I'm honored." I sat down beside him on the rug by the fireplace as he carefully opened the old lid.

The rusty hinges of the trunk creaked and groaned as the musty smell of long ago escaped into the great room. Peering inside, we found notebooks, photos, old diaries, and an assortment of photos documenting lives long since gone.

Like two kids in a candy store, we began extracting items. "Look at this!" we'd cry out as we discovered fascinating bits of history. We began sorting things into piles—one pile to read and review later, one for our book, another to donate to the library or museum, another for Paul to keep.

There were family photos and photos of other pioneers who settled in this area. My heart broke when Paul retrieved one lonely photo of a baby boy with his two young parents. He hung his head to hide the tears from me, but I knew.

"You and your parents?" I whispered.

He nodded, as I pulled him into my arms and held him, rocking him like a baby. He did not protest.

Finally he pulled away. "I'm sorry. It's just that I've never seen a picture of us together before. It must have been taken shortly before they dumped me on my grandparents' doorstep and left. I never saw them again. Perhaps that's for the best." He turned back to the trunk. The moment was over.

Hours flew by as we made some fascinating historical discoveries. Some of the old photos would also be perfect for our book.

Finally, I pulled an old tintype photo from the trunk—and almost fainted. I was face-to-face with Henry, Amelia's Henry. The man I'd loved when I'd traveled back into her lifetime. The man whose sketch hung in my loft. The one who had appeared to me at the Elling House.

Hands trembling, I dropped the tintype onto the rug.

"What is it?" Paul asked, alarm in his eyes. "Are you okay? You are pale as a ghost, Rose. Or have you just seen a ghost?"

I nodded as my head swam in dizzying circles. "Smelling salts..." I mumbled before I fainted.

≈≪

Disoriented, I opened my eyes in an unfamiliar room. Where was I? Focusing hard, I recognized Paul standing over the ornate loveseat where I lay. "Rose? Come back, Rose!" He was shaking me.

"What happened?"

"You just fainted. Here, drink some water." He helped me sit up and gave me a few sips of water. His eyes were full of questions.

"I'm fine. Where's that photo, the tintype?" I tried to get up as he held me down.

"Not so fast. I'll get the photo for you." He was examining it carefully when he returned and handed it to me.

"Who is this?" I whispered, holding my breath. I needed to know but was not sure if I was ready to handle the information.

"I think it's my great-great-grandfather," Paul replied, squinting hard as he read the faded label on the back of the print.

Trying to hide my shock, I asked, "Are you sure? Is there a name?"

"Yes, it is my great-great grandfather." He looked up, watching me closely. "Henry. Henry DuBois."

Oh my God! Henry? I began to tremble as it dawned on me that Paul's great-great grandfather had murdered my great-great aunt! Stay calm, Rose. Breathe deeply, I reminded myself. You need to find out as much as you can. Paul cannot know.

"Rose, what's going on?" Paul took my hand. "Why are you so shocked to see my great-great grandfather's photo?"

"I've seen him, Paul, several times. I can't talk about it. I'm...I'm just too upset."

"You know, there were probably a number of men who looked much like old Henry DuBois. They all wore those mustaches and top hats and had walking sticks in those days. If you saw a spirit that looks like this guy, it could have been anyone, Rose."

While Paul was trying to reassure and comfort me, I sensed a cloud of suspicion arising between us. Did he believe what he was telling me or was he trying to hide something from me? Did he know the truth about his great-great grandfather?

Do not trust this man, Rose, that little voice began to nag me once again. This time the voice was louder, demanding that I pay attention to it.

"Tell me what you saw. What are you thinking?" He was trying to pry into my mind, to crack open the vault where I'd buried all my secrets about Amelia and her life. I could not let him succeed.

"Perhaps you're right. The man I saw could have been any one," I lied in an attempt to buy myself a reprieve from his questions. However, there was no doubt in my mind whatsoever as to the identity of the man in the photo. Sitting up, I gulped down the rest of the water. "Tell me about your great-great grandfather, Henry." I almost choked as I spit out his name. "Did he settle here in Ennis, perhaps start a business here?"

"No, my great-grandfather, Henry's son, is the one who settled in Ennis, built this house and a profitable business."

My thoughts drifted back to the little boy Jonathan's age, the one I saw arrive on the stagecoach with his mother in 1868. Paul's great-grandfather?

"As for old Henry," Paul continued, "he was one of the first pioneers who settled in Virginia City after gold was discovered in Alder Gulch. He was a prominent banker there; in fact, he also owned more banks back in Illinois."

That cinched it. There was no doubt whatsoever that this was the man I'd been seeking, the one I planned to seek revenge upon for the desertion and death of Amelia. Paul's great-great grandfather? I could hardly believe the situation I'd gotten myself into.

My curiosity overtook my reeling emotions. I had to learn more. Perhaps I'd never have another opportunity to do so. "What else do you know about his life, or his children's lives?"

"Henry was a troubled and bitter man. They say he'd suffered a horrible loss of some kind and never got over it. He had money, a beautiful house, and a nice family. But he suffered from melancholy as they called it. He was not a happy man."

"What kind of loss could that be, Paul? It sounds like he had everything going for him."

"Nobody knows. It remains a mystery—something he apparently took to his grave with him. My grandfather never mentioned him. But my grandmother used to pray that his soul was finally at peace, and that he'd been released from the demons that tormented him in life."

What if he's not at peace? What if he still roams the earth, trying to complete his business, trying to find Amelia? I shuddered beneath Paul's watchful eyes.

"What, Rose? What are you thinking?" A flash of anger blazed through his dark eyes. He was angry that I refused to share my thoughts with him, refused to let him into my private world. The sparks disappeared within moments, but I knew they were there somewhere. I'd always known there was a dark side to this man, a side that he kept well concealed most of the time.

Dark shadows crept into Paul's gloomy mansion as the sun began to sink into the river. A penetrating chill swept through the room. There were only a few glowing embers left from the roaring fire in the great room. It was time to leave. I needed to get away, to be alone.

"Paul, I'm not feeling well. I really need to go home." I stood up to leave.

"I will drive you home," he offered, although my car was parked at the end of his driveway.

"No thanks," I protested. "I'm fine. Really I am. And I need my own car."

"Well, I will at least walk you out to your car." He took my arm and steered me down the driveway that wound through the woods, holding my arm a little too tightly. He tried to lighten the mood as he kissed me goodbye. "Do you still need smelling salts?" he teased.

"Smelling salts?"

"Right before you fainted, you asked for smelling salts. Don't you remember? I think you've had too much history today. You're slipping back into the good old days of fainting ladies and smelling salts."

I settled myself in the driver's seat and drove home in a trance. For some strange reason, all I could think of was Bob. He would know what to do. He was the only person in this world that I would trust enough to share everything—even the story of Amelia.

Oh, Bob, what have I done?

Chapter 34

June 10, 1868

Dear Diary,

Oh dear God, I am with child, and I do not know what to do! While this should have been a delightful occasion, one that Henry and I could share together, I am alone in this world. Henry cannot marry me as I always thought he would.

I have still not recovered from learning that the man I love deceived me in the worst possible way. I shall never forget the day I watched his wife and children step from the stagecoach into his arms.

I am not far enough along for anyone to notice that I am with child. I succumb to nausea in the mornings, and I dance nights at the hurdy-gurdy house. I pray to God that He will guide me since I know not what to do.

The only decision I have made is that I will keep this child, Henry's child. I will raise him or her by myself if need be. This child was conceived in love. It is a part of the man that I shall always love, although I do, of course, also despise him. I shall raise this child with my beloved Jonathan. I may need a miracle to make this happen...

"Oh, Amelia," I whispered into the loft where I was once again immersed in her diary. What did she do? Closing my eyes, I began to breathe slowly, letting go. I needed to return to Amelia's world so I could fully understand what happened to her.

ॐॐ

Suddenly I am there. It is 1868, and I am Amelia once again. This time, I'm lying on my bed in the log cabin I share with three other dancing girls. It's a warm day with a gentle breeze filtering in through the open window. My morning sickness is almost over, but the heartache that consumes me is my steady companion.

I have nothing to get up for, but I do. Perhaps a walk would be good for me and for the baby I now carry. Donning my sunbonnet, I step out into the dusty street as a horse-drawn carriage rumbles by.

"Mornin', ma'am," a cowboy tips his hat as I stroll down the street past the shops where the fancy ladies have their dresses and hats made. I wonder how much longer I will be able to fit into my dancing dress, how much longer I will be able to dance.

I have saved a great deal of money from this employment, almost enough for the house I planned to build for Jonathan and myself. I hope it will be enough to see me though my pregnancy and support the three of us.

I do not know if I will stay here in Virginia City. My heart is torn between staying so that I may once again see my cheating lover, and leaving so I shall never have to lay eyes upon him again.

It has been several months since I last saw him, since we last slept together. Of course, he does not know that I am with child. I have at times considered telling him. But what good would come of that?

Tonight I dance more quietly than I normally do, lost in my tormented thoughts.

"Amelia, there's a gentleman here asking for Rose, the smiling girl with the rose in her hair." The owner of the establishment glares at me. "He didn't recognize you."

"Oh, I guess I forgot my rose." I touch my hair.

"And your smile. You do not seem to be yourself these days," he growls at me. "Your dance numbers are down. How about adding a little life to this place, the way you always used to?" He turns from me and hikes back to the bar.

I plaster a smile upon my face for the rest of the night. I laugh at the stupid jokes that my partners tell. Nobody knows that I am crying inside. I no longer care to dance. Sometimes I am not sure that I care to live...but I must. I must live, and I must handle the disgrace that shall soon fall upon me. I must do it for Jonathan and the baby.

Finally, the evening is over. I am very tired as I slip out the side door by myself. I am startled when a man emerges from the shadows.

"Amelia?"

My heart begins to throb uncontrollably. It is Henry's voice. As he steps toward me, I put my nose in the air and walk on, pretending I have not seen him.

"Please, Amelia, I simply must see you. Do not turn me away."

Henry follows me down the street while I do my best to ignore him. Tears well in my eyes. After all this time, after all he has done to humiliate and deceive me, I still want nothing more than to fall into his arms.

"Oh, sweetheart, my heart still yearns for you. I am in agony without you. Please speak to me. Let me explain."

"There is nothing to say, sir. You are a married man, and you have deceived me. Leave me alone," I finally whisper, but my voice is not as firm as it should be.

"I shall not leave you alone, not ever," he insists, moving in closer as I walk faster. "We can find a way to be together. I will provide for you."

Was he asking me to be his mistress, a kept woman? What kind of a woman did he think I was?

"My answer is no. It will always be no. I shall not keep company with a married man," I cry out as I begin to run down the boardwalk. I hear him gaining on me, his footsteps getting closer and closer.

Suddenly he grabs me, spins me around to face him, and crushes his mouth over mine. I begin to protest, trying to shove him away from me, beating my hands against his chest. But he soon overcomes my resistance and I find myself helpless in his arms. I find myself kissing him back with all the passion and longing that has been growing within me for the past months.

Finally, he releases me and looks into my eyes. "I love you, Amelia. I told you I always would, and I have kept *that* promise at least. Can you honestly tell me that you do not love me?"

"Love is not the be all and end all. It does not matter when one is not free to declare his love for another."

"But you do love me. You cannot deny that, can you?"

Suddenly we both realize that we are not alone. Men are coming out of the saloons, some quite intoxicated. Several whistle and make crude comments as they pass by.

"This is not a good place to talk, but I have found a place for us to spend some time alone together. It's right on the Madison River. I will bring a picnic lunch and pick you up at noon tomorrow in my carriage. We may even take a boat ride if the weather permits." He does not ask; he assumes I will consent.

"But…that would not be proper." I wondered why I, of all people, should be concerned about how things may appear to others. He is the one who is married and has a reputation to uphold.

"I am willing to take that chance for you. Besides, my wife and children have taken the stagecoach to visit friends. They will not be back for a week."

Henry escorts me home, bids me good night with a low bow, and I sink down into my sagging bed. My head and heart are doing serious battle. I should not go with him tomorrow; perhaps I will be gone when he arrives to pick me up. However, my heart will not allow me to pass up an opportunity like this.

Although I am exhausted, tiring easily these days, I cannot sleep. I finally light the lamp beside my bed and pull my diary out from its hiding place. I begin to write:

June 12, 1868

Dear Diary,

My darling Henry has come back into my life, pleading with me, telling me how much he needs me. After one kiss, I fear that I shall once again become his. I know this is wrong in the eyes of the world, but I cannot deny my love for this man. He is, after all, the father of my unborn child.

Tomorrow he is picking me up in his carriage to take me out for a picnic on the Madison River, perhaps a boat ride as well. I must confess that I am looking forward to our time together. My heart sings once more. I have renewed hope for the future, whatever it may hold.

I shall perhaps tell Henry about the baby tomorrow. I pray to God that this tiny being may be the glue that holds us together forever.

I am happy at last!

Sleepy at last, I snuff out the candle and fall into dreams of Henry and me in each other's arms.

❧❦

Henry pulls up outside my door precisely at noon the next day.

"Thank the Lord you are here. I was so afraid that you would decide not to come, Amelia." He smiles that irresistible crooked grin at me as he helps me into the carriage. Two sleek black horses are hitched to his elegant carriage, anxious to be on their way.

"Perhaps I should not have come," I reply wistfully, "but it cannot hurt to talk and be friends, can it?"

He chuckles, a wicked gleam in his eyes. "Somehow I rather doubt that you will be content to remain my friend instead of my lover."

I stiffen as my smile disappears from my face.

"Of course, that is my lady's prerogative, if that is all that you desire. I am a gentleman, after all."

It is a beautiful drive over the mountains to Ennis. The mountain-sides are splashed with waves of colorful wildflowers. Today the sun shines as brightly as the love glowing within my heart. The world feels like it is almost right once again. Soon it will be almost perfect—complete with Jonathan, our new baby, and maybe…just maybe…I dare not think that far ahead. 'Tis best just to enjoy the day ahead of us.

I can see and hear the river calling from a distance. We drive through the town and take a wooded trail that winds along the banks of the river. Finally, Henry stops, waters and tethers the horses, and helps me out of the carriage. I follow him down a makeshift trail to a secluded spot beside the gently flowing river. He spreads a blanket for me and sets down the picnic basket.

After a leisurely lunch, he pulls me into his arms and down onto the blanket. His kisses are urgent. I cannot help but respond in like measure. Suddenly, he is unlacing my corset and removing my bloomers. I cannot resist. I find myself swooning as his lips move up and down the growing contour of my stomach.

His pent-up desire finally explodes as he slips forcefully into that place that he's long since claimed as his own. I shudder as waves of passion wash through my body, surrendering once again to the love of my life.

Luxuriating in the afterglow of our long-awaited reunion, I muster up the courage to boldly announce that I am with child. I wait for him to enfold me within his arms, telling me once again how much he loves me and cannot live without me. I expect him to be pleased with my news, perhaps because I am blinded by my own enthusiasm. Obviously, there are complications with his current situation. Yet I believe that this revelation may be enough to convince him to leave his wife and establish a real home with Jonathan, our new baby, and me. I am, after all, the woman he loves. I have no doubt about that.

"What the hell?" Henry hisses, pulling up his trousers. "How do you even know I'm the father of this bastard child? For Christ's sake, Amelia, you cannot have this child! Do something about it, do you hear me?"

My mouth drops open in shock. I cannot believe the stinging words from Henry's snarling mouth. Never before had he spoken to me in such a manner. A slap across the face would have been much kinder. I begin to weep, tears flowing down my cheeks.

Henry does not reach out to comfort me. Instead, he jumps up and begins pacing back and forth along the edge of the river, running his hands through his mass of windblown hair. Finally, he comes back and plops down beside me.

"Look, I'm sorry for what I said. It was cruel. All that matters is that you get rid of it right away. You know there are ways—abortifacients, herbal potions, those Portuguese Female Pills. Ask some of the other dancing girls."

"*It?* Get rid of *it?*" I find myself shrieking at him. "This is *your* baby, *your* flesh and blood, a baby conceived through our love for each other!"

"That may be true. But surely you cannot expect me to admit I am the father—which I may or may not be. There is no proof. Besides, it would destroy my career and my family."

I cannot believe what I am hearing. This cannot be the man I love. He would never speak to me this way. He would never think this way. Or would he? I had not yet encountered the dark side of Henry DuBois. Maybe this was the real Henry. I shudder at the thought. "And what about me? What about the fact that I desperately want this baby?"

"So you purposely got yourself with child, trying to trap me into matrimony, is that it?"

"I did not know you were married, did I? You were not honest with me, sir. Had I known—"

"I apologize. I was a cad. And you were wrong to get yourself in the family way. I do not want to fight with you, Amelia. Despite all of this, despite the cruel things that have been said this afternoon, the fact remains that we love each other. Nothing is going to change that."

I do not reply. How can he speak of love after the things he has said? I hold my hand over my stomach, gently rubbing the life growing within me. I know exactly what I am going to do.

"I will tell you about love, Henry, the greatest kind of love there is. It is my love for my little son, Jonathan, and for this unborn child of ours. That supersedes any other kind of love in this world. You know nothing of love or you would not have spoken to me as you have. You know nothing of love or you would not ask me to destroy our baby." Once again, I begin to shake and my tears flow freely.

"So I'm a bastard," he says softly, "and I apologize for that. Perhaps one of the other men you love to dance with will treat you better?"

I do not reply, so he goes on. "I've been watching you. How do I know you don't grant them special favors?"

"You know better than that. You are the only man I've ever loved. How can you possibly think such a dreadful thing?"

"So you've just admitted you do love me," he chuckles in an evil way. "Nevertheless, I've heard talk about you and other men."

"What? That is simply not true. Of course, I have had offers, but I swear to God I've never once been with another man."

"I shall not discuss this with you anymore. Just get rid of it and things will be fine between us again. We will go back to the way things were as if none of this ever happened."

"I shall not get rid of our child!" I scream hysterically as I run toward the river. "I shall not, do you hear me?"

I need to get away from this man, the one I thought I loved. Perhaps I still do in a twisted way that I am beginning to regret. Blinded with rage, I stumble along the rocky shoreline until I see a crude wooden boat pulled up onto the shore. I run through the water toward the boat, planning to make my escape.

I can't swim, but the river is fairly calm today. I shove the shaky boat out into the water, climb in, and settle myself on the front seat. I stretch my legs out to the sides of the boat to balance myself. I've never rowed a boat before, but I've seen others do it. My father used to take us for boat rides on the river back home in Galena.

I dip the oars into the clear water, splashing myself in the process. Suddenly, I hear a loud series of splashes coming up from behind me. Turning around, I see Henry jumping into the back of the boat.

"Are you crazy?" he shouts at me, water dripping from his clothing onto the rotting wooden planks covering the floor of the boat. "You know nothing about navigating this river. You will drown."

"As if you would care. Perhaps that would solve all of our problems." Tears spent and rage subsided, I am numb by this time. Nothing matters anymore.

"Damn it, I love you. Why can't you understand that?"

"You have a mighty fine way of showing it, sir," I sneer at him, staring straight ahead into the widening expanse of riverway.

"Women," he sighs loudly as he grabs the oars from me and begins to row. "Since you are determined to go for a boat ride, I shall take you. Just sit still so you don't tip the boat."

He rows harder, faster, becoming angrier with every stroke of the oars. Sneaking a glimpse back at him, I see his jaw set in a hard line. His eyes blaze with anger as he rows out into the churning rapids. The waves seem to build along with his seething anger. Who is this dark stranger? I do not know him.

I hold tightly to the sides of the boat as he maneuvers it through the rapids. My stomach lurches as we spin in a circle, barely missing a large boulder protruding from the shallows. Suddenly, an angry wave splashes over the bow, drenching me.

Henry pays me no mind when I gasp, wiping water from my face. A look of fierce determination plays across his face as the sky darkens and heavy banks of fog begin to roll in from the other side of the river.

I fear that he is trying to scare me into submission, into giving up the child growing within me. I am terrified, but I will not admit that. I will not speak to this man whom I no longer know. I cannot. I am frozen with fear.

߬s

Suddenly, I found myself transported back to my cozy loft and the year 2011. I wasn't ready to leave Amelia's world in the middle of this horrific scene. Terrifying as it was, I needed to know exactly what happened to her.

I shuddered as I realized that the words Henry spoke to Amelia after she'd told him about the baby were the same words I'd heard in my dreams. I emerged from the year 1868 with a powerful feeling of déjà vu.

I closed my eyes, breathing deeply, trying to go back to where I'd just left off. But I was unable to do so. "Amelia!" I cried out. "Help me go back. I need to know what happens next."

"You already know, my dear," her gentle words came to me. "It will all come back to you in time. This is not yet the time."

"What am I supposed to do? How am I going to resolve this impossible situation and find peace for you?"

"You must be patient. It will happen in a timely fashion." Then she disappeared, refusing to answer any more of my questions.

Frustrated, I grabbed her diary, turning to the place I'd left off. As I read on, I found that all these entries confirmed the experiences I'd just had on my trip into the past. The last entry intrigued me. Dated June 12, 1868, it contained the same words I'd found myself writing late that night in Amelia's bed:

Tomorrow he is picking me up in his carriage to take me out for a picnic on the Madison River, perhaps a boat ride as well. I must confess that I am looking forward to our time together. My heart sings once more. I have renewed hope for the future, whatever it may hold. I shall perhaps tell Henry about the baby tomorrow. I pray to God that this tiny being may be the glue that holds us together forever. I am happy at last!

I cautiously turned the page. It was blank, as were all the remaining pages in that journal. This June 12th entry was the last one Amelia ever wrote.

June 13, 1868 would have been the day Amelia went on a picnic and boating with Henry, probably the last day of her life. I was rapidly coming to the end of her journey through life. I prayed that the final pieces would come together soon—for her sake as well as my own.

I closed the journal, a profound sense of sadness washing over me. Amelia's life was over. In my hands, I held the proof of her existence. I would cherish this diary forever. But I would also make a copy for posterity, perhaps several copies. I'd wait until Sunday when the library was closed. Hopefully, Paul would not be there working as was his usual habit.

On a whim, Lucky and I hiked up to the cemetery. Along the way, I picked a bouquet of wildflowers for Amelia. Of course she wasn't there, as she'd taken temporary refuge in my house. But I still felt the need to run my fingers over the faded inscription on her tombstone.

Lucky and I walked through the open wrought iron gates and went directly to Amelia's grave. I arranged the flowers beside the crumbling headstone, promising myself that I would erect a new stone for her that would include her full name and dates of birth and death. "Amelia O'Brien Johnston," I whispered into the stillness of the cemetery. "Born February 1, 1840; Died June 13, 1868." I was as sure as I could be of those dates.

I settled down on the ground beside Amelia's tombstone, gazing out across the valley into the mountains. A sense of tranquility and peace engulfed me as the flowers on the graves swayed in the breeze.

I loved old cemeteries. A deep sense of history and permanence lived on amongst the graves. People were born, and then they died—a cycle of life that went on generation after generation. Was death really the end or was it the beginning of another phase of existence?

Perhaps it was a new beginning for many. That's what I'd always believed. But then there were spirits like Amelia who had not moved on into the light. "I will set you free soon," I promised her as I ran my fingers over the "Amelia 1868" inscription on her stone.

I felt a chill creeping up behind me. As I spun around, I saw a dark figure disappear into thin air. A sense of devastating grief saturated the air for a brief moment and then disappeared along with the apparition. It reminded me of the grieving person I'd seen by this grave the night Paul and I were here doing research. Whoever this spirit was, apparently he had not moved on either. He was still here paying his respects to Amelia. Still grieving

Then it hit me. Henry? Could it be Henry?

෴

On Sunday morning, I let myself into the library, breathing a sigh of relief that Paul was not there working. I started making two sets of copies of Amelia's journal. One would go to John the local historian who had been so kind to me. The other was a backup. Perhaps I'd give it to Paul someday. Maybe we'd use parts of it in our book. But I had to think about that. I was not ready to share any of this with him. Perhaps I never would be.

I couldn't put my finger on it, but there was something about Paul that I did not completely trust. Knowing that his great-great grandfather was the man who murdered my great-great aunt reinforced my feelings of mistrust for Paul. Not that he was responsible for what his ancestor did. Still, I had growing reservations about my relationship with Paul. Once again, I was shutting him out of my life. Once again, he was frustrated with the change in my affections. Lost in my conflicted thoughts as I pried the journal open and copied page after page, I almost didn't notice a tiny scrap of yellowed paper that fluttered from the journal onto the floor. That was strange. I'd never noticed anything like that in that journal before, and I had examined it carefully. Bending down, I retrieved a fragile yellowed newspaper clipping from *The Montana Post* dated 1868 that read:

A female body was discovered late the evening of the thirteenth of June on the Madison River. It has been identified as a hurdy-gurdy girl named Amelia. Cause of death was suicide by drowning.

Feeling faint, I stumbled into a chair and put my head down. Suicide by drowning? Where had they gotten that misinformation? Henry, of course. He had covered his tracks well. He was probably the one who supposedly "discovered" the body.

"Amelia?" I cried out, my eyes searching the library for some sign of her. "Where did this come from?"

"I thought you should see it," her tiny voice sighed. "But you must know that I did not die by suicide."

"I know that, Amelia."

"Jonathan's descendants do not even know what happened to me," she lamented sadly. "They need to know the truth. They need to know I did not desert my beloved son."

My mission was becoming clearer. It was more than finding a way to strike back at Henry for what he had done to Amelia. Perhaps I could also find Jonathan's descendants. First, I needed to travel back into her life to learn exactly what happened.

"Take me back, Amelia," I pleaded with her. "I need to find out exactly what happened that day."

"It is not yet time," she announced firmly. Then she was gone.

Chapter 35

Try as I might, I could not go back in time. It was as if Amelia had blocked all access to her life. Frustrated, I decided to take Mama's advice and "sleep on it." In other words, just let it go for a while. Instead of chasing that elusive butterfly, she always said that if you gave it enough freedom, it would come back to you when the time was right.

So I began planting a vegetable garden on the sunny side of my cabin. I'd have fresh vegetables and herbs this summer, just like back home on the farm in Walnut. Sometimes I missed my hometown. Spring on the farm was always an exciting time of the year, especially when calves were born and the sleeping world burst to life in shades of spring green. The farmers would be out planting their fields late into the night, the lights on their tractors lighting up the darkness.

Papa chuckled when I called to ask his advice on which varieties of plants and seeds to select. "Never thought you'd become a gardener like us," he lamented.

Of course, Mama kept asking when I was coming home for good. I'd always tell her, "Soon, Mama." No sense in upsetting her. Her days and nights were beginning to blur, her sense of time retreating into the fog of Alzheimer's. Papa said she liked to roam around at night while everyone else slept.

"I have a devil of a time waking her for church on Sunday," he confessed to me. That was the only day she had to get up before noon.

I enjoyed my talks with my father. Mama no longer monopolized all conversations nor stood firmly in the center of our relationship. She listened in the background, sometimes shouting out comments for Papa to relay to me.

One day I asked Papa how Bob was getting along. I'd been thinking of him lately and was hoping he was doing well. I wondered if I'd ever see him again, if we could ever be friends. Of course not, I reprimanded myself. Why in the world would he want to be my friend after what I did to him?

Papa did not seem surprised at my question. He sounded more pleased than anything else as he began updating me on what Bob was doing. "He's still hard at work on his house, night and day. I hear he's making a big garden out back. Saw him hauling one of those log lawn swings in his truck the other day. Said he was putting in a fire pit out there, even a waterfall."

I smiled to myself. Bob was creating the backyard we'd planned together. I'd been the one who wanted that waterfall. He didn't, but he'd given in to me. It surprised me that he hadn't scrapped that plan.

"...such a nice place. Just a shame he don't have nobody to share it with..." Papa lamented. "Oh, Rose, I'm sorry. Guess I shouldn't have said that. I didn't mean no harm."

"It's okay, Papa. I'm sure he will find someone soon. Whoever she is, she will be lucky to have a man like him," I mumbled as a pang shot through my heart.

Finally, Papa responded. "Guess he will. Mama says she heard he was seeing a nice lady from church. But you can't be sure if that is true or not, you know."

I went back to digging in my garden. Playing in the dirt was good therapy, I decided. It puzzled me, however, that I should care if Bob was finally seeing someone, as Papa put it. He deserved a good wife and a happy life. I had not been able to give him those things.

Chapter 36

I knew what I had to do next and when I must do it. It came to me one evening as I stood before my kitchen calendar, trying to decide when to schedule my first week of vacation. Perhaps I'd drive up to Seeley Lake to see my old friends. Lucky and I would hike the trails, canoe on the lakes, and camp out at the campgrounds we once called home.

Then it hit me. June 13th was rapidly approaching—the 143rd anniversary of Amelia's death by drowning. I felt compelled to get out on the Madison River that day. Hopefully, I'd recognize the places where she'd spent the last day of her life. Maybe I could slip back into her life one more time and find out how it really ended.

Paul had been asking to take me out in his canoe. Until now, I'd rejected his invitations and managed to create some well-needed distance between us. He didn't see it that way, obviously. He nursed his wounds in silence, watching me from a distance. Sometimes I felt smothered by him, as if I was drowning. What else was new? This had become the sorry and repetitive story of my life.

June 13th fell on the following Saturday. Paul readily agreed to take me canoeing that afternoon.

I drove to his place and met him in the driveway with the picnic lunch I'd packed. We hiked down the path to the river. It was a beautiful, sunny day although the weatherman had predicted possible rain or storms later in the afternoon.

"Why the sudden change of heart?" Paul asked as we devoured my homemade fried chicken. "I wasn't sure you'd see me again after you saw that photo of old Henry."

"It's not your fault that you're related to him," I replied half in jest.

"You really dislike him for some reason that completely baffles me. Do you even know why you have such a strong aversion to him?"

"Maybe. Maybe not. Let's not ruin the day talking about him, all right?"

"That's a deal. So tell me what you'd like to do today." He dove into the apple pie squares that were still warm and fresh from my oven.

"I'd just like to paddle around in the river, maybe even head out toward the rapids. Not through them, however. I'm not that brave."

"If you want to know the truth, neither am I. I must confess that I do not swim. Imagine that—having spent my life living on this river, I still seem to have a phobia about water. Have you ever dreamed you were drowning, Rose?"

"Why, yes, of course." I was surprised at his confession. "Doesn't everyone?" Visions of the past dreams I'd had of Amelia drowning in this river flitted through my mind.

"I don't think so. I thought I was the only one. Now there's two of us," he laughed. "Come on, let's go."

Paul grabbed two life preservers and the canoe paddles and steadied the canoe as I climbed into the front end. Wading into the water, he carefully pushed the canoe out before climbing into the rear seat.

We began to paddle in silence, our paddles dipping and slicing through the crystal clear water. Finding our rhythm, we spoke only to exclaim over an eagle soaring through the sky or one of the famous Madison River trout leaping into the air in pursuit of insects.

My mind drifted back to Amelia's boat ride 143 years ago. I wanted to go back in time, but I needed to do so without Paul's knowledge. I closed my eyes and laid the paddle across my lap.

"You look so relaxed," his voice broke through my reverie. I could hear and feel his love for me resonating in the air. He seemed happier than he'd been in weeks. "Rest awhile. I'll paddle," he offered as I began to relax to the soothing sounds of the lapping water. The canoe rocked gently on the waves as I basked in the warm sunshine.

I had no choice but to trust him, I decided. It was the only way I'd be able to lapse back into the year 1868. Letting go, little by little, I soon found myself disappearing back into Amelia's world, back to that fateful day on the river...

☙❧

Frozen in fear, I huddle on the floor in the front end of the boat as waves crash over the bow. I hear Henry laughing like a maniac, his laughter echoing as he rows the boat in circles.

I feel the sting of raindrops or perhaps sleet pelting my head, face, and arms. I am too terrified to look up. Am I going to die, to leave my son and my unborn baby behind? Oh dear God, I pray silently, please help me. Please forgive me for my sins and let me live.

Suddenly, the boat lurches up into the air in the midst of the swirling rapids and crashes back down. I'm thrown out into the raging waters. Struggling to stay afloat, flapping my arms and kicking my feet, I scream for Henry. He is the last hope I have left in this world.

"Henry! Please help me! Henry!" I scream into the rain and fog. I can barely see his boat. I'm gulping water as the waves toss me back and forth, dragging me into a clump of weeds and waterlogged branches from dead trees.

"Are you going to get rid of it, Amelia?" a harsh voice echoes through the fog.

"I will not!" I cry out defiantly before resuming my pleading. "Henry! I can't swim!"

"I know..." an eerie voice replies as Henry and his boat disappear into the fog.

Shrieking into the night, trying to free my hair and limbs from the dead branches that are dragging me down into the black waters, I fight with every ounce of strength I can muster. I must save my unborn baby. I must live for Jonathan. Over and over again, I try to climb onto the submerged rocks, only to slip back down into the churning rapids. I am dazed, exhausted. My lungs begin to fill with water. I know I am dying. Finally, I give up the hopeless fight as a bright light appears on the horizon, calling me home. I begin to float toward the light, leaving my body behind.

Hovering over my lifeless body, I decide to wait for someone to find and retrieve it. Hours later, about midnight, a boat with a lantern slips through the fog. Henry sobs as he gathers my body into his arms. "Oh my God, my Amelia," he croons as he rocks my lifeless body in his arms. "Please come back. Please. I love you, and I'm so sorry. You can even keep the baby if you like. Just come back to me, my darling."

He loads my body into his boat as my spirit turns away from him and floats into the blinding light. My time on this earth is over and strangely enough, I am at peace. Almost.

❧⟡

I awake from the dream to find a man gazing down at me, a look of concern clouding his dark eyes. Although my vision is blurred by the brilliant sunlight, I assume it is Paul. But on second glance, I am shocked to recognize Henry standing before me. He holds onto his glass-handled walking stick to balance himself in the canoe.

Anxiously looking around, trying to ground myself in reality, I find myself still sitting in the canoe as a speedboat cruises by. The year is 2011, according to the calendar in my purse. But I'm wearing a familiar long Victorian day dress and sunbonnet.

"Amelia?" Henry cries out in disbelief as our eyes meet.

"Henry?" My voice quivers as I find myself face-to-face with the man in my dreams, the one who let me drown an agonizing death in this river so many years ago.

Shaking our heads in disbelief, Henry seats himself across from me. Do we have anything to say to each other after all these years, after all that happened between us? What cruel fate has brought our souls together once more?

I seethe with anger, recalling the cruel death I suffered at the hands of this man, the one who swore he'd love me forever. I see the familiar sparks of anger also flashing in his eyes. Finally, he breaks the silence as the canoe drifts into the open waters of the river. "It is a pity that we had to part as we did." He clears his throat the way he always did when he spoke of an uncomfortable subject.

"Part ways?" I finally find my voice. "You drowned me in this river, Henry DuBois."

"That most certainly is not the way it happened. You fell from the boat, apparently intent on drowning yourself and that baby you carried."

His eyes of steel pierce my soul but not my heart. I feel nothing, no trace of the all-consuming love I once felt for this man. All that is left now is pent-up anger crying out for release and justice after all these years.

"That is not true! I had no wish whatsoever to drown. I had much to live for. Why did you not save me?" I glare at him, clenching my fists to keep myself from striking out at him.

"Because you betrayed me, and I was not about to claim a child fathered by another man. Why should I?"

I gasp in horror. "Where did you ever get such a crazy notion? I swear I was always true to you. Where did you hear such lies? I deserve to know the truth."

"From my wife, of course. She knew everything that happened in old Virginia City."

"From your *wife*?" I am horrified at his stupidity. "Think about the words you have just spoken. Did it never occur to you that she knew of your love for me? Perhaps she followed you and saw us together. The only way she could keep you for herself was to discredit me in your eyes."

"Nonsense!" he explodes, pounding the tip of his cane against the bottom of the canoe. "My wife had no idea how I felt about you. I was very careful to protect her and to be a good husband. She was not the kind of woman to follow me anyplace. She trusted me."

"Is that why she'd walk past my place of work, her head lowered, looking for me? Is that why she'd turn away angrily when I'd catch her watching me? Was she looking for you, Henry, perhaps thinking you were with me? If she didn't have suspicions about us, why did she ask my regular customers and friends about me and if I had a beau?"

"I don't believe you. You never told me anything like that before!"

"Of course not! Why should I? I was foolish enough then to want you for myself."

Henry's eyes are now ablaze with anger.

"One more thing, Henry. Do you know that you talk in your sleep?"

"Nonsense!"

"And do you know what you say in your sleep? You call out my name as you reach for me. I do not believe for a moment that you ceased talking in your sleep just because your wife was beside you. Of course, she knew you were in love with an Amelia, and she made it her business to find out who I was."

"Oh dear Lord," he buries his face in his hands, finally recognizing the bitter truth. He begins to weep. "I have been such a fool. I was deceived and look what happened as a result of my wife's deceit."

As if he had not first deceived and betrayed his wife. As if he had not surrendered his heart and soul to another woman. What did he expect?

"Can you find it in your heart to forgive me, my darling?"

I cannot believe he is foolish enough to think that I'd ever forgive him. I take no pity on the man who weeps before me. My heart has grown cold as if it were encased in a tomb of ice. Silence stretches between us as we drift along. Once his sobs subside, he wipes his eyes and looks up at me. The steel in his eyes is gone, replaced by pools of agony and repentance. The same look I've occasionally seen in Paul's eyes as he watches me from a distance at the library.

"Despite what happened between us, my dear Amelia, you must know that I've always loved you." Henry crosses his heart with his hand. "I still do. I spent my life in agony, grieving over you. I wept at your gravesite the rest of my days. Even now, my spirit returns often to sit beside your grave, trying to find you. And I finally have."

Images of the shadowy figure I'd seen lurking at the cemetery beside Amelia's grave, my grave, flash through my mind.

But Henry's words no longer touch my heart any more than his tears. As I think of Jonathan and my unborn baby, a blind rage builds within me, a fury I've never before known. A thirst for vengeance surges through my body as the sun disappears behind threatening clouds. The wind picks up suddenly, tossing the canoe to and fro in the churning waves. I watch in amusement as terror plays upon Henry's face. He reaches for the life preserver Paul had thrown into the boat and misses it as I begin to rock the canoe from side to side.

"How does it feel, Henry?" I mock him, remembering the last day of my life.

"Stop, Amelia! For God's sake, you will tip the boat." His face turns white as waves splash into the canoe. We are heading into the rapids. Now the canoe is swirling in circles and we are crashing over the rocks.

I tip the canoe into the churning rapids, spilling us both out into the water. I swim with powerful strokes through the rapids into an eddy of calmer water. Stopping to look back, I see Paul's canoe pounding against the rocks, splintering into pieces. The river is taking it away, bit by bit. Henry's head bobs up and down, his arms flailing, his feet kicking. He is trying to swim.

"Help me, Amelia," he pleads. "I can't swim!"

"I know," I sing out as I watch him treading water. "Neither could I." My voice echoes through the banks of fog rolling in between us.

Henry is thrashing about in the waves, trying to climb up onto a slippery rock and then slipping back down into the choppy waters rushing over his head.

Sweet revenge, I think to myself. Finally, after all these years.

My mind is reeling, flipping back and forth between my lives as Amelia and Rose.

A vision of a black-robed nun suddenly floats through my mind. Snapping out of my trance, I manage to free myself from Amelia's grasp. Rose is back. Horrified, I realize that the man I've left behind to drown is Paul, not Henry! Paul does not deserve to die for Henry's sins!

ॐॐ

I plunged back into the rapids, swimming with all my might, consumed with my need to save Paul, who was clinging desperately to a submerged rock when I arrived. Waves washed over him as he gulped mouthfuls of river water. His eyes were crazed, perhaps as wild as mine had been the day I drowned in this river.

He did not protest or move as I flipped him onto his back and put him in a headlock. Thank God I had trained on the swimming team and was a strong swimmer. If I had not been, we both would have drowned.

Finally, I dragged him up onto the shore, and rolled him over on the rocky beach to drain the water from his lungs. He began to cough, spitting out the river water. Although he was dazed, he was breathing. He would be all right.

I collapsed beside him, suddenly exhausted once my rush of adrenaline had expired. Although my first reaction had been to run as far and as fast as I could, I was unable to move. More importantly, I couldn't leave Paul like this, not without saying good-bye. We'd been cast into this strange situation together. We needed to resolve it together.

Panting, breathing deeply, and counting to ten over and over again, I finally calmed myself down as I watched Paul's every movement, praying he would be all right. Sitting close beside him, staring out into the wild river, I tried hard to make sense of what had just happened to us and to figure out my next move.

I watched him breathing slowly, his powerful chest moving up and down, his eyes closed. Was this the man I loved or was he simply the manifestation of Henry, the man Amelia had loved? Had Paul and I merely been playing out roles from our past lives so we could find closure together?

Finally, Paul opened his eyes, staring at me in bewilderment. He was pale as a ghost. "What the hell just happened out there?" He pulled himself upright, staring at me as if he'd never seen me before.

"I think the old score between Henry and Amelia has finally been settled," I began softly, reaching out to touch his hand.

"I was Henry out there." He shook his head in disbelief. "I really *was* my great-great grandfather Henry."

"I know, and I was Amelia, my great-great aunt—the one Henry drowned in this river in 1868. The woman I've been obsessing over since I came to Virginia City."

"Oh my God, Rose." Paul shivered as he put his arm around me. "It's as if they used us to settle their differences."

"I think they've finally found peace and closure, Paul. Maybe they're ready to move on."

"I sure as hell hope so. We don't need any more experiences like this one." Looking into my eyes, he added, "You know a lot more about all of this than you've told me, don't you?"

"I do," I admitted. "I think it's time to level with you. It's all documented, Paul. I even have Amelia's old journal and letters."

"What? How can that be?" The researcher and paranormal investigator in him came alive with excitement. "Can I—"

"I've already made copies for you. I hope you can use them in your book or in your research."

I felt his eyes watching me intently, suspiciously, sensing that I was drifting away from him. *Our* book had become *his* book.

"What about us, Rose? Has something changed between us today— aside from the fact that you almost drowned me before deciding to save my life? And I thank you for that, by the way."

My eyes filled with tears as I met his gaze. "I'm sorry. I wasn't the one who tipped the canoe and left you, Paul. It was Amelia seeking revenge against Henry."

"I know that, but you haven't answered my question about us."

"I don't know yet, Paul. I don't know any more than you do if we really love each other or if we were just pawns in their ill-fated game. Is our relationship real or not?"

His jaw tightened. He did not speak.

"Maybe we need time to figure this out—time for each of us to free ourselves from the ghosts of the past. To be honest, I feel I've finally been freed from something that's haunted me all my life."

He remained silent, staring out into the river as if lost in his own thoughts.

"Tell me what you're thinking, Paul." I touched his hand. He did not respond.

"Maybe you're right," he said at last. "But I do love you."

"And I feel the same way. I'll never forget you."

"That sounds pretty final to me, more than a time out." He stared straight ahead.

"It doesn't have to be. I'll stay in touch," I promised, although I began to doubt my words as they flittered from my mouth. Something had changed between us. Without Henry and Amelia, things were different. It seemed to me that Paul also recognized this.

"You're leaving."

"Yes, I need to go home for a while to help out with Mama," I lied, trying to make an excuse, an easy way out for myself. "I may be back someday."

He did not protest as I stood to leave. Perhaps he also needed time to think this through. Pulling himself up to face me, he folded me into his arms and held me close. "I'll never forget you, little one. If we are meant to be, it will happen someday. If not, I wish you life's very best."

"And I hope you will find peace at last and release from the things that have tormented you for so long."

"I think I already have," he smiled broadly as a tear dribbled down his cheek.

I wiped tears from my eyes as I turned away from Paul DuBois for the last time and began to climb the steep riverbank. I glanced back to find him sitting beside the river.

"Good-bye, dear Paul. Good-bye, Henry and Amelia," I whispered as I begin breaking my way through overgrown brush, wild raspberry bushes laden with thorns, and fallen trees.

A transparent image of a black-robed nun appeared once again. Sister Irene smiled down upon me proudly.

"I'm free at last," I whispered to her.

And so is he, her words penetrated my mind.

Chapter 37

I could hear a few cars passing nearby, so I figured I must be near a road. Moving slower now, starting to feel the aches and pains from my ordeal, I found the road. Thankfully, I recognized it and realized I was not that far from Paul's house.

I pushed on, hiking along the roadside. Drivers in several cars stopped to offer me a ride, which I refused. I needed to be alone.

Once I found my car, I drove back to Virginia City, impulsively planning my next move. I must move fast. If I waited too long, I might give in and decide to stay. I might be swept away by memories of the past. I needed to forget Paul's kiss, to convince myself that what we had was probably not real. I could, after all, come back someday once I'd had time to figure things out.

By the time I pulled up at my home, the place I loved and hated to leave behind, I was in whirlwind mode. Karen was out in the garden trimming her roses. She waved when I got out of my car. "What happened to you?" she asked right away. "Are you all right?"

I was a mess with scrapes and dried patches of blood on my arms and legs. My shorts and tank top were ripped in places. "I'm fine, just took a tumble while I was hiking," I lied. "But I am really sorry to tell you that I have an emergency in my family. My mother...you know, I've told you about her?"

"Oh, dear, I'm sorry." Karen apparently assumed she had died.

"No, she's still alive, but I need to leave at once. She's in critical condition, and I need to rush home now. Not sure if or when I'll be able to come back. She's going to need long-term care."

"But of course. You must go, I understand. Can I help you pack?"

Karen helped me lug my things out to the car. I thanked her profusely and told her I'd be in touch, but when she asked for my address, I put her off. I wasn't sure where I was really going. I had not thought that far ahead. One step at a time. That's all I was capable of.

The last things I removed from my place were Amelia's diary, my journal, and the copies I'd made of both. After loading Lucky into the car, I stopped at the library. First, I made sure that Paul's truck was not there. It was hard enough to tell someone good-bye once. But, of course, he wasn't there. He was probably still sitting beside the river, thinking about all that had happened.

I rushed past the librarian and into my office with the two manila envelopes containing the copies of Amelia's journal and my documentation. I scribbled a cover page, which I inserted into each envelope that read simply, "The journal of Amelia O'Brien Johnston. Born February 1, 1840. Died June 13, 1868. Buried in Hillside Cemetery, Virginia City, Montana. Grave marked 'Amelia 1868.' "

I addressed the first envelope to John. Someday I would contact him again to clarify that Amelia had not committed suicide and the circumstances of her death. For now, I tucked a copy of that yellowed death notice into the envelope and gave it to the librarian. "It is very important that you give this to John," I told her.

She looked at me with a puzzled expression. Of course, she may also have been surprised at my appearance. Although I'd changed into jeans and a short-sleeved shirt, my arms and face were still scraped and bruised.

"I need to leave for a while. Going on vacation," I lied.

I looked around the library one last time, knowing I would never return. Then I walked into Paul's office, holding my breath. Carefully placing the envelope in the center of his desk, I began to walk out, but I soon returned to scribble a note on the outside of the envelope: "Wishing you peace and happiness. Always, Rose"

As I closed the library door behind me for the last time, I marveled at the rugged beauty of the mountains that surrounded me. I breathed in the tantalizing scent of the fresh spring air and the wildflowers blooming throughout the valley.

Lucky and I had one final stop to make: Amelia's grave. I laid one perfect red rose upon her grave.

"Rest in peace, my dear Amelia," I whispered into the winds that rustled the spring green leaves shimmering throughout the cemetery. A new season was beginning. I felt Amelia smiling down upon me as I walked away from my life in Virginia City.

"Where to now, Lucky?" I patted his head. He didn't seem to care where we went. He merely licked my hand, letting me know that he was content to go wherever I decided to take him.

I headed east this time. I was tired of running. I suddenly realized that I no longer felt a need to escape from whatever demons had possessed me in the past. All I wanted was to go home to my sleepy little hometown of Walnut, Iowa.

A profound sense of peace settled over me as if I'd accomplished my mission, thereby freeing myself from a past life that had held me hostage for so long. I was free to move on with my own life.

I thought of Paul, the man I once thought I loved. Strangely enough, those feelings had dissipated in the midst of the Madison River. I shivered to think how close I'd come to giving myself to a man whom I had not really loved. Still, he would always hold a special place in my heart. Looking back upon the good times we shared, I hoped that Paul would also find peace so he would no longer need to carry around the burdens of his Henry persona.

As the miles flew by, my thoughts turned toward Walnut. It was time for me to go home so I could help Papa with Mama. But as I got closer, my mind kept drifting back to Bob, to what we'd once shared and what I dared to hope we might share again someday. Of course, he may have already found another woman. I shuddered at the thought.

By the time I reached my hometown, after several days on the road, I knew what I must do as soon as I arrived.

Taking the familiar exit off Highway 80, I drove out toward Prairie Rose State Park. Rolling down the windows, I breathed in the sweet scent of clover and marveled at the sight of wildflowers spilling across the rolling fields.

I pulled off onto the shoulder of the country road as the sun was setting in the West. Slipping off my shoes, I brushed out my hair, added a dash of lipstick, and straightened the yellow sundress I was wearing. Bob's favorite. I walked barefoot through the grass, the way I always did as a child, toward the house perched on the knoll overlooking the park. The house Bob had built for the two of us.

There should be two rockers on the porch, the ones we'd planned to sit in side by side as we watched the sun set together. My greatest fear was that my chair would be occupied by another woman. Still, I hoped with all my heart as I tiptoed through the fields of daisies.

In the past, just thinking about spending the rest of my life rocking on the porch instead of exploring the world and running from place to place had made me claustrophobic. But something had changed. Today I could think of nothing I'd like more—as long as Bob was the one rocking beside me.

Bob—a kind and gentle soul who had loved me forever, at least until the day I stood him up at the altar. Bob was a hardworking man with calloused but gentle hands. He loved nature, farming, and fishing. Down to earth, he didn't have a fancy education or a college degree like I did. But he had a brilliant mind. He loved reading books, building things, landscaping, and discussing philosophy and politics. He was the rock, I now realized, that a free spirit like me needed to find some balance in life.

You have no right to expect him to forgive you, I reminded myself. Do not be surprised if he has found someone new.

Slipping quietly through the grass, I could finally make out one chair rocking on the porch. My heart leaped as I realized the other chair was empty. I stopped, gazing into Bob's face. He seemed to be lost in thought, rather sad and very much alone. I watched him for a while, my heart stirring with something I'd never before allowed myself to feel for any man.

Finally, Bob startled, jolted out of his reverie. His mouth dropped open in amazement as he looked in my direction. I walked to him as if in a trance, the evening breeze blowing my long hair in all directions.

Bob's eyes sparkled with love, tears glistening in his eyes, as I came closer. "Prairie Rose?" he called out as he ran to meet me, his arms outstretched.

Prairie Rose. The name I'd hated all my life. But now it felt right. It made me feel loved—and finally at home.

"Prairie Rose is home, if you still want me," I smiled through my tears as I rushed into the arms of the man I will always love.

Epilogue
One Year Later

June 13, 2012

Today is the 144th anniversary of the tragic death of Amelia O'Brien Johnston and her unborn child.

As I write, I am sitting in our backyard beside the waterfall, my baby girl asleep on my lap. The sound of the bubbling water lulls her to sleep. Her name is Amelia Rose—we call her Melia. She is beautiful. She has those Irish green eyes, my dark hair, and Bob's smile. I never thought I could be this happy. Life has been good to us.

The only difficult part has been watching my mother disappear into the world of Alzheimer's. She was, however, able to hold her first grandchild in her arms before that cruel fog closed in. She was radiant, so pleased that Bob and I had married and given her the grandchild she always wanted. I treasure the photo I took of Mama holding her newborn grandchild, gazing so lovingly at our little bundle of joy.

I take little Melia to the nursing home to visit Mama. She seems to enjoy our visits sometimes. Other times she does not know us. It's hard for Papa. But, again, Amelia has been a blessing to him also. While he's never been a man of words, I know how much it means to him to have us living close by. I have him over for dinner often.

Bob and I were married shortly after I returned from Montana. This time we had a simple wedding ceremony beside the waterfall in our backyard. This time, I did not run. I have found peace and the love of my life.

While I no longer dwell upon the past, I must tell you, dear diary, what I've done. For Amelia's sake, I spent many hours researching family genealogical records. While doing research at the Walnut Library, I actually found Jonathan's living descendants. My long lost relatives…

Bob and I made a trip before the baby was born to the charming historic town of Galena, Illinois. Amelia's descendants still live there. I shared her story with them and gave them a copy of her journal and letters. They were pleased to find out what had happened to their long-lost ancestor and especially happy to learn that she had not deserted her beloved Jonathan..

They had a surprise for me also—a tintype photo of Amelia. Holding it in my shaking hands, I was shocked to discover that she wore the same elegant dress she'd worn back in Virginia City when I'd traveled back into her lifetime. More shocking yet was the fact that my antique cameo brooch, the heirloom necklace Paul had given me, graced her neckline. I still have that necklace tucked away in my jewelry box at home. So Henry had given it to Amelia after all! I found some satisfaction in knowing that.

Turning the photo over, I found the words "My Mommy" written in a faded childish handwriting.

"Oh, Jonathan," I whispered as tears filled my eyes, and I grew pale.

"Are you all right, Rose?" Bob put his arm around me.

"You look like you've seen a ghost," one of my newfound relatives chimed in. "But I must say that you look so much like Amelia that I am stunned."

I nodded, finding it difficult to speak. Bob stepped up to the plate on my behalf. "We're pregnant!" he beamed proudly. "Sometimes she gets a little emotional about things, don't you, honey?"

They gave me this cherished old photo, after making a copy for themselves. "It belongs to you, Rose. I sense that Amelia would want you to have it," the oldest of my new relatives told me with tears in her eyes. That photo is one of my most prized possessions.

No, I did not tell them of my experiences as Amelia. Bob is the only one I've shared this with. He has been a wonderful support as I worked through my feelings and moved into the future.

As for Amelia, she disappeared shortly after our visit to Galena. The last time I saw her was in one of my dreams. "Thank you, my dear," she beamed at me, her face radiant. "You have completed our unfinished business. Now it is time for me to go—and for you to find peace and happiness in this short lifetime of yours." Then she was gone. I miss her. It feels as if a part of me has disappeared into a foggy past.

As promised, I had a new gravestone made for Amelia. My friend John, the historian in Virginia City, had it erected in the cemetery where Amelia lies. I decided against going back for the ceremony. It is best that I not see Paul again. My old friend Maria recently wrote me that Paul is dating again. He seems happy, as if he's been transformed and released from a heavy burden that he has carried silently for many years. I wish him the best. I will never forget all that we shared, but it is the past. It was not meant to be. Our book has been published, and he credited me as coauthor. I recently received a copy in the mail, postmarked Virginia City, Montana, with no return address.

Do I ever think of Paul or Henry? Of course I do. Their memories have been imprinted upon my soul. I cherish the good and have forgiven the bad. I've learned that forgiveness is the key to letting go and freeing oneself of the burdens of the past.

While I no longer dwell upon the strange things that happened to me, I still wonder sometimes why Amelia chose me to complete her unfinished business, or if I am her reincarnated spirit. I've wondered if souls sometimes leave part of their energy behind on the spiritual plane before reincarnating into a new body. Maybe that explains how Amelia and I could have co-existed together for those memorable days in Virginia City, Montana. All I know for sure is that my supernatural experiences have freed me from the past and given me a new perspective on life.

Thank you, Amelia. Until we meet again, may you rest in peace.

ABOUT THE AUTHOR

Janet Kay

Janet Kay lives and writes on a lake in the woods of Northwestern Wisconsin. Drawn to nature since she was a child, she sees its wonders as a source of renewal, reflection, and connection with something greater than oneself. She is also strongly drawn to the Victorian era and its fascinating history. Her lifelong passions include creative writing, travel, photography, and spending time with family and friends.

Her first novel, *Waters of the Dancing Sky,* continues to earn excellent reviews and has a five-star rating on Amazon.com. Her new novel, *Amelia 1868,* is already creating a buzz. Future plans include a sequel to *Waters of the Dancing Sky,* and a paranormal novel to be set at Galveston Island, Texas.

She encourages her readers to check out her website at http://www.novelsbyjanetkay.com.

WHAT THEY'RE SAYING ABOUT AMELIA 1868

"This is a dynamic tale of a bright, free-spirited young woman who is driven to complete an unknown mission that has dominated many aspects of her life. Kay is a remarkable storyteller who adroitly combines fiction and history to create stories with depth and meaning. This story highlights the author's ability to use place as a technique for fleshing out the human experience. Kay's descriptions of the places in her novel were so vivid and enticing I needed to see them with my own eyes. She simply has a gift for putting readers in the scenes of her stories and in the middle of her characters' lives. Amelia 1868 combines history, romance and the supernatural in an elegant tale of love, loss, and purpose. I highly recommend it."

Melissa Brown Levine
Independent Professional Book Reviewers

ॐ◌ॐ

"Amelia 1868 has all the elements of great storytelling—intrigue, drama, conflict, and romance. I love how the author incorporated the spiritual/intuitive realm into both the plot and characters in a practical, very credible fashion, which adds richness and depth to both. Amelia 1868 is a real page-turner!"

Diana Schramer
Freelance Copyeditor

RESOURCES

Walnut, Iowa – Iowa's Antique City	http://www.iowasantiquecity.com
Seeley Lake, Montana Alpine Artisans, Seeley Lake	http://www.seeleylakechamber.org http://www.alpineartisans.org
Ennis, Montana	http://www.ennischamber.com
Virginia City, Montana	http://www.virginiacity.com
Rank's Mercantile, Virginia City, MT	http://www.ranksmercantile.com
Big Sky Resort, Montana	http://www.bigskyresort.com
Diamondback Dave	http://www.diamondbackdave.net

BOOKS

Cabin Fever, A Centennial of Stories about Seeley Lake by Seeley Lake Historical Society	ISBN # 0-9620902-47
Spirit Tailings – Ghost Tales from Virginia City, Butte & Helena by Ellen Baumler	ISBN # 0-917298-91-8
Witness to History, The Untold Story of Virginia City & Nevada City, Montana by John D. Ellingsen	ISBN # 978-1-59152-089-4
Images of America – Virginia City by Evalyn Batten Johnson	ISBN # 978-0-7385-8205-4
Ghost Stories of Montana by Dan Asfar	ISBN # 978-976-8200-36-5